What Hides Inside

Ally Blue

A Samhain Publishing, Ltd. publication.

Samhain Publishing, Ltd.
512 Forest Lake Drive
Warner Robins, GA 31093
www.samhainpublishing.com

What Hides Inside
Copyright © 2007 by Ally Blue
Print ISBN: 1-59998-417-2
Digital ISBN: 1-59998-484-9

Editing by Sasha Knight
Cover by Vanessa Hawthorne

First Samhain Publishing, Ltd. electronic publication: April 2007
First Samhain Publishing, Ltd. print publication: October 2007

Dedication

To the girls of Just Between Us Ladies, the wonderful critique group who helped knock this book into shape. I love you guys!

Chapter One

Mobile Press-Register

Wednesday, Nov. 17th, 2004

MOBILE—South Bay High has been ordered closed by the chief of police following another student disappearance during school hours.

Junior Arlene Ray was last seen leaving her first period Civics class on Tuesday November 16th, on her way across the sprawling campus to the auditorium basement for second period Theater. She never arrived. When she neglected to return home on the bus after school, her mother called the police. A search of the campus and the surrounding area failed to turn up any clues to her whereabouts.

Arlene Ray is the third student to have vanished between classes at South Bay High in the past month. The other teens, Patrick Callahan and Susie Hutchins, remain missing. The police and Alabama State Bureau of Investigation have no leads in any of these cases, although Mobile Chief of Police Gloria Modesky says that they have so far found no clear signs of foul play.

According to Principal James Innes, the school continues to...

"Sam?"

Sam Raintree set the morning paper on the desk, open to the place he'd been reading, and glanced at his boss. "Yeah, Bo?"

"Could you come into my office for a moment, please? I need to discuss something with you."

Flipping his hair out of his eyes, Sam leaned back in his chair and gave Bo a more thorough look. Dr. Bo Broussard, founder and lead investigator of Bay City Paranormal Investigations, stood in the doorway of his private office. His deep brown gaze darted from Sam to the front door and back again. One hand tugged at the end of his waist-length black braid in a nervous gesture Sam had come to know well in the last three months.

Sam knew exactly what the man wanted, and it had nothing to do with talking.

"Sure," Sam said, managing to sound casual. "Be right there."

Bo gave a curt nod, turned and strode back into his office. Adjusting his swelling crotch as discreetly as he could, Sam stood and followed him, watching the rest of the team from the corner of his eye.

They didn't seem to notice anything out of the ordinary. Cecile Langlois, resident psychic expert, was giving someone on the other end of the phone directions to the BCPI office in downtown Mobile. David Broom and Andre Meloy huddled over one of the new cameras they'd bought. None of them even looked up as Sam sauntered toward Bo's office.

Probably used to it by now. Sam wondered sometimes if they were really as oblivious as they seemed, or if they were simply pretending not to notice for Bo's sake. He strongly suspected the latter. There was no way anyone with half an eye could fail to notice Sam's mussed hair and swollen lips every time he stumbled out of Bo's office after one of their frequent "discussions". And how could they miss the dazed look in Bo's eyes, or the way his cheeks reddened as if he'd been out in a cold wind?

Of course, if his coworkers noticed, the things they most likely imagined happening were way off the mark. Sam wished they weren't. Not that he minded hand jobs, especially accompanied by needy kisses and Bo's soft, sweet moans. But he ached for more. And he was sick of skulking around like a teenager breaking curfew. He understood Bo's hesitation about telling people—coming out was never easy—but he didn't know how much longer he could remain patient with the lack of progression in their relationship.

Inside the office, Sam shut the heavy wooden door and leaned against it. "You wanted me?"

"I did." Bo pulled the dark green curtains closed across the big bay window, shutting out the deepening darkness and the glow of the downtown streetlights, then turned to Sam. "Come here."

Sam crossed the tiny room in two long-legged strides and went straight into Bo's arms. Bo met him in a deep, urgent kiss, fingers threading through Sam's hair. As usual, Sam's frustration melted like spun sugar in the blast furnace intensity of their mutual desire.

The kiss went on for long, wonderful minutes. When they broke apart, Sam buried his face in the curve of Bo's neck, arms tightening around his waist.

"Mmmm," Sam hummed, drawing a deep breath scented with Bo's skin. "I like this kind of discussion."

Bo didn't say anything, just held Sam closer. Sam frowned, noticing for the first time the tension in Bo's body. "Bo? What's the matter?"

7

"Not now," Bo whispered, cheek pressed to Sam's. "Just kiss me again."

Sam did, but the joy had gone out of it. In the two months they'd been together—if you could call this furtive sneaking around "together"—Bo had never been like this. Like someone had just pulled the rug out from under him. Even when Bo's friend and business partner, Amy Landry, died in the investigation of Oleander House, Bo hadn't seemed this lost and forlorn.

When Bo slipped a hand between their bodies and started unbuttoning Sam's pants, Sam grabbed Bo's wrist and pushed him back so he could look him in the eye. "Tell me what's wrong, Bo."

For a second, Bo's eyes snapped with anger. Then he sighed and leaned against Sam's chest. "It's Janine."

"Again? What'd she do this time?" Sam didn't even try to keep the anger out of his voice. Janine, Bo's wife, hadn't taken Bo's announcement that he was leaving her well. Ever since they'd separated, she'd done everything in her power to hurt him.

Sam cringed to think of what she'd do if she knew the real reason why her marriage had fallen apart. Bo hadn't told her he was gay and had been in the closet all their years together, or that he was seeing Sam. He'd blamed the breakup on the stress of Amy's violent and unexpected death. Sam couldn't help wondering if Janine bought that story, or if she knew the truth and was punishing Bo for it.

"She's taking the boys to her parents' for Thanksgiving. They live in Ohio. I was hoping to spend some time with the kids while they're out of school. Talk to them, you know? Let them know I'm still there for them. That just because Janine and I are breaking up doesn't mean I'm deserting them." Bo shook his head, his expression sorrowful. "She promised they'd stay home for Thanksgiving. I was planning to have the boys all day on Friday."

An all-too-familiar fury coursed through Sam. He'd only met Janine once, a brief "hello" when she'd come to the office one day to take the house key from Bo, but he'd already learned to hate her. Four times in the past month and a half, she'd agreed on a date for Bo to spend some real time with his sons, Sean and Adrian, only to change it at the last minute. A weekend became an afternoon, an all-day trip to the Gulfarium became a hasty dinner with Janine frowning over him the whole time.

Sam had watched the woman tear Bo down bit by bit, and felt helpless to stop it. What was worse, he strongly suspected she blamed the constant changes of plan on Bo, planting the idea in the boys' heads that Bo didn't want to be with them. What kind of mother, he wondered, would deliberately set out to make her children think their father didn't care for them?

"Bo," Sam said, keeping his voice calm with a monumental effort, "I've said it before and I'll say it again. That woman is a class-A bitch. You're their *father*, for fuck's sake. You have just as much right to see them as she does. Can't you go to a lawyer or something?"

"I don't want to put the kids through something like that. Besides, I'm not sure there's anything a lawyer could do."

"They could if you'd file for divorce."

Sam tried not to sound bitter, but he couldn't help it. The fact that Bo hadn't yet asked Janine for a divorce stung more than his reluctance to go to bed with Sam, or even his refusal to see Sam openly. Even though Bo and Janine were separated, Sam knew that he and Bo had no chance for a real relationship until the marriage was dissolved.

"You think I've got a chance in hell of getting custody?" Bo barked a short, sharp laugh. "Hardly. She's holding all the cards. She brings in seventy thousand a year, while I barely make enough to keep this business going. She works at home, I work all kinds of weird hours and I'm out of town all the time. And if I asked for custody, her lawyer would find out that..." Biting his lip, Bo looked away.

"They'll find out you're gay," Sam finished for him, "and use it against you."

"Don't think they wouldn't." Bo's eyes flashed with helpless anger. "You have no idea how ruthless Janine can be. And there are still judges here who believe that...how we are is a good enough reason by itself to deny custody, or even visitation."

"Why can't you even say it? We're homosexual, Bo. Gay. Queer." Sam shook his head. "You didn't have any trouble saying it before, at Oleander House."

Bo stiffened in Sam's arms. "Things were different then."

"Oh, I see. It was just me that was queer then, not you." Pushing Bo away, Sam started pacing the floor, arms crossed over his chest in what he knew was a defensive posture.

"It's not like that." Letting out an irritated breath, Bo sat on the edge of his desk. "Christ, Sam. I thought you understood how hard this is for me. My life's been turned completely upside down here."

"I know that. I understand, truly."

"Then why are you acting like this? What the fuck do you want from me?"

That stopped Sam cold. What did he want, really? Sex? The freedom to not hide how he felt? Yes, and yes, but he knew those things weren't the cause of his unease. The root of it all was both simpler and more complex than either. All Sam's anger and hurt and frustration drained abruptly away, and a soul-deep sadness welled up inside him.

Walking over to Bo, Sam stood between his parted knees and put his arms around him, pressing their foreheads together. "Are you ever going to really accept this, Bo? Or is it going to be this way forever?"

Bo didn't answer right away. Cupping Sam's face in his palms, he planted tender kisses on Sam's cheeks and chin. When their lips met and Bo's mouth opened to him, Sam knew. He could taste Bo's fear and confusion in his kiss.

"I want to make this work with you, Sam," Bo whispered, fingers stroking Sam's hair. "I do. But I don't want to lose my children. Can you hold on a little longer? Just until Janine and I are divorced, and I can prove to a judge that I'm a good father?"

"So, you're going to ask for the divorce?"

"Yes. You're right, I have to do it. Janine and I both know we're never getting back together, so I suppose there's no real reason to wait. But I can't let Janine or anyone else find out about you and me. Not yet." Bo kissed Sam again, his desperation crystal clear. "Please, Sam. Please. Just give me a little more time."

Looking into Bo's pleading eyes, Sam wanted to lie. He longed to say all the things Bo needed to hear, to promise he'd wait forever if that's what it took. The problem was, it just might be forever. Bo hadn't yet accepted his own nature, and until he did, he would find excuse after excuse to keep his relationship with Sam hidden. And Sam wasn't sure he could deal with that on a long-term basis.

Laying a hand on Bo's cheek, Sam tried to find the right words to say what he had to say. "Bo, I—"

A knock at the door interrupted him. "Who is it?" Bo called without looking away from Sam's face.

"It's Cecile. There's a client here to see you."

Bo shot a frustrated glance at the door, then wound a hand around Sam's neck and kissed him hard. "This conversation is not over," he murmured.

Sam said nothing as he pulled out of Bo's embrace and straightened his clothes. He waited until Bo was seated behind his desk, then went to open the door. Cecile's eyebrows went up, but she made no comment. Sam stood aside, allowing Cecile to enter, followed by a slender black man with graying hair and a stern expression.

"Bo, this is James Innes, he's the principal of South Bay High." Cecile nodded toward Bo, who was already rising to his feet. "Mr. Innes, this is Dr. Bo Broussard, our lead investigator."

"Dr. Broussard." The principal reached across the desk to shake the hand Bo offered. "Thank you for seeing me, I know this is short notice."

"Not a problem," Bo answered with a smile. "Please, have a seat." He glanced at Sam. "This is Sam Raintree, a very valuable member of our technical team."

"Nice to meet you, Mr. Innes," Sam said, offering his hand to shake. The older man had a firm grip and a direct, no-nonsense manner Sam liked. "Bo, you want me to send Andre in?"

Since Amy's death, Andre had become Bo's business partner, managing a great deal of the day-to-day running of Bay City Paranormal. He was always present for client interviews, though Sam sometimes wondered if that was a good idea. Amy had been his longtime lover, and losing her had caused the once open and friendly Andre to become withdrawn, moody and often surly. His friends and coworkers understood, but clients were sometimes intimidated by the big man silently glowering at them.

"Andre and David left just a few minutes ago." Cecile glanced at her watch. "Actually, I was planning to head home myself, if that's all right?"

Bo nodded. "Sure, go ahead. I'll see you in the morning."

"Okay. Oh, by the way, Bo, you have an interview tomorrow morning at ten."

For the tech position, Sam remembered with a sharp pang. With Amy gone and Andre taking over her previous position in the company, they were short a tech person. Even though he knew it wasn't his fault, Sam couldn't rid himself of the smothering sense of responsibility. He'd opened the dimensional doorway in Oleander House, however unintentionally, and Amy had died as a result. No one else blamed him, not even Andre, but he figured he blamed himself enough for them all. Sometimes he wondered if he'd ever be rid of the guilt.

Bo smiled at Cecile, neatly concealing the pain Sam knew he felt. "Thanks."

"Sure thing." Cecile turned to their client. "Good night, Mr. Innes. See you soon."

"Certainly, Ms. Langlois. Thank you." Mr. Innes shook Cecile's hand, then settled into the plush leather chair in front of Bo's desk.

Sam started to follow Cecile out the door.

"Sam, since Andre's not here, could you stay?"

Forcing himself to relax, Sam turned around. "Sure, Bo."

Sam dragged the extra chair out of the corner and up to the desk, trying to ignore the tension between himself and Bo. Thankfully, Mr. Innes didn't seem to pick up on it.

His most winning smile in place, Bo rested his elbows on the desk and clasped his hands together. "What can we do for you, Mr. Innes?"

"I'm sure you've heard by now about the students who have disappeared from my school," Mr. Innes said.

"Yes," Bo answered. "Terrible thing. The paper said the police had no leads."

"That's true." The principal stared at his lap for a moment, then raised his head. His gaze was direct and a bit defiant. "Let me be blunt, gentlemen. I need you to investigate South Bay High."

Sam and Bo glanced at each other. Bo's expression reflected the question in Sam's mind—*Why?*

"I hope this doesn't sound rude," Bo said, brows drawing together, "but I'm not sure we're the right people to help you. It seems more a matter for the police. It may take a while, but I'm sure they'll find out something eventually. There's always evidence to be found, somewhere. People don't just disappear without a trace."

Except when they do. Sam darted a pointed look at Bo, and saw the man's eyes widen a little as he remembered what Sam just had. Josephine Royce, who'd vanished off the face of the earth after the death of her lover, Lily. Vanished, most likely, into the same world from which Lily's killer had come. Almost twenty-five years later, her whereabouts remained a mystery.

Not again. Not another Oleander House. The thought formed a hard knot of dread in Sam's guts. They'd been hired to investigate several suspected cases of dimensional gateways since word of the events at Oleander House got out, but so far all had ended up having more mundane explanations. Sam breathed a frantic prayer to whoever or whatever might be listening that this was another such case.

Mr. Innes shifted uncomfortably in his chair. "I know it seems like a strange request. And to be perfectly frank, I agree with you. I don't expect you to find anything out of the ordinary at my school."

"But?" Bo prodded when Mr. Innes hesitated.

"But," the principal continued, "the students are terrified. Not that I blame them, but their fear is misdirected."

"And how can we help you fix that?" Sam asked, trying not to sound as on edge as he felt.

The man glanced at him with a frown. "Wild rumors have been circulating at South Bay. Rumors of...things, creatures, living in the tunnels beneath the school. The students are saying that these beings are taking unwary students in between classes and dragging them into the tunnels."

Bo's eyebrows shot up. "Tunnels?"

"Yes. South Bay was built in 1901, and was originally a monastery. The tunnels started out as simple cellars, built to store food and wine. The monastery was converted into a school in 1922, after the monks left. In the 1950s, the tunnels were expanded and designated as bomb shelters. They were sealed up in 1977, when their use by students for drugs and romantic trysts and such became a problem. They've been closed ever since."

Bo's expression gave nothing of his thoughts away, even to Sam's practiced eye. "Did the police search the tunnels for the missing students?"

Mr. Innes nodded. "The seals on the one remaining accessible door had been broken somehow, and there was evidence of student use. Condoms, beer cans, things like that. There was no sign of the missing students, however, or of what may have happened to them. There was evidence that the place is infested by unusually large rats, but that isn't terribly surprising."

"So what you'd like us to do," Bo clarified, "is to investigate the school, specifically the tunnels, in order to put your students' minds at ease by proving to them that there are no supernatural beings hiding there and abducting people."

"Exactly. Your company has quite a stellar reputation in this town, after the case you solved in Mississippi. If you say that nothing unnatural is happening at South Bay my students will listen to you." Mr. Innes smiled, relief written into every line on his face. "You can start immediately. As you know, Chief Modesky has ordered the school to close, but only long enough for her to put protective measures in place. We are planning to reopen South Bay as usual after the Thanksgiving holidays. That gives you more than a week to perform the investigation. Will that be enough time?"

Bo licked his lips, which had the effect of tightening Sam's jeans. As casually as he could, Sam crossed his legs, hoping Bo wouldn't notice the flush he felt creeping into his cheeks. Why did Bo's every unconscious movement have to affect him this way? Especially since their relationship seemed to have no future. Sam blinked away the sudden stinging behind his eyelids and forced himself to focus on business.

"What if we do find evidence of paranormal activity?" Bo asked.

"You won't." Mr. Innes seemed absolutely confident.

"Most likely not," Bo agreed. "But before we consent to investigate your school, I need to know that you'll take our findings seriously, no matter what they are. We're professional scientific investigators, and we never declare a place haunted or otherwise paranormally active unless we have hard evidence and we've ruled out every other explanation. If you're only here to find unquestioning confirmation of what you've already decided is the truth, you'll have to find someone else to investigate the school. We at Bay City Paranormal stand by our methods and our results."

Sam managed to swallow the triumphant cackle that wanted to come out. Evidently Bo had come to the same conclusion as Sam—that Mr. Innes was only prepared to hear one result of an investigation. Bo was unfailingly polite to most clients, but he refused to tolerate those who came to him looking only for someone to tell them they were right.

To Sam's surprise, the school principal threw his head back and laughed. "Dr. Broussard," he said, still chuckling, "I think I like you."

Bo grinned. "Are we agreed, then?"

"We are. Can you start tomorrow?"

"Sorry, no. The rest of the week is completely full." Pursing his lips, Bo tapped a finger on his chin. "What about Saturday?"

"Saturday would be fine." Mr. Innes reached a hand across the desk. "Oh-eight-hundred?"

"We'll be there." Bo shook the principal's hand, and all three of them stood. "We'll bring the necessary paperwork with us."

"Very well." Mr. Innes held a hand toward Sam. "Mr. Raintree."

"Mr. Innes." Sam shook the man's hand, quirking an eyebrow at Bo. "See you Saturday."

"Yes." Mr. Innes paused at the door. "You won't find anything."

"Let's hope not," Bo answered mildly.

The corner of Mr. Innes' mouth turned up in a wry smile. "Thank you for your time, gentlemen. Good night."

Mr. Innes strode out of Bo's office. The front door squeaked open and rattled closed as he left.

Sam stood in Bo's office doorway, gazing out the front window at the headlights of the cars passing by on Dauphin Street. A few seconds later, Bo's arms slid around his waist from behind, Bo's body pressing warm and solid against his back.

"What are you thinking, Sam?" Bo kissed his neck, soft lips lingering on his skin.

Sam let himself relax into Bo's arms. "South Bay. Wondering what we're going to find there."

"Mm." Bo's tongue traced the shell of Sam's ear. "I hope Mr. Innes is right and we don't find anything out of the ordinary. But I have this feeling..."

"Yeah. Me too." Turning in Bo's embrace, Sam tugged the rubber band off the end of Bo's braid so he could bury his hands in all that thick, silky hair. He never tired of the feel of it, slick and heavy between his fingers. "Bo, what we were talking about before—"

"Please, don't decide yet, okay?" Bo's wide-eyed, pleading gaze bored into him. "Please just...just give me a little time." Laying both hands on Sam's cheeks, Bo kissed him, tongue flickering over his lips. "Please, Sam, I need you right now, please..."

Sam didn't have it in him to refuse Bo anything when he begged like that, fear and confusion and need raw in his voice. With one arm snug around Bo's waist and the opposite hand tangled in Bo's hair, Sam shut his eyes and let Bo's kiss carry him away. This time, when he felt Bo's fingers unbuttoning his jeans, he didn't stop him.

Chapter Two

Sam usually arrived at work early. Mostly because he loved his job, but he couldn't pretend Bo being there had nothing to do with it. Especially when Bo would push him against the wall and kiss him until he was dizzy.

This Thursday, however, he slept in, lingered over his coffee, and walked the two miles to work instead of taking the bus. The morning was bright and inviting, and unusually warm for November. Mobile had endured cold, dreary rain nearly every day for the past two weeks, and Sam found the pleasant turn in the weather irresistible.

He tried to tell himself he was going in late simply so he could enjoy the beautiful morning before starting his day. It almost worked, too. He bounded up the steps of the old Victorian home that housed the BCPI office and opened the door.

Bo was standing beside Cecile's desk, reading a sheet of paper. He glanced up, his gaze locked with Sam's, and Sam instantly knew the real reason for his lazy morning.

He was avoiding being alone with Bo. Distancing himself in an effort to prevent being hurt should Bo cast him aside.

Sam closed the front door, carefully schooling his face into a casual expression. "Morning. Sorry I'm late. It's so nice out, I decided to take my time and walk."

"Not a problem." Bo's tone was light, but Sam could hear the hurt in his voice.

He knows I was avoiding him. Shit. Sam stifled the urge to sweep Bo into his arms and kiss away that mournful look. It wouldn't help either of them in the long run.

"Bo, I can't find the file from the Sanders case," David said, coming in from the back room at that moment. He grinned. "Hi, Sam."

"Hey, David." Looking around, Sam noticed Andre's desk was empty. "Where's Andre?"

"He's gone to check out that storage building in Tillman's Corner. The owners claim it's haunted by the ghost of a German shepherd that died in there last summer." Cecile spun her chair to face David. "Oh, and I already filed the stuff from the Sanders case. It's closed, right? We shouldn't need to keep it with the active cases."

"Oh yeah, I forgot we'd closed that one. Thanks, babe." David leaned over and kissed the top of her head. "A dog ghost, huh? That's a new one."

"Hopefully Andre will be able to tell us whether or not it's worth pursuing," Bo mused, twirling the tail of his braid around his finger. "His abilities have become pretty impressive."

Sam nodded his agreement. In the few months since Oleander House, Andre's newly discovered psychic talents had grown by leaps and bounds. He'd been working closely with Cecile, honing his perceptions and learning how best to use them. The results so far had been stunning. Cecile still knew more about psychic phenomena in general and how to control and direct it, but Andre's actual abilities now outstripped hers and Sam's.

"Yes, he's better than me now." Cecile shook her head. "Pretty soon there won't be any need for me here."

David took her hand in his and squeezed. "Hey, we'll always need good investigators, and you're good at way more than just that mumbo-jumbo shit."

"Thanks, I think." Cecile laughed. "Speaking of good investigators, Bo, your interview'll be here any minute, is there anything you need?"

"No, I'm good." Bo held up the sheet of paper he'd been reading. "His resumé is far and away the best we've received. He has a great deal of experience, in research as well as investigative techniques."

"Sounds good," Sam said. "Hopefully this one'll work out. How many interviews is this so far, Bo?"

"Twenty-five." Bo glanced at Sam, that one look overflowing with a sadness that tore at Sam's heart. "Sam, would you mind starting on the planning for Saturday? I'd like to see if Mr. Innes has any sort of map of the tunnels, including any entrances that are still sealed, ventilation system, any other openings of any sort. I'd also like for you to get some names of students and staff we can talk to if need be. We might need to know precisely where those missing students were last seen."

"You got it." Sam stared at Bo as hard as he could, trying to tell him without words that it didn't have to be over between them.

Bo blinked and looked away. "Okay. Thanks. Um, David? Could you sit in on the interview? If we hire this guy, you'll probably be training him, so I'd like your opinion."

"Sure thing, boss-man." David kissed Cecile's fingers and let her hand drop, then started toward the back room. "Let me finish up this paperwork real quick and I'll be right in."

As David and Cecile went back to their tasks, Sam tried to catch Bo's eye again. Bo clearly wasn't having it. He strode into his office without looking Sam's way. Sighing, Sam shuffled across the room to his desk and plopped into his chair.

He'd barely booted up his computer when the front door opened, letting in the sounds of traffic and conversation before it swung shut again. Sam glanced up in time to see their visitor unzip his jacket and hang it on the coat tree beside the door.

Sam wondered if this was the person Bo was interviewing for the tech position. He couldn't help noticing how attractive the man was—lithe and slender, with pouting lips and big gray-green eyes, brown hair streaked with blond falling in an elegant sweep across his forehead. His snug charcoal gray sweater and well-fitted black pants emphasized rather than hid his slim, toned body.

The rush of heat that shot through Sam as those pretty eyes met his was as unwelcome as it was unexpected. Ignoring it as best he could, Sam stood and came forward.

"Hi." He smiled in what he hoped was a casual way. "Can I help you?"

Grabbing Sam's outstretched hand in a firm grip, the young man shook it. "I'm Dean Delapore, I'm here for an interview with Dr. Broussard." Dean flashed a grin Sam was willing to bet got him into—and out of—a whole lot of trouble. "Are you Dr. Broussard?"

"No, I'm Sam Raintree. Nice to meet you, Dean." Sam retrieved his hand. "Bo's in his office, he'll be ready for you in a minute."

"Okay." Dean's eyes shone with a teasing light. "So, what do you do here, Sam?"

Sam licked his lips, trying hard not to notice the openly appraising way Dean was looking at him. "I'm part tech assistant, part investigator, and part psychic-in-training. We all do a little bit of everything around here."

"Do you? Hm. I see." Dean quirked an eyebrow at Sam, then sauntered over to Cecile's desk. He held a hand out to her, that thousand-watt smile still in place. "Hi, I'm Dean, what's your name?"

With an amused glance at Sam, Cecile stood and shook Dean's hand. "I'm Cecile Langlois, we spoke on the phone yesterday."

"Oh yeah, I remember. Nice to meet you in person, Cecile." Dean let go of her hand. "Don't think I'm being forward, but you're a very beautiful woman."

"Isn't she?" David came strolling in from the back room at that moment and walked up to Dean with a grin. "I'm David Broom. Don't flirt with my girl."

Dean laughed as he shook David's hand. "Duly noted. Good to meet you, David, I'm Dean Delapore."

"Yeah, Bo's interview." David clapped Dean on the shoulder. "C'mon, Bo's expecting you. I'll be in on the interview."

"I hope you won't hold my behavior against me," Dean said, though he didn't sound worried.

"Naw, it's cool. Who could help it?"

Sam watched the two of them enter Bo's office, already chatting like old friends. He shook his head.

"Okay, what was that?" Cecile asked after David shut the door. "Is it my imagination, or was he just flirting with you and me both?"

"I don't think it was your imagination." Sam laughed. "Should be entertaining if Bo hires him."

Cecile gave him a sharp look. For a second, Sam was sure she knew all about him and Bo. A thrill of fear went through him. Then she smiled and sat back down.

"You want me to help you with some of the research and stuff for Saturday? I'm done with the last of the paperwork I had."

Sam swallowed and managed a smile. "That'd be great, thanks. I'll call Mr. Innes if you can do an internet search for the history of the school."

"I'm on it."

Cecile turned to her work, and Sam let out a silent sigh of relief. While part of him realized Cecile and the others must at least suspect what was going on, he wasn't sure he was ready for them to know for certain. Or rather, he wasn't ready for Bo's reaction if he found out their relationship was common knowledge in the office. Bo was so skittish, the slightest thing could make him push Sam away right now.

He still wasn't sure what his friends did or did not know, and he didn't feel like thinking about it right then. Forcing the worry to the back of his mind, he picked up the phone and dialed Mr. Innes's number.

♋

Forty-five minutes later, the door of Bo's office finally opened again. Bo and David followed Dean out into the main office. Sam glanced away from his computer, trying to read Bo's face, but Bo wouldn't meet his gaze.

"Thank you for coming in, Dean," Bo said, shaking Dean's hand. "We'll give you a call when we decide."

"Great, thanks." Letting go of Bo's hand, Dean flashed a blatantly flirtatious smile at Sam. "I hope I can come to work here. I think we could be really good together."

Sam blinked, startled by the man's boldness. He was so busy staring at Dean that he almost missed the angry flush rising in Bo's cheeks.

"Yes, well. We'll let you know." Bo crossed the room and opened the front door. "Thank you, Dean."

Dean's eyebrows went up. He glanced at Bo, then back at Sam, eyes glittering in a way that made Sam distinctly nervous. "All right. Nice to meet you all. See you soon, I hope."

Sam watched thoughtfully as Dean shrugged his jacket on and left the office. He wasn't sure which unsettled him most—Dean's shameless flirting, or the fact that the man had clearly noticed the tension between Sam and Bo.

He's around Bo and me together for two minutes, and he already sees it. There's no way the others haven't noticed.

Of course, Dean had no preconceived notions about either of them. Maybe it was easier for a stranger to see. Sam decided to believe that version of events, for now.

"Well, I guess we've got a new tech guy." David leaned against the wall, grinning from ear to ear. "Bo, you still gonna do any other interviews, or stop here? 'Cause I gotta tell you, I don't see the point in talking to anybody else."

Bo shook his head, lips pressed into a stubborn line. "No, he's not the one. I've still got a few resumés on my desk, I'll start making calls."

David gaped at him. "What?"

"You heard me. We're not hiring him."

"Why not?"

"Because..." Bo's gaze darted around the room, settling on Sam just long enough for Sam to see the jealousy in his eyes. "I just don't think he'll fit in, that's all."

David glared. "Bo, we have to hire this guy. He's perfect. He knows all the equipment, he's got close to sixty in-depth investigations under his belt, and hell, I like him. Besides, you know as well as I do that no one else who applied is anywhere near as qualified as he is. We *need* him, Bo. We're drowning in new cases since Oleander House, we need help, and he's a fucking wet dream for this job. Come on."

Bo tugged on the end of his braid. "It doesn't bother you that he flirted with Cecile?"

For a second, Sam felt as if all the air had been sucked out of the room. Bo's real reason for not wanting to hire Dean was crystal clear. To him, anyway. He wondered just how obvious it was to everyone else.

"It didn't bother me, so whether or not it bothered anyone else is pretty much immaterial." Cecile crossed her arms and gave Bo a stern look. "Anyway, he didn't do it again after he found out David and I are together, so I don't see how that would affect whether or not you hire him."

Grinning, David elbowed Bo in the ribs. "It's not bugging you that he flirted with Sam, is it?"

Bo's blush was answer enough. He stared at a spot on the far wall and said nothing. David's jaw dropped, and Sam bit back a groan.

Huffing impatiently, Cecile smacked David's arm. "Will you stop? Bo's probably worried that Dean's going to spend more time flirting than working. Or maybe he's worried that Dean and Sam'll start dating and it'll interfere with work." She turned a wide-eyed look to Bo. "Is that it, Bo?"

Bo blinked and stuck his hands in his pockets. "Uh. Yeah. That's pretty much it, yeah."

David laughed. "Is that all? Shit, Bo, have you even been paying attention to this place? Me and Cecile? Andre and...."

Sadness filled David's eyes. "Yeah. Well, anyway, I don't think it'll be a problem if Sam and Dean hook up, and that's a big if."

"David's right, it won't be a problem." Sam stared hard at Bo, willing the man to look at him. "Dean's nice, but he's not my type anyway."

The glance Bo gave Sam was brief, but enough to tell Sam that he'd gotten the message. Bo held up both hands in a gesture of surrender. "Okay, y'all talked me into it. I'll hire him."

"Hallelujah, the man sees reason at last." Picking up a pen from Cecile's desk, David twirled it between his fingers. "Gonna call him today?"

"I guess so," Bo said, sounding less than thrilled. He pointed a warning finger at David. "You'd better be right, David. I am not going to be happy if I hire this guy and he turns out to be more interested in dating the entire office than getting his work done."

"Boss-man, you can drag out the thumb screws if I'm wrong. But I'm not." David set the pen down, leaned over and tilted Cecile's chin up to kiss her. "Mmmm, office romance. Tastes like chicken."

Sam laughed as David deftly dodged the smack Cecile aimed at his head and sauntered into the back room. The laughter abruptly stopped when Bo stepped close and laid a hand on his shoulder. Mouth dry and heart racing, Sam looked reluctantly up into Bo's dark eyes.

For a second, he was positive Bo was going to kiss him. He couldn't decide whether to be relieved or disappointed when it didn't happen.

"Sam, did you get hold of Mr. Innes?"

"Yeah, I did." Sam wished his voice didn't sound so rough. So dripping with lust. Ignoring Cecile's curious gaze, he plowed on. "He said he has a map of the tunnels, he's gonna email it to me. He also said he'd talk to the kids who claim to have seen things at the school and see if they'd be willing to talk to us."

Bo nodded. "Good. Thanks for doing that."

"No problem." Reaching under the desk, Sam adjusted his swelling crotch. He wondered if Bo realized he was stroking Sam's neck, thumb teasing his earlobe.

A glance at Bo's face told him probably not. Bo was a million miles away, staring into the middle distance with knitted brow and bottom lip caught between his teeth. His fingers crept into Sam's hair, and Sam had to bite his tongue to hold back his moan of pleasure. *Damn.* Not for the first time, Sam wished Bo would stop trying to hide their relationship from their friends. Maybe then he wouldn't have the subconscious need to touch Sam like this every time he started thinking.

Sam let himself lean into the caress for a second before clearing his throat. "Um, Bo?"

"Hm?" Bo curled a finger around a hunk of Sam's hair, pulling just a little too hard.

"Ow. Bo, uh..." Casting frantically about for something—anything—to say, Sam blurted out the first thing he thought of. "Want me to get out the paperwork for Dean?"

Behind him, Bo stiffened and yanked his hand away. "Yeah, that would be a big help. Thanks."

Bo turned and hurried into his office, slamming the door behind him. Closing his eyes, Sam leaned back in his chair and drew a deep breath. *That was close.* Part of him hated Bo for making him think that. For hiding what they were to each other, even from their closest friends.

And just what are you to him? The question rose unbidden from the dark corner of his mind where a lifetime of loneliness and self-doubt lurked. He didn't want to face it.

"Sam?"

Opening his eyes with great reluctance, Sam met Cecile's concerned gaze. "Yeah?"

"I asked if you had all the forms on your hard drive, or if you need me to print them off for you."

Sam shook his head, feeling slow and stupid. "Forms?"

"For Dean." Cecile frowned. "Are you okay? You're not getting sick, are you? The flu's been going around lately."

"No, I'm fine. Just thinking." Sam forced a smile. "I think I've got all the forms. I'll let you know if I'm missing anything."

"Okay." Tilting her head to one side, Cecile fixed him with a penetrating stare. "You know what, I hope you don't take this the wrong way, but lately I've been wondering—"

The trill of the phone ringing cut her off. She frowned at it, glanced at Sam, then snatched up the receiver. "Bay City Paranormal, this is Cecile, how can I help you?"

Sam turned away as Cecile grabbed a notepad and started scribbling furiously, the phone tucked between her ear and shoulder. He could practically feel her watching him, the weight of her gaze pressing on the back of his neck.

She knows about Bo and me. She's been watching, and she knows.

Cecile was by far the most intuitive person in the office, so he wasn't surprised she'd been the first to figure it out, but the others wouldn't be far behind. The thought made him feel oddly calm. His colleagues at BCPI had become very important to him over the past few months, and he knew he could trust them. Bo knew it too, if he'd just let himself move past the fear of discovery and learn to open up to the people who loved him.

Maybe if he could do that, he could finally open himself completely to the one who loved him most of all.

The one who loves him...

Sam blinked, startled. It was the first time he'd truly admitted the depth of his own feelings, even to himself. He had a strange urge to laugh. Of all the men in the world to fall irretrievably in love with, he *would* have to pick one still halfway closeted. One who he was beginning to fear would never see him as anything but a shameful secret.

Shoving the bitter thought to the back of his mind, Sam opened the "forms" folder on his computer desktop. He had work to do.

♋

"Turn here."

"Here?"

"Yeah. No! No wait, my bad, it's the next one."

Andre glared at David, who sat beside him in the front seat of the SUV. "You sure about that?"

"Yeah, it's Pierre Avenue." David frowned at the crumpled piece of paper in his hand, where he'd scribbled the directions to South Bay High. "Yeah, that's right. Sorry, man."

Andre shook his head and turned onto the indicated road without a word. In the backseat, Sam snickered. "What's wrong, David, couldn't read your own writing?"

"That's what y'all get for making me answer the phone." Twisting in his seat, David grinned over his shoulder at Sam. "How come you didn't wait and ride with Dean?"

Dean had called earlier that morning, as the rest of the group stood waiting for him to arrive, to say his car had broken down and would they mind coming to get him. Bo and Cecile had volunteered to pick him up in one of the SUVs. Since Dean was the only one who already knew how to get there, he'd given David directions, then the group had split up to get started. Sam had elected to go with Andre and David. He was a bit surprised it had taken David this long to start teasing him about not waiting to ride with Dean.

"I didn't want you and Andre to get lonely without me," Sam answered, fluttering his eyelashes at David.

Usually a little low-key flirting was enough to make David blush, grumble and stop teasing. This time, he just smirked. "Thought I caught some chemistry between you two yesterday."

Sam blushed in spite of himself. Dean had come in to the office the previous day to fill out the necessary paperwork for the hiring process. His flirting was far more subtle than it had been on Thursday, but there was no mistaking the lusty gleam in those gray-green eyes.

For his part, Sam had no idea how to react. He loved Bo, but Bo obviously didn't return those feelings. Maybe he never would. In any case, Bo still wanted to keep their relationship under wraps. Confusing things further was the fact that Dean was so hot, and clearly interested in Sam. It all made for a complex tangle of emotions, which made Sam tired to think about.

"I told you before, Dean's not my type," Sam insisted.

"Yeah, whatever."

Leaning forward, Sam smacked the back of David's head. Andre laughed, something he hadn't done much since Amy's death. It was a sound Sam was glad to hear.

David whistled as they rounded a curve in the road and the school came into view ahead and to the right. "Damn. That's a school?"

"No kidding." Sam leaned forward in his seat, staring at the five white, Spanish style buildings spread out across the expansive grounds. Tremendous oaks draped with Spanish moss shaded the buildings and walkways. "This place is huge. Hey, I wonder if any of the original monastery's left?"

"I talked to Mr. Innes yesterday on the phone," Andre said, slowing down to pull the SUV into the wide drive leading to the front of the central building. "He told me that the walls of the main building, the one there in the middle, are the original ones. They're foot-thick stone."

"Couldn't build that nowadays." Glancing at the paper in his hand, David pointed to the cul-de-sac at the end of the drive. "We can park here, right?"

Andre nodded. "Mr. Innes is meeting us in the office. It's through the front door and to the right."

They parked the SUV and piled out into the early morning sunshine. Sam lifted his face to smile at the pale blue sky. The weather was still unseasonably warm, and supposed to continue that way right through Thanksgiving.

Within a few minutes, the second SUV rolled to a stop. Cecile hopped down from the driver's seat while Dean stepped out of the passenger side. Bo slid out of the backseat, looking unbearably hot in snug black jeans and a form-fitting long-sleeved red T-shirt. Sam licked his lips, wishing the sight of the man didn't make his skin tingle. Not when he couldn't do a damn thing about it.

Dean sauntered toward Sam. "So, what do you think of the place?"

"It's gorgeous," Sam answered, truthfully enough. "I can't believe this is a public school. It looks more like a private college or something."

"Yeah, but don't be fooled. There's no air conditioning and it floods every spring."

Sam gave Dean a curious look as they followed the rest of the group up the steps to the archway leading inside. "Cecile said you went to high school here, is that right?"

Dean laughed. "Yeah. Of course, I graduated twelve years ago, so I'm sure some things have changed, but I'm betting there's still not air conditioning. It'd be a real bitch to install here."

"So, did you ever hear anything about these tunnels when you were in school here?"

"Yeah, everybody knew about 'em. Hell, I lost my cherry there."

"No way."

"It's true. The baseball team's pitcher nailed me during gym in tenth grade."

"Doesn't sound very romantic," Sam mused, holding the front door open for Dean to pass through.

"Oh, and I suppose your first time was on a moonlit beach, with wine and roses and violins?" Dean arched an eyebrow as he brushed past Sam, so close Sam could smell his musky cologne. "Spare me. Besides, it took me weeks of plying the boy with my considerable charm before he caved. Major closet case, that one was."

Sam grinned. "Something tells me you were never a closet case."

"Right you are. I proudly swing both ways." With a quick glance at the group a few paces ahead, Dean leaned close, voice dropping low. "You're not, are you?"

"What, a closet case? No, I'm out."

"I figured. I can always spot the bent ones, if they're my type." Dean flashed a wicked smile. "And you are *definitely* my type."

A spike of pure lust shot up Sam's spine at the suggestion in Dean's voice. Hot on the heels of his physical reaction came a wave of horrified guilt. *I love Bo. How could I want Dean?*

The answer, of course, was clear. Sam's feelings for Bo couldn't overcome his need for a warm, willing body between his legs and a hot, hard cock pounding him into blissful oblivion. Much as he wished it wasn't true, he craved sex, and Bo wasn't ready to give it to him. The fact that Dean was willing and able was terribly tempting.

"Would you two care to join the rest of us now?"

Bo's irritated voice shook Sam out of his thoughts. He looked over to where Bo stood in the open doorway of the principal's office. Bo's cheeks were flushed, his dark eyes snapping with transparent jealousy. Sam didn't know whether to be flattered or aggravated.

"We're coming," Sam said, ignoring Dean's barely stifled giggle. "We were talking about the tunnels."

"Yeah," Dean chimed in. "They're really hot and tight."

Sam cringed. Bo gaped. Dean plowed on, apparently oblivious to them both. "I was telling Sam how I'd been down there in high school. The tunnels are narrow and low-ceilinged, and warmer than you'd think."

"That's true," Mr. Innes added as they stepped through the door. "As a matter of fact, some scholars have speculated that the unexpected heat in the tunnels may have been the reason the monks abandoned the place. Evidently the original cellars didn't turn out to be cool enough to store their wine and perishables for any length of time."

"They didn't tell anyone why they left?" David wondered.

Mr. Innes shrugged. "If they did, it was never recorded. The monks simply disappeared, without leaving any record as to where they were going."

Andre's eyebrows went up. "That's interesting. Can you tell us any more of the property's history?"

"I'm afraid I've already told you all I know." The principal frowned. "Is it important?"

"It could be." Bo glanced at Dean, dark eyes cool now. "Dean, on Monday I'd like for you and David to go to the main library and see what else you can find out about this property."

"Okay." Dean gave Bo a winning smile. "Anything in particular you want us to be on the lookout for?"

Bo tugged on his braid, his expression thoughtful. "Keep an eye out for any other disappearances especially, but you'll want to look for anything unusual. I wish I could be more specific, but I can't. You'll both just have to use your judgment."

"Got it, boss." David nudged Dean's elbow. "You'll be training with me, by the way."

Dean nodded. "Bo told me. I'm looking forward to it."

Glancing at Bo, Sam was relieved to see the man's eyes gleaming like they always did on an interesting case, all traces of jealousy gone. Sam caught Bo's gaze and held it, letting his love shine through. Bo cast a furtive glance around the room, then flashed a brief, brilliant smile that made Sam feel hot all over.

Bo cleared his throat. "All right, let's get started. Mr. Innes, what we'll need to do first is tour the school, including the tunnels. After that, we'll regroup here in your office, if that's okay, and decide on an investigative plan for the day."

"Very well. And what do you need me to do, apart from showing you the school?"

"Nothing, really," Andre answered. "We may have more questions for you after the tour, though."

"And we'll need to know where the electrical outlets are," Sam added. "In case we need to set up cameras."

"I can show those to you as we go." Fishing in his desk drawer, Mr. Innes pulled out a hefty ring of keys and pocketed it. "Shall we go?"

"We're ready." Bo started toward the office door, then turned around again. "Who's got the notepad?"

"I do," David said, pulling a small notebook and a pen from his jacket pocket.

"Oh, no." Andre snatched the items out of David's hand and passed them to Sam. "We need notes that someone can actually read later."

David pressed a hand to his heart. "I'm wounded, man. Wounded."

Rolling his eyes, Andre gave David a shove toward the door. "I'll show you wounded, smart-ass. Move it."

Still playfully bickering, Andre and David followed Mr. Innes out of the office, with the rest of the group trailing behind. As they headed down the first floor hallway, Sam found himself walking between Bo and Dean. He couldn't help wondering just how prophetic that position would turn out to be.

Chapter Three

It took the better part of two hours to tour all the school buildings and grounds. The place was a marvel of Spanish style architecture, with its whitewashed stone walls and the roof of red Spanish tiles. The entryways were shaded by arched alcoves paved in earthy red. Inside, huge fans set at intervals along the high ceilings lay idle. Mr. Innes told them the fans were used to cool the place in the stifling heat at either end of the school year.

When they'd covered the entire campus, Mr. Innes led them back to where they'd started. "The only unsealed entry into the tunnels is here in the main building, underneath the central stairwell. You have flashlights, correct?"

"We do, yes." Bo glanced around at the BCPI team. "Okay, everybody, you know what to do. Sam, can you continue to take notes?"

Sam brandished his pen. "Yep."

Bo flashed him a warm grin, then turned to Dean. "Dean, today I want you to start learning how BCPI runs an investigation. I don't think you'll have any trouble picking it up, considering your experience. And feel free to speak up if you have anything to add. Okay?"

"Got it." Dropping his voice to a whisper as Bo turned to speak to the principal, Dean leaned close to Sam. "I'll show you the best make-out spots, if you want."

Sam nearly jumped out of his skin when Dean's fingers traced up his spine, the touch light and teasing. He glanced at Dean as they followed the rest of the group to the stairwell. Dean's eyes shone with what could only be termed lust. With a wink, he slid his hand down to cup Sam's ass.

"Dean," Sam breathed. "What are you doing?"

"Groping you." Dean's hand squeezed, and Sam bit back a yelp.

"Um, Dean, I don't—"

"Hey, it's okay." Darting a sly smile at Sam, Dean stuck both hands in his back pockets. "I know I'm a hopeless flirt, but I figure if I'm interested, I let 'em know. No hard feelings if you don't share my interest."

"It's not that exactly, it's just...well..."

"You're seeing someone?"

"Kind of." Too late, Sam remembered he was supposed to be single as far as the office staff knew. "Well, not exactly, I mean we see each other sometimes, but it's not... I mean, we don't... Shit. Forget I said anything."

Dean gave him a considering look. "Take my advice, Sam, don't date a closet case. It never works."

Sam gaped at him. "How did you know?"

"Been there, done that. Trust me here, save yourself the aggravation."

Swallowing, Sam stared at the floor. "It's not that easy."

"It never is." Dean patted Sam's shoulder, and this time it was comforting rather than flirting. "If you ever get this guy out of your head, you know where to find me."

Sam didn't answer. The offer was a little too tempting for comfort.

The group's arrival at the entrance to the tunnels was a welcome distraction. A rather forbidding metal door was set in the shadows underneath the large stairwell in the center of the first floor hallway.

"Watch your footing on the stairs," Mr. Innes said as he pushed the metal handle down and heaved the door open. "They're narrow and steep, and the lights don't always work like they should down here."

As if to prove the principal's words, the light over the stairs went out halfway down. Sam switched on his flashlight and played it along the stone walls as they descended. Moisture seeped through cracks in the rock, making dark gray spots. The rough arch of the ceiling hung mere inches above Sam's head.

Instead of growing cooler as they descended, the air became close and hot. By the time they reached the bottom of the stairs, Sam's shirt clung damply to his back and sweat dewed his face. He wiped his forehead on his sleeve.

"Good grief, it's hotter than f...um, heck down here." David wrinkled his nose. "Smells too."

"Yes, it's rather damp." Mr. Innes flipped a switch on the wall. A row of dim yellow light bulbs flickered to life, illuminating a cramped hallway stretching out left and right from the stairs. "There seems to be a mildew problem as well."

"Wow, it's even warmer down here than I'd remembered." Frowning, Dean wandered a few feet down the hallway. "And it's awfully clean."

Cecile shot him a surprised look. "You've got to be kidding."

"No, I'm serious." Dean reached up and ran a fingertip across the ceiling. "When I used to come down here, there were spider webs everywhere, and roaches and stuff. Plus it was dusty. There's none of that now."

Like Oleander House. No birds, no crickets... Apprehension shivered up Sam's spine. He glanced at Andre, and saw that he had made the same connection. Sam hoped they were both wrong.

Andre ran a hand over his close-cropped hair, which brushed against the stone ceiling. "Mr. Innes, how far do these tunnels go?"

"The main tunnel runs the length of this building. There are—or rather, were—two side tunnels, one branching off from each end of the main tunnel."

"What do you mean, 'were'?" Bo asked. "What happened to them?"

"As I understand it, they both underwent partial collapse just before the tunnels were sealed in 1977." Mr. Innes started down the hallway to their right, motioning the others to follow. "The city had particularly heavy rains that spring, and the walls of the side tunnels weren't reinforced with stone like those of the main tunnel. The saturated ground caused a large portion of the side tunnel walls and ceiling to collapse. The entrances were filled in and bricked over."

"I see." Bo swung around in a slow circle, nodding to himself. "Okay, let's do this. David and Dean, head down to the left, check out the lighting and general condition of the corridor and look for the best places to put cameras if we need to do that. Sam and Cecile, y'all do the same down the right side. Andre, you and I will go back to the office so Mr. Innes can fill out the paperwork. When the rest of you get done, come on back up and we'll unload the equipment and get started."

"Got it." David nudged Dean's ankle with a grungy sneaker. "C'mon, Apprentice O' Mine, let's do this. You tell me what you think as we go, and I'll tell you if you're right or not."

"Sounds delightful." Grinning, Dean brushed past Sam a little closer than was necessary. "Meet y'all back here at the steps?"

Cecile nodded. "Sure. Do you guys need some paper or anything, to take notes?"

"Naw, I can keep it right here." Dean tapped the side of his head. "See you in a bit."

"Y'all be careful," Bo cautioned as he started up the stairs behind Mr. Innes and Andre.

"We will," Sam promised.

"Good." Bo stared at him for a moment, his dark gaze heated, then turned and jogged to the top of the steps.

"So," Cecile said as she and Sam walked down the hallway. "What do you think so far?"

Sam shook his head. "I hope Mr. Innes is right about this place, but something tells me he's not."

"I know what you mean. The kids disappearing like that, and the stories about the things in the tunnels? And what Dean said about it being too clean?" Cecile shuddered. "I don't like it, Sam. Not a bit."

"Neither do I." A light bulb went out with a loud pop overhead, and Sam jumped. "Shit like that isn't helping."

"No kidding." Cecile switched her flashlight on, sweeping the beam into the dense shadows between the puddles of faint, sickly light. "I think we should both keep our senses on high alert, especially down here."

"Absolutely. Andre too."

Cecile gave him a long, solemn look. "Sam? Are you scared?"

"Yeah." Another light bulb blew, and he fought not to flinch. "I am."

"Me too."

Cecile's voice was soft and calm, but Sam heard all the things she wasn't saying. The memories of Oleander House, and the cold dread of having it happen all over again. He slipped an arm around her shoulders, pulling her against him in a brief, comforting hug. She hugged him back and gave him a wan smile.

They didn't mention it again during their exploration of the tunnel. Sam felt a mixture of relief and dismay knowing Cecile shared his impressions of the school. He tried not to think of what could happen if South Bay High turned out to be a true dimensional gateway.

I won't let it happen again, he promised himself. *Never again.*

He hoped it was a promise he could keep.

♋

Half an hour later, the group stood on the steps in front of the school, a pile of equipment at their feet. Sam squinted against the brightness, trying not to get distracted by the way Bo's ebony braid gleamed in the sunlight.

"All right," Bo said. "Here's the plan. David, Dean and Andre, take the left-hand side of the tunnel. Sam, you and Cecile will come with me down the right-hand side. One person mans the video camera, one does EMF and temp readings, the other takes notes and carries the recorder for EVPs. Andre,

Cecile and Sam, all three of you keep your psychic senses open and record any and all impressions. Got it?"

The group answered with a chorus of yeses and nods. Mr. Innes looked puzzled. "Would you mind explaining those terms to me? I'm not familiar with them."

"EMF is electromagnetic field," Andre answered. "The EMF often spikes during paranormal activity, though spikes can be caused by other things too so you have to be careful how you interpret it. EVP stands for electronic voice phenomena. That's when you get voices or other unexplainable sounds on tape, stuff you didn't hear at the time."

The principal's eyebrows went up. "Do you get these findings often?"

Bo shook his head. "No. We do frequently pick up sounds on the recorder that we are able to explain away later, or things that we actually heard at the time of recording, but it's not usual to get true EVPs."

"And we should be able to determine which EMF spikes are caused by electrical equipment and stuff, now that we know where the fuse boxes and things are," Sam added.

"Hm. I see." Mr. Innes gave them a tight smile. "Well. Madam, gentlemen, I will be in my office. Please take as much time as you need."

"Oh, hey, wait a sec." David dug through his backpack and pulled out an extra walkie-talkie. He turned it on and handed it to Mr. Innes. "Take this. That way, we can call you if for some reason we're trapped in the tunnels."

The principal frowned as he took the radio. "Surely you don't expect such a thing to happen."

"Nope, but it pays to be careful." Hefting his backpack, David swung open the front door and grinned over his shoulder at the rest of them. "Well? What are y'all waiting for, an engraved invitation?"

Hoisting his own pack onto his shoulder, Sam followed the others inside. Mr. Innes parted ways with them at his office, and the BCPI group continued down the hall to the tunnel entrance.

Bo stopped as they reached the little alcove. "Okay, everyone, check your radios. We're on channel two."

Sam flipped his on and glanced at the display. He had the correct channel and a full battery bar. "I'm good."

"Me too," David answered. Andre, Dean and Cecile echoed him.

"All right." Bo turned to look at Sam. "Do we have extra batteries?"

Sam nodded. "I've got several in my bag."

"So do I," Andre said, peering into his leather satchel.

"Good." Drawing a deep breath, Bo grinned. "Okay, let's get busy."

Getting a firm grip on the handle, David hauled the heavy door open. It was surprisingly quiet, swinging against the wall with only a slight squeal. *The students must keep the hinges oiled, so no one can hear them sneaking in here.* The thought made Sam chuckle.

Bo led the way down the steps, the rest of the team trooping single file behind him. Sam brought up the rear, with Dean right in front of him. It disturbed Sam immensely that he couldn't seem to stop staring at the strip of creamy skin showing between the man's low-slung jeans and snug sweater.

It's just physical, he told himself. *It doesn't mean anything, except you desperately need a good fuck.*

The tension in Sam's shoulders relaxed somewhat when they reached the bottom of the steps and Dean moved away to talk to David. Sam didn't like the attraction he felt for the newest member of the BCPI team. Even though he had no intention of acting on it, his body's reaction still seemed like a betrayal of his feelings for Bo.

Setting his bag on the floor, Sam crouched down and rifled through it. "Bo, what do you want me to do?"

"I'd like you to handle notes and the audio recorder, if you don't mind." Bo strolled over and stood close enough to make Sam's pulse speed up. "That way you'll be better able to concentrate on feeling the place out psychically speaking."

Sam rose slowly to his feet, slinging his bag over his shoulder again. "You want me to see if I feel what I felt in Oleander House, don't you?"

"Yes." Bo held Sam's gaze, his expression full of concern. "Can you?"

Savagely suppressing the part of him that wanted to scream *no*, Sam nodded. "Sure, no problem."

"I'll take the video," Cecile said.

With one last half-worried, half-grateful glance at Sam, Bo turned to Cecile. "You don't have to do video all the time, you know. You've become very proficient with the EMF detector."

"I know. But I was thinking I could let my psychic senses guide how I take video. Like if I get a sudden sense of presence from a certain spot, I can quickly turn the camera to that area. Seconds count when we're talking about paranormal phenomena, right?"

"Absolutely." Grinning, Bo squeezed Cecile's shoulder. "This is one reason I was so glad you decided to accept my offer to work with BCPI permanently. You come up with some fantastic ideas."

Cecile's cheeks went pink. "Thanks. I had lots of good reasons to accept." She smiled fondly at David's back, where he stood talking animatedly with Dean and Andre.

As if he felt her watching him, David turned around and winked at her. "So, do we have a time limit here or what?"

"No, take whatever time you feel is necessary." Bo switched on the EMF detector and thermometer, holding one in each hand. "Cecile, go on and start the video."

Sam heard the soft chime of the camera switching on. Glancing at his watch, he wrote the date and time at the top of a clean notebook page. He turned on the audio recorder and hung it on his belt.

"Saturday, November twentieth, two thousand and four, ten-forty-five a.m.," Cecile said, for the benefit of the recordings. "South Bay High School underground tunnel, South leg."

"EMF's steady at three. Temp, eighty-four degrees." Bo glanced over at Andre, who was doing baseline measurements of his own. "What've you got?"

"Same," Andre answered without looking away from his instruments.

"Are you feeling anything here?" Cecile asked.

"No." Andre frowned and looked up. "Wait, yes. Kind of. I don't know, it's very strange. Just this vague sense of...wrongness, for lack of a better word."

Cecile was silent, and Sam knew that she was stretching out her own psychic senses, seeing if she could pick up what Andre had. Closing his eyes, Sam did the same. And after a groping moment, he felt it. A jarring sense of something out of place. Similar to what he'd felt in Oleander House, but not exactly the same.

"It's more focused, isn't it?" Cecile whispered. "At Oleander House, you got that weird feeling everywhere. I didn't sense this upstairs. Only here. And it's very faint."

"I agree." Forcing his eyes open, Sam jotted down Cecile's impressions and his own. A few feet away, Dean scribbled on the extra notepad Sam had given him, presumably writing down what Andre had said. "Let's try to see if we can pinpoint where this unsettled energy is coming from, okay?"

"Yeah, good idea." Andre gave him a worried look. "I didn't feel that intelligence like we felt at Oleander House. Did you?"

"No, not really." Sam figured it wasn't really a lie. He didn't feel that sinister presence here, though he sensed something he couldn't quite put his finger on. An elusive and uncomfortably familiar vibration in the back of his skull, subsiding as soon as he tried to focus on it.

Don't jump to conclusions, he reminded himself. *Observe, record, and analyze later.*

Easier said than done.

Bo started moving slowly down the hallway, sweeping the EMF detector back and forth in a smooth, steady motion as he went. Cecile followed with the camera. Pushing his uneasiness aside and concentrating on keeping his senses open, Sam trailed after them.

It took about forty minutes to cover every inch of the South tunnel between the stairs and the other end. The EMF reading remained steady at a mildly elevated level, but the temperature rose as they went. By the time they reached the cracked and stained stone wall at the far end, Bo's thermometer read ninety-two degrees.

"I wondered if I'd imagined it getting hotter before as we got near the end of the tunnel," Sam said as he jotted down the unbelievable reading. "Guess not."

Bo frowned at the irregular rectangle of rough brick on the wall to his left. "Do either of you remember Mr. Innes saying anything about any electrical equipment in this blocked-up side tunnel?"

Cecile glanced at Sam, who shrugged and shook his head. "No," she answered. "Why, what are you getting?"

"The EMF goes up a bit right next to the bricks." Holding the detector with the display outward so they could see it, Bo swung the instrument away from the bricked-up entrance, then back again. The reading went from three-point-two to five. "See?"

Sam laid a palm against the bricks. They felt warm and clammy, almost like flesh. He pulled his hand away, fighting the urge to shudder. "If it's electrical, the source is either a little ways off or pretty weak."

"Let's ask Mr. Innes for a blueprint of the school's electrical system," Cecile suggested. "And a list of any electrical equipment on, what, the first floor of this building?"

Bo nodded. "That'll be good. We shouldn't be picking up anything on the second floor."

"We need to find out more about these side tunnels, too," Sam added. "They weren't on the map he sent me, just this main tunnel was."

"Right." Bo's sharp gaze flicked between Sam and Cecile. "Do either of you feel anything different here?"

Drawing a deep breath, Sam let his mind float the way Cecile had taught him, detaching himself from the physical world just enough to let himself sense what lay beyond. What he felt was a palpable wave of menace that knocked the wind from him.

"Oh, shit," Cecile gasped. "Sam, did you feel that?"

Sam nodded, leaning against the wall and waiting for the world to right itself. "Yeah. Fuck."

Moving closer, Bo brushed a hand down Sam's arm. Sparks crackled in the wake of his fingers, drawing Sam back to solid reality. He was grateful that Bo's touch grounded him this time instead of throwing his mind and body into turmoil like it usually did.

"Are you all right?" Bo's question was directed at them both, Sam knew, but those deep brown eyes were only for him. Slipping a hand into Bo's, Sam gave his fingers a quick squeeze that said everything he couldn't voice right then. Bo smiled, looking relieved.

"We're okay. Just kind of shaken up." Cecile's voice quavered a little.

"What was it?" Bo asked, resting his back against the wall next to Sam. His position effectively hid the fact that his hand still clutched Sam's.

Sam glanced at Cecile. She looked as puzzled as he felt. "I don't know," he answered. "It had the same sort of underlying feel as what I sensed in Oleander House, but it was different somehow. I can't really explain it."

Bo stared into space, teeth worrying his bottom lip. His thumb rubbed tiny circles on the back of Sam's hand. It took every ounce of control Sam had to resist the urge to pull Bo into his arms and kiss him. He settled for sliding infinitesimally closer to Bo, until only a breath separated them.

"Is there anything else we need to do right now, Bo?" Cecile peered at them with wide, nervous eyes. "I feel very uncomfortable here. I'd like to get outside for a while."

Shooting Sam a brief, sidelong glance, Bo let go of Sam's hand and pushed away from the wall. "That's a good idea. Let's meet up with the rest of the group, then we'll head back upstairs and work out a plan for the rest of the day."

"We're not leaving?" Cecile's expression didn't change, but Sam heard the plaintive note in her voice. He understood perfectly.

"It's kind of freaking me out, too," Sam said. "But I guess we need to set up cameras, which means we'll have to stay. Right?"

"I suppose we could leave the equipment here," Bo mused, sounding apologetic, "but I'd rather not. We can't afford to replace any of it right now, and I feel like we're too vulnerable to theft if we leave the cameras unguarded down here."

"Yes, that makes sense." Cecile sighed. "Well, if I need to stay down here, I will. Just don't make me stay alone."

Sam stepped forward and kissed the top of Cecile's head. "Don't worry. You'll have me for company, at least."

Cecile laughed and hugged him. "Thanks, Sam."

"Why is it," David called from somewhere behind them, "that everyone's always hitting on my girl? Even the gay guy, for Christ's sake."

"It's a secret woman-power," Cecile answered dryly. "What are you guys doing here? Shouldn't you be investigating the North leg of the tunnel?"

"Yeah, well, we're done." David glanced at Andre, who looked tense and shaken. "We didn't find anything as far as EMF or seeing anything, but Andre had one of his feelings. Y'all weren't back at the stairs yet, so we figured we'd come find you."

Cecile trembled against Sam's side, her arm tightening around his waist. "Sam and I felt something too. What did you experience, Andre?"

The big man pressed his lips together for a moment before answering. He seemed almost angry. "It was kind of like Oleander House, but not as strong. Just a feeling of some sort of intelligence nearby."

Sam and Cecile glanced at each other. "That's exactly what Cecile and I felt. Only I had to concentrate and put effort into picking it up this time, rather than it just hitting me out of the blue."

"Like it was more focused this time. More controlled." Andre's brown eyes burned with the light of discovery. "Y'all, we need to go more in-depth here. Set up cameras, do some concentrated research. And frankly, I'd like to open up these side tunnels and check 'em out. What I felt seems to have its origin in there."

"I agree." Bo twirled the end of his braid, his expression thoughtful. "I have no idea if we'll be allowed to open the side tunnels, but we can try. I'll speak with Mr. Innes while y'all set up the cameras."

"Find out if he's got the names of students we can talk to," Sam added. "We need to find out what, if anything, the students have seen down here."

"Are we staying here in the tunnels for the rest of the day?" Dean asked. The idea didn't seem to make him nervous. Probably because he'd been here before, Sam figured.

"No," Bo said after a moment's thought. "I think we need to film the tunnels without our presence disturbing things. We'll take shifts guarding the door."

"I'll go get us all some lunch," David offered.

Andre chuckled. "That's smooth, man."

David widened his eyes in an utterly ineffective attempt at looking innocent. "What're you talking about?"

"Getting out of first shift guard duty." Letting go of Sam, Cecile slipped her arms around her boyfriend's neck and kissed him. "Don't worry, dear, you'll get your turn."

"I'll take the first shift," Sam volunteered. "I don't mind."

Dean flashed a flirtatious grin. "Want some company?"

Sam's mouth went dry. He was saved from having to answer by Bo.

"I'll take the first shift with Sam. I have some things I need to discuss with him anyway." Bo's voice was firm. "Okay, here's the plan. We'll go get the equipment, and I'll talk to Mr. Innes while y'all set everything up. David and whoever wants to go help him can grab lunch and we'll all eat, then Sam and I will pull guard duty for a while. Say we run the cameras until midnight, that'll be about twelve hours, and there's six of us, so that's four hour shifts. So Sam and I will stay until four, then Cecile and Andre until eight, then David and Dean until midnight. Sound good?"

Everyone nodded, though no one looked particularly enthusiastic.

"Great," Bo said. "Anyone who's not on guard duty is free to leave or stay, whatever you want to do. We'll all keep our cell phones and radios on, just in case."

"Gotcha." David kissed Cecile's forehead, then drew away and put his video camera in his bag. "Let's get out of here, it's fucking hot."

"You got that right." Switching off his EMF detector and thermometer, Andre started down the hall toward the steps.

The rest of the group followed. Dean, Cecile and David had their heads together, all talking at once. Bo lagged behind, and Sam found himself slowing his own pace to match.

"I hope you don't mind me taking watch with you," Bo murmured. "I really do want to talk to you."

"Of course I don't mind." Sam glanced at Bo, who was looking straight ahead as they walked. "Why do I get the feeling it's not about work?"

"Because you know me so well it's scary."

They traveled the remainder of the tunnel and up the stairs in silence. As their coworkers emerged into the relative brightness of the first floor hallway, Bo grabbed Sam's wrist, holding him back. Sam started to ask what was wrong, but his words were cut off by Bo's lips on his.

The kiss went deep, Bo's arms clutching Sam close, one leg bending to slide their thighs together. Surprised, Sam could do nothing but answer Bo's passion with his own. Not that there was anything else he wanted to do. As always, Bo's kiss brought Sam's world to a screeching halt. Nothing existed at that moment but Bo's mouth hot and hungry against his, their bodies wound together.

It felt like ages before they finally pulled apart, though Sam knew it couldn't have been more than a few seconds. He could still hear the rest of the team talking, their footsteps echoing in the hall. "What was that for?" Sam whispered, leaning his forehead against Bo's. "Not that I'm complaining, of course."

The corners of Bo's mouth turned up in a sweet, sexy little smile. "Just because I felt like it. Sometimes I want you so much I can't stand it."

Sam's throat went tight. He wished it meant more than lust, but he wouldn't count on it. Couldn't. Pressing a light kiss to Bo's lips, Sam forced himself to let go. "We should catch up. They'll wonder what happened to us."

"I don't—" Bo broke off, biting his lip. He whirled around and strode out into the hall before Sam could utter a word.

Sam trailed behind, his mind in turmoil. For one white-hot moment, he'd been sure Bo was going to say "I don't care." The feverish desperation in those dark eyes spoke volumes.

But he didn't say it, Sam thought bitterly. *He never will. He'll never stop being afraid.*

The thought was too depressing. Angry at himself for being so morose—and for letting himself fall foolishly in love—Sam shoved his fears and doubts to the back of his mind and tried to concentrate on the job at hand.

Chapter Four

It didn't take long to run into the first snag. The tunnel's single electrical outlet refused to work properly, and the closest outlet to the door was almost one hundred feet down the first floor hallway. After a brief discussion, Andre, David and Dean were sent out to buy more extension cords and pick up lunch.

The group ate on the run, grabbing bites of subs and gulps of soda as they worked to get the equipment set up. Sam and Bo remained upstairs, sitting in two borrowed chairs in front of the folding table they'd placed just outside the tunnel door. They watched the pictures from the seven cameras come up one by one on the powerful laptop Bo had finally bought the previous month. The display was crystal clear, every crack in the stone visible.

"Okay, that's the last one," David's voice crackled over the radio. "How's it looking?"

"Perfect." Sam glanced at Bo. "What do you think, lights or night vision?"

Bo pursed his lips. "Hm. Night vision, I guess."

"Use the night vision, David," Sam repeated into the radio.

"'Kay. Andre, Dean, you got that?"

"Got it," Andre answered.

"Yep," Dean echoed. "Done."

Rising to his feet, Bo thumbed his radio on. "Okay, turn the lights off, let's make sure we're getting good pictures with the night vision."

Sam heard muffled voices, then the camera displays went dark. In the blackness, the stairs and tunnel walls glowed an eerie green.

"That's good," Bo said. "Come on up."

The gleam of flashlights showed on the computer screen, followed by the three men climbing the stairs.

"Damn, it's like a fucking sauna down there," David complained, mopping the sweat from his forehead as he emerged into the hall. "Feels good up here."

"It sure does." Lifting his sweater up to his armpits, Dean fanned his belly. "I think next time we come here, I'll wear a T-shirt."

Sam tried not to look, but he couldn't help it. Dean's pale skin shone with sweat, putting sleek muscles and hipbones in sharp relief. His cheeks were flushed red, his hair clinging in damp tendrils to his neck and forehead. For once, he didn't seem to be purposefully flirting. He pulled his sweater back down without a hint of his sly, seductive smile. Sam licked his lips, fiercely turned on by the unconscious sexiness Dean exuded when he wasn't even trying.

"There's water bottles in the bag there." Andre gestured toward the plastic bag sitting beside the wall. "Figured we might need them, with the heat down there."

Dean lunged for the bag, grabbed three water bottles and tossed Andre and David each one. Twisting the cap off the third bottle, he downed half of it in one breath. "Oh God," he gasped. "I needed that. Thanks, Andre."

"No problem." Andre took a long swallow of his own water. "All right, I'm off for a while. Who wants a ride home?"

"Me," Cecile said, coming down the hall from the ladies' room. She'd offered to stay upstairs and talk with Mr. Innes about opening the side tunnels since Bo's help had been needed with the equipment set-up. "I have some errands to run before Andre and I have guard duty. Are we leaving the cameras up until one a.m. since we got started late?"

"Yes, I guess we should." Bo glanced at his watch. "Well, Sam? You ready to get started?"

The fevered look in Bo's eyes went straight to Sam's crotch. He didn't think Bo was talking about guarding the equipment, or monitoring the cameras.

"Um, yeah." To Sam's relief, his voice sounded normal.

"Okay, we're off then." Andre jerked his head toward the front entrance of the school. "Come on, I have things to do."

Sam watched as Andre stalked off without a backward glance. His heart ached for his friend. It couldn't have been easy for Andre to experience the sort of sensations he'd had in Oleander House, bringing back memories of that horrible night. If he closed his eyes, Sam could still see Amy's lifeless body. How much worse must it be for Andre, who'd been her lover and partner for years?

"Is he all right?" Dean asked, gray-green eyes full of concern as he watched Andre walk out the door, David and Cecile following arm in arm in his wake.

"He will be." Bo sighed. "I'll tell you about it sometime soon. Right now, it's enough to know he's going through a tough time. He closes up sometimes. Don't take it personally."

"Okay, sure. See y'all later." With a quick wave, Dean trotted after the rest of the group.

Sam glanced around the suddenly quiet hallway. Mr. Innes had left while they were setting up the cameras, saying he would be back in a few hours. The knowledge that he and Bo were alone in the building hit Sam like a hammer.

Sam cleared his throat. "Okay. So. What did you want to talk about?"

For a moment, Bo said nothing. Then, just as his silence started to make Sam nervous, he took Sam's hand and pulled him into the shadows under the stairs.

"Bo, what—"

Bo's hand against his lips cut him off. "Shhh. Don't say anything. Just touch me."

"But—"

"But nothing." Pressing close, Bo rolled his hips against Sam's. The unmistakable hardness in Bo's jeans sent Sam's head spinning. "I need you to touch me, right now." Bo's voice was a rough whisper, his lips warm and silky on the skin of Sam's neck. "Please. There's no one here to see. Please."

Sam wanted to protest, if for no other reason than Bo's resolute refusal to see him openly. Then Bo's mouth found his, Bo's hand slipped between his legs, and all thought melted in a scorching wave of desire.

Whimpering into the kiss, Sam cupped Bo's head in one hand and fumbled Bo's jeans open with the other. Bo shuddered against him when he wrapped his fingers around Bo's erection and squeezed.

"Oh God," Bo whispered, his breath hot on Sam's lips. "Yes."

"Yeah." Sam licked Bo's ear. "Bo…"

Even as Sam spoke, Bo's fingers yanked open the button on his jeans and tugged down his zipper. Sam's legs turned to rubber at the feel of Bo's hand on his cock, the shy yet eager touch he'd become addicted to over the past few weeks. Letting the last of his reservations fall away, Sam closed his eyes and gave himself up to his need.

The uncomfortable angle soon had Sam's wrist cramping, but he couldn't bring himself to care. Not when Bo pushed rough moans into his mouth every time his thumb pressed into Bo's slit. Bo's fingers twisted around Sam's shaft, sending tingling tendrils of pleasure snaking down his thighs. The kiss turned hungry and harsh, both men groaning as they fucked each other's hands.

"God, Sam," Bo panted, and bit Sam's lower lip. "Close."

Sam nodded, stroking Bo's prick faster. "Love how you touch me."

Bo went still, his cock pulsing in Sam's hand. When he spoke, his voice was barely audible. "Sam, oh my God..."

"Come on," Sam growled, pulling back enough to see Bo's face. "Let me feel it."

Bo stared, eyes wide and unguarded as he came all over Sam's hand, his body shaking. Sam thought he'd never in his life seen anything so sexy. It was enough to push him right over the edge. His orgasm followed hot on the heels of Bo's, his semen coating hands and clothes already sticky with Bo's release. Something about the thought of their seed mingling made him ache inside.

"Oh. Wow." Bo leaned against Sam's chest, his breath coming in rapid gulps as if he'd been running. "Jesus, I can't believe what you do to me."

Keeping his fingers coiled loosely around Bo's softening cock, Sam stroked his free hand down the length of Bo's braid. "Have you talked to Janine yet?" He nuzzled Bo's flushed cheek, pressing a soft kiss to his temple.

Bo tensed. Sam held on, soothing Bo with tender touches and tiny, sweet kisses, letting him know there was no anger or judgment in the question, just the honest need to know.

"Haven't had time yet," Bo told him, relaxing a little. "I asked her to meet me for lunch tomorrow. I'm going to tell her then."

"Good." Sam drew back to meet Bo's worried and slightly defensive gaze. He touched Bo's cheek. "It's the right thing to do, you know. Even if things don't work out with us, you have to do this for yourself."

"What do you mean, if things don't work out?" Bo demanded, sounding tense.

"I'm just saying," Sam answered, choosing his words carefully, "that even if we weren't together, you'll never be happy as long as you're living a lie. And I want you to be happy, more than anything else."

He hadn't intended to imply that they were breaking up. He'd only meant to let Bo know, as gently as possible, that he realized the possibility existed.

Bo evidently didn't take it that way. Shoving Sam away, he zipped his pants and started pacing like a caged panther. "Don't you tell me you don't want to see me anymore. Don't you *dare,* not after you fucking *seduced* me and changed my whole life!"

"That's not what I'm saying at all. I don't want to stop seeing you." Tucking his softened prick away, Sam fastened his jeans. Clumps of congealing spunk smeared across the fabric. He thought idly that he should clean up, but it didn't seem very important just then. "But you're not ready to come out yet. Not even to our friends. I'd be stupid if I didn't see what that might mean for us."

Bo stopped pacing in mid-step, whirled and glared at Sam. "Oh, I see. It's not good enough for you that I'm divorcing my wife, breaking up my family? It's not good enough that I've broken every professional rule there is by having sex with you at the office? If we can't skip down the goddamn street hand in hand, then we can't be together at all? Is that it?"

Something inside Sam snapped. Before he could stop himself, all the venom he'd bottled up for months came flooding out.

"Most people in their thirties and forties don't have to sneak around like kids to see each other," he shot back. "I think I deserve to be more than someone's nasty little secret. And you know as well as I do that there hasn't been any sex. We've never even seen each other naked. Is that your idea of an adult relationship? Because it sure as hell isn't mine."

The second the words were out, Sam wished he could take them back. The brief satisfaction of telling Bo exactly how he felt would never be worth the hurt and shame and despair in Bo's eyes at that moment.

Taking a tentative step forward, Sam reached for Bo, wanting more than anything to make it better. "Bo, I'm sorry."

Bo danced out of reach, shaking his head. Turning without a word, he fled down the hall. Sam watched him disappear into the men's room. He ached to follow, to hold Bo and kiss him and touch him until those vicious words were forgotten. But he knew neither of them could possibly forget what he'd said. It would hang between them like a lead curtain until the problem was resolved. Until either Bo decided to take the plunge and out himself, or he and Sam broke up for good.

Sam knew which outcome was most likely, and it tore him up inside.

Fifteen minutes later, Bo emerged from the bathroom, his shirt and jeans splotched with water. His face was blank, lips pressed together. He wouldn't look at Sam, but Sam saw the redness rimming Bo's swollen eyes. Sam wondered if Bo would ever forgive him. He was pretty sure he'd never forgive himself.

Sighing inwardly, Sam shuffled down the hall to the restroom to get himself cleaned up. If he did his own crying and cursing and wishing things were different, he figured it was his own business. Bo didn't need to know.

♋

Sam ran, the cold air burning his lungs, sweat trickling down his back as his feet pounded the pavement. Bienville Square slipped slowly past on his right. The gnarled old oaks loomed half-seen through the early morning fog, bare branches dark and sinister. Sam imagined they were reaching for him, grasping vainly at his clothes as he passed.

Normally, he wouldn't be out this early on a Sunday. He preferred to laze around his little apartment on his mornings off, curled in the chair in front of the window, sipping his coffee and watching the city come alive. Today, however, he'd woken before dawn after a few hours of restless sleep, with a smothering sense of being caged. Unwilling to examine the cause of it too closely, he'd pulled on sweats, gloves and a knit cap, and gone for a run.

He'd set out in the gray stillness before the sun rose. An hour had passed, the fog beginning to glow as golden light filtered through the trees, and he still hadn't run far enough to escape the previous day.

Bo had spent the afternoon acting as if nothing had happened between them. If it hadn't been for the tension in Bo's shoulders and his carefully neutral expression, Sam would've doubted his own memories. They'd parted with a terse goodbye in the late afternoon, and Sam hadn't seen or spoken to Bo since.

Vaulting a tree root protruding from a crack in the sidewalk, Sam veered down the narrow path into the midst of Bienville Square. The usually bustling little park was empty and quiet. The melancholy feel of it fit Sam's mood.

As he rounded a corner in the path, Sam saw a figure sitting on a bench on the edge of the park. The person was bending forward, elbows on knees, head resting in his hands. Sam slowed to a jog, wondering what had brought this solitary wanderer here. Some personal sorrow, no doubt. It seemed to be the morning for it, Sam thought with a wry smile.

The figure drew clearer as Sam got closer, the shrouding fog thinning, but Sam didn't recognize him until he lifted his head and stared straight into Sam's eyes.

"Hey, Sam," Andre called as Sam came to a halt next to the bench. "Thought I'd be alone out here."

"Yeah, me too." Sam plopped onto the bench, panting and wiping the sweat from his forehead. "You okay?"

"No."

"The school was hard, huh?" Sam guessed, watching Andre's unrevealing profile. "Too much like Oleander House."

Andre's silence was answer enough. Sam brushed his fingers over his friend's hand. "You want to talk about it?"

"No."

Andre's voice was flat and emotionless, but Sam wasn't fooled. He'd learned a lot about Andre in the past few months, and he could see how badly the man was hurting. He wished, not for the first time, that he could go backward in time and bring Amy back. Sometimes, he felt he'd give his soul to have Amy alive again, smiling and laughing in Andre's arms.

Not knowing what to say, Sam settled against the bench, offering Andre his silent support. They sat there for another half hour, neither speaking, just watching the day brighten and burn away the fog. When the first early riser appeared on the paths, jogging along with a Rottweiler on a leash loping beside her, Andre rose to his feet.

"Thanks," he whispered. Taking Sam's hand, he squeezed it hard, then walked away without looking back.

Somehow, the fact that his presence had helped Andre melted away some of Sam's own sadness. Nodding to an elderly couple who were strolling hand-in-hand along the sidewalk, Sam turned and began the long run home.

♋

Back at his apartment, Sam started the coffee brewing, then went to take a shower. He couldn't help imagining Bo there with him, wet and naked. Holding him, kissing him, running soapy hands over his bare skin. The mental image of Bo's bright, loving smile made Sam's chest constrict. He scrubbed himself until his skin was red, trying to wash away the feel of Bo's arms around him.

He spent the next couple of hours prowling his apartment, trying to find something to occupy his mind. To make him forget what he'd said the previous day, and the hurt in Bo's eyes. Nothing worked. By ten, he'd had enough. Shrugging on his jacket and shoving his wallet and keys in the pocket, he headed out the door.

The day had turned fine and breezy, the wind chilly enough to sting but not unbearably cold. A perfect day for wandering the shaded sidewalks, taking in the sights and sounds of the lovely old city. Sam strolled along through the growing crowd, face turned up to catch the afternoon sunshine. Just being outside eased some of the tightness inside him.

He had no particular destination in mind, but it didn't surprise him when he found himself standing in front of the Bay City Paranormal office. Walking up onto the front porch, he peered in through the bent spot in the window blind. The office was dark, which did surprise him a little. One or more of the BCPI team would frequently show up on Sundays, to get ahead of the week's work.

"Guess you didn't really want to be alone after all," he muttered as he unlocked the door and let himself inside. "And didn't that work out well?"

Just like everything else, he thought morosely, shutting the door behind him.

He hung up his jacket and looked around. The place seemed small and a little sad with no one in it. Sighing, Sam decided to go to the back room and dig out the video from South Bay High. Might as well get started on it.

He'd just booted up the laptop and started the video from camera one when he heard the front door open. Taking off his headphones and leaning back in his chair, he craned to see through the door into the office lobby. "Hello? Who's there?"

"Sam, is that you?" Andre came into view as he rounded Cecile's desk, a hulking silhouette against the brightness of the front window. "You following me?"

Sam grinned at the teasing tone in Andre's voice. The big man must be feeling less down now, he realized with relief. "I got here first. So what're you doing here?"

Grabbing a chair, Andre rolled it closer and sat down. "Got bored. Figured I'd come in and watch some of the video from the school. You?"

"Same. Obviously." Sam gestured to the computer screen, where he'd paused the video. "I just got started on camera one, the one from the north end of the tunnel. Which one you want?"

"Guess I'll take the south end. Might be a good thing to compare the two ends to each other, see if anything matches up."

"Great idea." Reaching for the box of cables and headphones, Sam snatched a pair of headphones and handed them to Andre. "Here. You want to watch the digital file or the tape?"

"Digital." Rolling over to the desktop computer, Andre booted it up. "None of the files are copied to the other computers yet, are they?"

"Not unless someone else came in at a truly ungodly hour and took care of it."

Andre's laughter was cut short by a huge yawn. Sam knew how he felt. They'd all met back at the school at one a.m. to break down the equipment and take it back to the office. Between that, his restless thoughts and waking up before dawn, Sam doubted he'd gotten three whole hours of sleep. Andre looked like he hadn't gotten any more than that himself.

"Nope," Andre said, scrolling through the list of files on his computer. "They haven't been copied. Send me the camera seven file."

"Okay." With a few clicks, Sam sent a copy of the video to Andre's computer over the wireless network. "You think we should leave it until tomorrow? I'm pretty sure David hasn't shown Dean any of this equipment yet."

Andre shot him an amused look. "Dean's got a degree in computer science. I think he can figure it out."

Heat crept into Sam's cheeks. He turned back to his computer screen, put his headphones on and started the video again, mortified that his attraction to Dean was so obvious. If they knew how Dean affected him, David and Cecile and possibly even Andre were sure to try to get them together.

Would that be so bad? the troublemaker in his head whispered. *Dean's hot, and he wants you.*

But I can't, Sam argued silently, frowning at the black-and-green picture on his monitor. *I love Bo.*

Of course you do. But what rule is there that says you can't want anyone else? Bo will never feel about you the way you do for him. Why torture yourself?

Sam shook his head, forcing himself to concentrate on the video. He refused to listen to the seductive little voice in his head, telling him to give in to his physical needs and damn the consequences. He'd already hurt Bo enough. If they stood any chance at all as a couple, the one thing Sam absolutely couldn't do was let his libido have its way.

"What'd you say?"

Startled, Sam glanced over at Andre, who'd pulled his headphones off and was looking curiously at him. His friend's face wore a puzzled frown, and Sam abruptly realized that he'd been muttering out loud. "Nothing. Sorry, just talking to myself."

Andre cocked a skeptical eyebrow at him, but didn't say anything. He slid his headphones back into place and restarted his video. Letting out a sigh of relief, Sam returned his attention to his computer.

For the next couple of hours, Sam and Andre sat silently watching the video they'd shot the day before. It was tedious work. The picture never changed. If it weren't for the time display ticking the seconds away in the bottom right corner, Sam would've thought it was a photo rather than video. The absolute stillness gave him an uncomfortable feeling in the pit of his belly.

"Weird, isn't it?" Andre asked, echoing Sam's thoughts.

Sam nodded. "Yeah. Not even a spider anywhere. Nothing. It's not normal."

"Only one other place I ever saw anything like that."

Sam swallowed. "I don't want to go through that again."

Grief filled Andre's eyes, and Sam mentally kicked himself. *As if what Andre went through wasn't ten times worse. As if it wasn't all your fault anyway.*

Andre gave him a tiny smile. "Stop it."

"I'm sorry," Sam blurted out. "I didn't mean to bring it all back. I shouldn't have said that."

Shaking his head, Andre removed his headphones, shut off his video and reached over to stop Sam's as well. He turned in his chair and pulled Sam's headphones off.

"I don't need you to remind me," he said softly. "I think about Amy every single day. I see her dying every time I go to sleep."

"I'm sorry," Sam repeated, wishing he could do more than apologize. "I'd go back and change that whole fucking week if I could."

"I know. But you can't, and neither can I." Giving Sam's shoulder a shake, Andre pinned him with an intense stare. "You have to stop blaming yourself, Sam. What happened wasn't your fault."

To his horror, tears stung Sam's eyelids. He blinked rapidly a few times, and managed to keep any from falling. "Wasn't it? I was the conduit. The gateway only opened because of me."

"Yes, you were the conduit, but you didn't have any control over it." Taking his hand off Sam's shoulder, Andre leaned back in his chair. "I wanted to blame you at first. I tried to. But there was nothing you could've done to prevent what happened. It just took me a little while to see that. I expect it might take you longer, but you have to see it eventually. You're too much of a scientist not to."

Though he'd known intellectually that Andre didn't hold him at fault for Amy's death, this was the first time Sam had heard Andre say it. The first time, in fact, that he and Andre had talked about that night at all. Knowing Andre not only didn't blame him, but still respected him professionally, lifted a huge weight from Sam's shoulders.

"Thank you," he said. "You don't know how much that means to me."

Andre nodded. Sliding his headphones on again, he swiveled around to face his computer and started the video. Sam followed his lead, feeling lighter than he'd felt in a long time.

♋

The next few hours passed more quickly for Sam than the previous ones had. Keeping his mind focused on watching the video effectively kept him from thinking of Bo, and what the next day might hold. Even the endless tapes from Oleander House had been exciting compared to the video from the school. Glancing at the window, Sam stifled a yawn. The last rays of the setting sun poured through the cracks in the closed blinds, striping the darkened office with golden red.

He almost missed the change when it came. A faint vibration, blurring the picture for a moment before clearing again. Leaning closer, Sam rubbed his eyes, wondering if he'd imagined it. The picture shook again, more noticeably this time, accompanied by a barely audible rasping sound that seemed to come from behind the bricked-over portion of tunnel wall. Sam let out a surprised gasp.

"Hey, Andre." Reaching over without looking away from the screen, Sam nudged Andre's arm. "Andre, look."

Andre glanced at Sam. "What?"

"The video moved."

"Moved? What do you mean?"

"I mean it moved. It vibrated, like..." Sam stopped, frowning. "I don't know. Like an earthquake almost, only not nearly so strong. And there was a noise."

Andre made a soft, shocked sound. "Like this?"

Pausing his video and taking his headphones off, Sam leaned over just in time to see the picture on Andre's screen tremble the same way Sam's had a moment before. Sam's stomach lurched when Andre unplugged the headphones and he heard the same odd, rusty sound as he'd heard on his own video. "Oh, shit."

"What time do you have on yours?" Andre asked, stopping his video.

Sam looked. "Seventeen-thirty-four. What about yours?"

"Seventeen-thirty-four." Andre set his headphones on the desk and stared at Sam. "What the hell, Sam?"

"I don't know." Wrapping his arms around himself, Sam glanced from one computer screen to the other. "Okay, let's look at this logically. Is there any possibility that it really was an earthquake?"

Andre shook his head. "No idea. I'll look into it."

"You and Cecile were there guarding the door when that happened, did either of you feel anything?"

"No, I don't—" Andre's eyes went wide. "Wait. We did. We both had kind of a strange sensation not long after we got there."

"When? Was it the same time as what's on the tape?"

"Could be. Hang on, I'll look it up." Jumping to his feet, Andre hurried across the room and snatched a notebook off the shelf. He hooked a finger behind one of the yellow tabs, opened the book and scanned the page. "Yeah. Seventeen-thirty-four exactly."

A chill raced up Sam's spine. He and Andre stared at each other.

"It might not mean anything," Andre said eventually, drumming his fingers on the top of the bookshelf.

"That's true."

"Cecile's told me lots of times that she picks up all kinds of different psychic energy, and she figures I do too."

Sam nodded. "Yeah, same here."

"A place as old as that school, who knows what all's floating around there?"

"Absolutely."

"It could've been some form of residual haunting."

"It could've been, yeah."

"Only it wasn't." Shoulders sagging, Andre shuffled over and dropped into his chair. "Fuck, Sam. It was too much like Oleander House not to be related. I've been trying ever since yesterday to convince myself that it wasn't, but it was."

Sam was silent for a moment, gathering his thoughts. "What about Cecile? What does she think?"

"She tried to tell me it was too similar to what we felt before to ignore it." Andre sighed and rubbed a hand across his forehead. "I didn't want to listen. But she's right. Damn."

A sudden thought struck Sam. "Hey, why didn't either of you mention this last night, when we were taking down the cameras?"

Dropping his gaze to the floor, Andre twisted his fingers together. "I asked her not to say anything. I wanted some time to think about it first."

Sam didn't need to ask why. Rolling his chair closer, he laid a comforting hand on Andre's knee. "Gonna tell the others tomorrow?"

"Yeah." Andre looked up, his troubled gaze locking with Sam's. "If you can open a gateway, I bet you can close it. We need to figure out how."

The thought of facing another dimensional gateway and the things waiting on the other side twisted Sam's insides with fear. Not so much fear of pain or his own death, but fear of failure. Of another person dying because of him. The thought was unbearable.

"Hey." Grabbing Sam's upper arms in both big hands, Andre gave him a gentle shake. "What'd I say before, huh? Stop blaming yourself."

Sam laughed bitterly. "I'm trying, but it's not that easy."

With an irritated huff, Andre let go of Sam and crossed his arms. "I know it's hard. Lots of things are hard. There's no room for your fear right now. If we've got another one of these damn gateways, you're the key to controlling it. I know you're scared, and I know *why* you're scared. But if we're dealing with what we think we are, you're gonna have to try and use your psychokinetic powers to shut the fucking thing down. You know that, right?"

For a second, anger flared inside Sam. It died away as quickly as it appeared, leaving him feeling tired and drained. In spite of his harsh words, Andre was right, and Sam knew it.

"Yeah, I know." Sam sighed, running a hand through his hair. "I've been researching it a little in my spare time."

Andre's eyes lit with interest. "Have you found out anything?"

"Not yet. But I'll keep trying."

"Good. I'll help you however I can."

"Thanks." By way of changing the subject, Sam gestured toward the computers. "Want to watch some more of the videos?"

"Sure. I've got nothing better to do."

Without another word, Andre plugged the headphones back in and started his video. Sam sat staring blankly at the paused picture on his own monitor, wishing he had a pause button for his life. He'd give anything to avoid facing the coming week. He dreaded it all—the school and what they might find there, and especially the icy mask he knew Bo would hide behind after what had happened between them.

"Fuck," he whispered with feeling.

Shaking off his rising trepidation as best he could, Sam focused on his computer screen and hit play.

Chapter Five

On Monday morning, Sam arrived at the office early, hoping to talk to Bo before the others got there. Bo was nearly always the first person to arrive. Sam wanted to catch him alone and apologize for the things he'd said on Saturday. Bo might not listen, but Sam knew he had to try.

To Sam's surprise, the office was dark and empty when he got there. Fishing his key out of his jacket pocket, he unlocked the door and slipped inside.

"Dammit, Bo," he muttered, slamming the door shut and flipping the light switch with more force than was necessary. "Just when I really need you to be here. Fuck."

With a deep sigh, Sam booted up his computer then shuffled into the back room to start the laptop. He could transfer some of the video to his computer, he figured, and start going over it. Get some of the work out of the way, and keep his mind off Bo at the same time.

He refused to acknowledge the niggling voice in the back of his brain reminding him that he hadn't gone more than a few minutes without thinking of Bo since they'd first met.

When the door squeaked open twenty minutes later, Sam paused the video he was watching and looked up eagerly. His shoulders sagged when he saw Dean standing there.

"Morning, Sam." Dean swayed over and sat in the chair next to Sam's, bumping their knees together. "So what're you looking so glum about?"

One thing Sam definitely did not want to do was discuss his current relationship troubles with Dean. He plastered on a smile. "I'm not glum, just a little tired."

Dean arched an eyebrow at him. "Yeah, right. Your closet case boyfriend being difficult?"

It was uncomfortably close to the truth. Sam felt the heat rising in his cheeks and didn't know how to stop it. "Can we not talk about this, please?"

Raising his hands palms-out in a gesture of surrender, Dean turned his attention to the computer in front of him. "Have you started on the video from Saturday yet?"

"Yes," Sam said, relieved at the change of subject. "Andre and I watched one and seven yesterday."

Dean glanced at Sam, eyebrows raised, as he booted up the computer. "I hope showing up on Sundays isn't a requirement of the job."

"Don't worry, it's not."

"Good. I'd hate to think I had to stay home and behave on Saturday nights because I had to work Sundays."

Sam laughed. "I was just restless at home yesterday. Guess Andre felt the same way."

"Restless? Why?"

The question sounded innocent enough, but Sam knew better. He shook his head. "Dean, thank you for caring, really, but I don't want to talk about...about him."

A swift, sympathetic glance from Dean was enough to tell Sam that his voice had given away the extent of his suffering.

Groaning, he rested his elbows on the desk and buried his face in his hands. "Shit."

The chair creaked as Dean rolled closer, and Sam felt a warm hand grip his shoulder. "Sorry, Sam. You know they'll leave you eventually, but it always hurts if you felt anything for 'em at all."

Sam wanted to be irritated with Dean for thinking he and Bo had broken up, but he couldn't. Dean couldn't be expected to know the truth. Sighing, he rubbed the back of his neck where a tense ache had begun. "Yeah, it hurts. Can we drop it now?"

To his relief, Dean didn't argue. "Sure. If you want to talk, you know where to find me." Patting Sam's shoulder, he rolled back to the other desk and busied himself with the computer.

Sam went back to the video with a sense of profound relief. "So. What are you doing here so early?"

"I just wanted to play with the hardware for a little while before David and I head to the library." Dean's fingers flew over the keyboard. From the corner of his eye, Sam saw a black-and-green picture with the words "camera 3" come up on the screen. Dean laughed like a child. "Oh, man, this is great. Y'all have a terrific computer network here."

"Thanks." Sam looked away from his video to grin at Dean. "Andre and David had most of it in place before they hired me, but I'm the one who talked Bo into getting the laptop and the DV format cameras."

"Excellent move," Dean said, nodding. "I know most serious investigators like to use regular videotape, but the way it's set up here is best. You get the digital file to work with, but you've got the tape as a backup."

"Exactly what I told Bo." Sam swallowed, fighting a sudden tightness in his chest. The memory of that afternoon, the way

Bo's body shook when he came in Sam's hand, was as vivid as if it had just happened. Sam liked to think Bo had agreed to buy the new equipment because it was a good idea, not because Sam had made the suggestion in the post-orgasmic afterglow. "He agreed with me."

Tucking one foot underneath him, Dean stopped his tape and gave Sam a long, considering look. For a moment, Sam was positive Dean was going to confront him with his all-too-obvious feelings for Bo. He schooled his face into a blank mask, his gaze fixed on the screen in front of him.

Eventually, Dean started his tape again. Sam was happy enough to watch the videos in silence.

♋

Andre came into the office at a few minutes after eight. With a grunt which Sam assumed was meant to be a greeting, he went directly to his desk and sat with his back to Sam and Dean.

Dean glanced at Sam, a question in his eyes. Sam shrugged. He didn't think Dean knew the whole story about Amy yet, and this sure as hell wasn't the time to tell it. Dean accepted Sam's reticence without comment, tossing one more concerned look at Andre before going back to his video.

David and Cecile showed up at eighty-thirty on the dot, looking worried and uncomfortable. Bo trailed silently behind them. Pausing his tape, Sam stared at Bo, unable to help himself. The man seemed not merely tired, but exhausted. His dark eyes had lost the lively sparkle Sam loved, and his shoulders slumped. Even his hair seemed defeated somehow, the normally glossy locks tangled and dull. And unbraided, Sam

77

noticed with a shock. He'd never seen Bo wear his hair down at work.

"Hey y'all." David's cheeriness rang false, the tension pouring from him in waves. "Dean, the library opens in half an hour, we'll head on out in a little bit."

"Okay." Dean stopped his video, leaned back in his chair and gave David a cautious grin. His gaze followed Bo to the coffee maker in the corner, where Bo poured a mug and stood quietly sipping it. "I started reviewing the camera three video, I hope that's okay. I know I'm supposed to be in training."

"No problem." Giving Cecile a quick kiss, David wandered over to lean on the back of Dean's chair. "Find anything yet?"

"Not a thing." Dean frowned. "In fact, it's abnormally quiet. I swear, when I was in school, that tunnel crawled with bugs. It's weird that they're not there anymore."

Sam turned to look at Andre. He sat perfectly still, his back to the room. Cecile walked over and laid both hands on his shoulders. "Andre?"

The big man sighed, then swiveled around to face the others. His expression was hard and resolute, but his eyes brimmed with grief. Sam knew he was thinking of Amy. "Cecile and I both felt something when we were pulling guard duty. It was very similar to what we sensed at Oleander House. Too similar not to be related."

A pregnant silence followed as David, Bo and Dean processed that information. Bo was the first to speak. "Andre, why didn't either of you say anything before?"

"I didn't want to," Andre answered. "I...I just needed time to think first."

Bo nodded, his eyes softening with sympathy for his friend. David squeezed Andre's shoulder. Glancing between his coworkers in evident confusion, Dean crossed his arms over his chest.

"Okay," he said. "Is anyone ever going to tell me what this is about, or not?"

Sam shot a questioning look at Andre. Scowling, Andre jumped to his feet and stomped toward the door. "Tell him," he growled. "Just somebody fucking tell him already. I'm going for a walk."

He yanked the door open and slammed it shut behind him as he left. Dean stared after him, looking utterly stricken. "Oh God, I'm sorry. I didn't mean to upset him."

Sighing, David ruffled Dean's hair. "Not your fault, Dean. Hey, why don't we go to that new coffee shop down the street before we go to the library? We can grab some espresso and I'll tell you the whole story of Oleander House."

"Okay." Dean bit his lip and rose to go with David. He looked very young and uncertain at that moment, and Sam's heart went out to him. Incorrigible flirt though he may be, Dean clearly had a great deal of empathy for others and wanted to help whenever he could. It must kill him to think himself the cause of someone else's pain.

Acting on impulse, Sam reached out and grabbed Dean's hand as he went by. Dean blinked down at him in surprise, and he smiled. "Don't worry, Dean. Andre's not mad at you, and he'll be okay. This is just how he copes."

Dean returned his smile. "Thanks, Sam. See you later." Giving Sam's fingers a light squeeze, Dean let go and followed David out the front door.

For a minute, no one said anything. Then Cecile shuffled over and dropped into Dean's chair. "Well. Must be Monday."

Sam sighed. "With a vengeance. Want to help me review videos?"

"Why not?" Twirling the chair around, Cecile nudged Bo's leg with her foot. "Hey, would you grab me some headphones, please? Andre's got an extra pair in his desk drawer."

Bo stared blankly at her for a second, then lowered himself into Andre's chair. Opening the drawer, he found the headphones and handed them to Cecile without a word.

Cecile exchanged a worried look with Sam before reaching out to brush her fingers against Bo's arm. "Bo, are you okay? You're not yourself this morning."

Bo's gaze locked with Sam's for the space of a breath, and Sam's insides twisted. He had a feeling he knew what Bo was going to say.

"I had a talk with Janine yesterday." Bo looked away, one hand fiddling absently with a lock of hair trailing over his shoulder. "It wasn't pretty."

The sorrow in Bo's eyes made Sam ache for him. Sam longed to wrap Bo in his arms and just hold him, touch him and kiss him and let him know he was loved. But Sam didn't think Bo would accept comfort from him, even if they were alone. Not after Saturday. That hurt more than anything else.

Cecile took Bo's hand and pressed it between hers. "I'm sorry, Bo. Is there anything we can do?"

"No. But thanks." The corners of Bo's mouth lifted in a wan smile. "Let's get some of this video knocked out. I'd like to get through as much as we can before David and Dean get back."

"You think Andre's coming back today?" Sam told himself he wasn't just talking so Bo would look at him. He wasn't sure he believed it.

Bo shrugged. "I don't know. If he doesn't, we'll manage. I don't want to push him."

"Yeah." Shaking her head, Cecile turned back to the computer. "Poor Andre. I wish I could help him."

"So do I."

Bo's voice was soft and sad. Sam knew how he felt. Not a day went by that he didn't wish he had the power to take away Andre's pain. Staring at Bo's profile, Sam fought to maintain his composure as a familiar wave of guilt washed over him. *I've ruined both of their lives. Andre and Bo. How can they stand to look at me?*

The logical part of Sam's mind knew he was being overly dramatic. Andre had suffered a terrible loss, but he was dealing with it. Bo was coming to terms with something he should've faced decades ago. Sam's words had been hurtful, but essentially true. Surely Bo would come to realize that eventually.

Sam knew blaming himself was counterproductive. If only his emotions were so easy to convince.

Whirling his chair around, Sam started his video again. Beside him, Cecile did the same. The tapping of keys behind Sam was followed by a faint static hiss as Bo started the video Andre had abandoned.

Although he wouldn't have called the silence between them comforting, Sam preferred it to stumbling his way through a conversation at that point. The things he felt were far too close to the surface, and he didn't trust himself to speak without breaking down, falling at Bo's feet and confessing his love and begging Bo's forgiveness. He didn't think Bo would appreciate that, especially now.

Get it together, Sam, he ordered himself. *You've got work to do.* Forcing his whirling thoughts into stillness, Sam focused his attention on the green-lit darkness on the screen in front of him.

♋

The three of them worked in silence, occasionally leaving their places to stretch or get a cup of coffee. After a while Sam's eyelids began to droop. He glanced at the time display on his monitor. Eleven forty-five. Yawning, he leaned back in his chair and stretched his arms overhead.

He had just about decided to turn the video off and go for a walk to clear his head, when the first vibration came. The time on the tape, Sam noted without surprise, read seventeen-thirty-four. Mentally cursing himself for having forgotten to tell the others before, Sam stopped the video and nudged Cecile's arm.

"Cecile, look at this," he said when she hit pause and took off her headphones. "Bo, you need to see it too."

"What is it?" Cecile rolled closer, peering at Sam's screen. "I don't see anything."

"Let me rewind a little. It's not very noticeable, but it's definitely there." Sam's hands trembled on the mouse as he went back to the place where he'd seen the vibration. He could feel Bo behind him, could smell the spice of his skin, and it did nothing at all for his concentration. "And the thing is, Andre and I saw the same thing on the tapes we watched yesterday, at the exact same time."

"Let's see it." Bo's voice was flat, without inflection, but the soft caress of his fingers on the back of Sam's neck gave away his excitement and nervousness. "And why the hell didn't either of you say anything before? I don't like that y'all are hiding things from the rest of the team."

"It wasn't intentional," Sam protested. "I'd forgotten, to tell you the truth."

Cecile raised her eyebrows at him. "You forgot something that potentially significant? Bo, I think you should give him a vacation. He's obviously been working too hard."

"I had other things on my mind," Sam mumbled, fighting the urge to squirm under Cecile's piercing gaze. "Can I show y'all what we found now?"

Behind him, Bo was silent. His fingers slid away from Sam's skin, and Sam mourned the loss. "It's right here," Sam said, starting the video again. "At seventeen-thirty-four. Same time as on the ones Andre and I saw yesterday."

Cecile sucked in a sharp breath, but didn't say anything until the two vibrations had come and gone. The strange sound from the other tapes, Sam noticed, was absent on this one.

"Sam, that's exactly the same time as Andre and I sensed...whatever it was." Cecile's voice shook. She twisted around to look at Bo. "I don't like this, Bo. I think maybe the rumors those kids are talking about are true."

Bo patted her arm. "Let's not jump to conclusions, Cecile. The fact that this phenomenon has so far shown up on three tapes out of seven is significant, but it doesn't have to mean that South Bay High is another gateway."

Sam hated to say what he had to say next. "There's something else."

"Something else you forgot?"

Surprised by the venom in Bo's voice, Sam stood and faced Bo. The man's eyes snapped with anger and fear and frustration. Sam couldn't decide if he'd rather hit him or kiss him. He gritted his teeth and forced both contradictory urges down.

"There was a sound," Sam said, keeping his voice deliberately calm and measured. "A sort of raspy sound. It was faint, but Andre and I both definitely heard it on both videos."

83

Cecile made a small, frightened sound. "It was like what we heard at Oleander House, wasn't it?"

"Yeah," Sam answered, still staring at Bo's face. "It was."

"I didn't hear any sound on this one." Bo held Sam's gaze, dark eyes full of sorrow.

Sam shoved his hands in his pockets to keep himself from reaching out and pulling Bo to him. "No, neither did I."

"Which tapes did you and Andre watch yesterday?"

Sam answered Cecile's question without even looking at her. "One and seven. The ends of the tunnel, where the bricked-up places are."

"And this one is"—Cecile's chair creaked as she leaned over to peer at Sam's monitor—"camera five."

"Close to the middle." Bo's gaze flicked down to Sam's mouth, and he licked his lips. "Maybe it came from one of the side tunnels."

"We heard it equally from both cameras." Without thinking of what he was doing, Sam leaned closer to Bo. They stared at each other, their fingers brushing together. Heat stirred in Sam's groin.

"Um. Okay." Cecile rose to her feet, walked over to her desk and pulled her purse out of the bottom drawer. "It's nearly lunchtime. I'm going to Fontaine's, who wants burgers?"

Clearing his throat, Sam forced himself to smile at Cecile. "Will you get me a black bean burger and seasoned fries?"

"Sure thing. Bo, you want anything?"

"No thank you. I'm not hungry."

"You sure?"

"Yeah."

"Okay." Hoisting her purse over her shoulder, Cecile started for the door. Her arm brushed Sam's as she passed. She gave him a pointed look, and he wondered once again just how much she'd figured out about him and Bo. "See you guys in a little while."

The door opened, hinges squealing, and Cecile walked out into the sunshine. Sam waited until the door shut behind her before giving in to his desires and pulling Bo into his arms.

Bo melted against him, mouth opening to his kiss, fingers fisted in the back of his shirt. They both moaned when Sam's hands slid down to cup Bo's ass.

When the kiss ended, Bo drew back enough to look into Sam's eyes. "I'll miss this," he whispered, tracing the line of Sam's jaw with his fingertips. "It's so good with you, Sam. I'm sorry I can't give you more."

In the flood of relief that Bo wasn't still angry about Saturday, Sam almost missed what Bo had said. "No, I'm sorry. I promised to wait, to not push you, and I ended up pushing you anyway, I shouldn't have—" He stopped as Bo's words sank in. "Wait, what? Why would you miss it?"

Bo pushed him gently away and stepped back. "Because we can't do it anymore. This isn't working."

Sam felt like he'd been kicked in the stomach. He couldn't pretend Bo's decision was a surprise, but it still hurt worse than anything he'd ever felt.

"Why?" He ran a hand over his face. "Is it what I said Saturday? Because I've regretted it ever since. I never should've said that to you. I'm sorry."

A faint smile curved Bo's mouth. "But you were right, Sam. This isn't an adult relationship at all. You deserve better."

A sick feeling rolled in Sam's belly. "I want to be with you. Whatever that means, whatever it takes."

"I believe you mean that. But it's not enough." Bo shoved his hair impatiently out of his face and wrapped both arms around himself. "I don't think I can come out, Sam. Not even to our friends. And you may think you can live with that, but you won't be able to forever. You already resent me for it."

"Does this have anything to do with Janine?" Stepping forward, Sam grasped Bo's upper arms and stared into his eyes. "What did she say to you, Bo? You said it wasn't pretty. What did she do?"

Bo's cheeks flushed like they always did when Sam was close. He licked his lips. "I told her I wanted a divorce. She didn't like it. We said some ugly things to each other. She threatened to keep the boys away from me entirely."

Fury bubbled up in Sam's chest. "She can't do that. You're their father. You have rights. Don't let her threaten you."

"That's more or less what I told her. But it doesn't matter. She told me she'd find a way to keep me from seeing them. She said 'Everyone's got skeletons, Bo. I'll find yours.' You know what that means."

Sam did know, and he didn't like it. "There's only so far she can go without crossing some legal line. We'll be even more careful than we already are. We'll make damn sure she doesn't find out."

"For how long, Sam? The rest of our lives?" Twisting free of Sam's grip, Bo started pacing the room. "Even I can't deal with that. No. As much as it kills me to say it, we have to break this off. Now."

I will not beg. I won't. "Please don't do this." Sam reached for Bo, barely holding back a frustrated shout when the man stumbled out of reach. "It won't matter. She'll just find something else. You won't ever be able to date anyone, including women, without her twisting it somehow."

"God, Sam. This isn't just about Janine." Bo stopped and pinned Sam with an angry glare. "Even if she wasn't in the picture, I still wouldn't be able to see you openly. I'm not ready, I'm not sure I'll ever be ready, and it's killing us both to keep hiding it. Go find someone else. Date Dean, if you want. God knows he wants you."

The bitterness in Bo's voice was impossible to miss. Sam stared hard at him, trying to read his face. That beautiful, heartbreakingly closed-off face, hiding an equally beautiful soul Sam had begun to realize he'd never be able to share. All the fight drained out of Sam in a rush that left him weak.

"I don't want to date Dean. I want you." Sam sighed and sank into the nearest chair. "I wish you'd try. I wish you'd give us a chance out in the open. But I can't make you."

"I'm sorry, Sam," Bo said, his voice soft and shaky. "You'll never know how much. But it's better this way, and we both know it."

Sam shook his head. "Maybe so. But I don't have to like it."

"No, I don't guess you do."

Silence fell. Sam stared at the floor, refusing to meet Bo's gaze. After a long, tense moment, Bo turned and went into his office. The door closed quietly behind him. Dropping his head into his hands, Sam closed his eyes and breathed deep. When the urge to scream and cry and throw things went away, he moved back to his desk and started the video where he'd left off.

He may have lost Bo as a romantic partner, but Bo was still his boss, and he still had a job he loved. A professional relationship might not be the same, but it was better than nothing. Sam was determined to hang onto that.

Chapter Six

Cecile returned twenty minutes later. With a mumbled thank-you, Sam took his burger and fries and handed her a five dollar bill, keeping his face turned away. She didn't comment, but Sam knew she had to wonder what had happened. He was grateful when she put her headphones on and returned to the video she'd been watching before, nibbling chicken strips as the file played.

Bo stayed in his office. Sam wasn't surprised.

At three o'clock, the front door banged open. Looking up, Sam saw David and Dean enter the office. They were talking excitedly, their voices stumbling over each other.

Arching an amused eyebrow, Cecile paused her video and got up to greet David. "That must have been some trip to the library."

"You have no idea." David swooped Cecile into his arms and gave her a resounding kiss. "Amazing the stuff you can find out if you dig a little."

"And we didn't even have to dig all that hard." Dean glanced around the room. "Where's Bo and Andre? We want to tell y'all what we found out."

"Bo's in his office." Sam glanced at the closed door, his chest constricting. "Andre hasn't come back yet."

"Oh." Some of the light went out of Dean's eyes. "I hope he's okay. I feel really bad about this morning."

Letting go of David, Cecile took Dean's hand and squeezed it. "Please don't feel bad. He gets like that sometimes. He took Amy's death pretty hard."

"Yeah, David told me what happened." Dean glanced at Sam, and Sam knew instantly David had told him everything. The mingled sympathy and curiosity in Dean's eyes made it crystal clear. "Y'all think maybe South Bay High is another dimensional gateway, don't you?"

"It's possible, yes."

Sam hadn't even heard Bo's office door open. Turning toward Bo's voice, Sam forced his face into a blank mask. He knew he wasn't acting normal, he knew the others would notice, but it was the best he could do. If he tried to talk to Bo, he'd lose it completely.

"We have no solid proof, of course." Bo pushed away from the doorframe and walked into the main room. His eyes cut sideways for a second, giving Sam a look he couldn't decipher. "But there are too many similarities to Oleander House for us to discount the possibility. Not that we ever had any real proof of Oleander House being a gateway either."

David plopped into a chair and put his feet up on his desk. "Well, the things we found out about South Bay wouldn't count as proof, but I think they strengthen the circumstantial case."

"So stop teasing and tell us what you learned," Sam demanded, congratulating himself when his voice didn't quaver.

"Okay." Hurrying around behind Cecile's desk, Dean sat next to Sam and leaned forward, his face lit with excitement. "Listen to this—"

At that moment the front door opened. Andre sidled in, watching the huddled group warily. "Um. Hi. Sorry I've been gone so long, I, uh...I had things to do."

No one questioned this declaration, though Sam could tell he wasn't the only one who wanted to. "Forget that," David said, grinning. "You're just in time to hear what me and Dean found out researching today. Sit down, shut up and listen."

Andre's relief was palpable. He laughed as he sat at his desk and swiveled around to face the room. "Okay, I'm listening. Shoot."

David and Dean looked at each other. "You start," David offered, waving a hand at Dean.

Flashing a blinding smile at David, Dean began to speak. "We figured the best place to start researching the site would be with records from the monastery. So we asked if they had those, and they said yes."

"The originals are locked up under glass in the display section," David added. "But they had everything on microfiche. We went through most of the records from the first six months at the monastery."

When David paused, Dean jumped in again. "Most of it was pretty dull. Stuff about who joined up, who died, how many prayers they had, junk like that. But there was also an account of finding and purchasing the property, complete with a hand-drawn map and description of the topography of the area."

"And a blueprint of the original building," David continued. "And here's where it starts getting interesting—"

"There was a house already on the property when they bought it," Dean interrupted, eyes shining.

David smacked Dean's leg. "It was pretty much a ruin, mostly just a foundation and some walls. The roof had fallen in."

Sam bit back a laugh as David and Dean started talking at once, their excitement spilling over to infect the rest of the group.

"When they went to take down what was left of the house," Dean said, "they found a pit in the ground underneath it—"

"—the pit was about twenty-five feet underground, with a slanted passageway to the surface—"

"—but it didn't look like it had been dug from the surface down—"

"—but rather from the pit up."

Surprised silence greeted this breathless declaration. Everyone else's faces reflected the same mixture of skepticism and interest that Sam felt.

"What made them think so?" Andre asked, frowning.

David and Dean both started to answer at the same time. Dean gestured toward David. "Go ahead. You're the one who found this bit."

With a nod at Dean, David continued the tale. "The floor of the house was still mostly intact when the monks found it, good solid hardwood planks. Between that and the piled-up rubble from the roof, the ground underneath was pretty well protected from the elements. According to the monk writing the account we read, the pattern of scratches and furrows in the pit and the passageway seemed to suggest digging from the inside. And listen to this. He said there was dirt piled at the bottom of the pit, as if it had been flung there during digging. Which of course wouldn't happen if you were digging from the surface down."

Goose bumps raised the hairs on Sam's arms. "What did they think did it? And why'd they buy the property after that? I sure as hell wouldn't have."

"They blamed demons." Dean leaned on his elbows on the desk behind him and gave Sam a wry smile. "They performed an exorcism and declared the place clean."

"Wow." Cecile rubbed her arms. "That's creepy."

Rolling over to her, David put an arm around her shoulders. "Wait, it gets better."

Andre's eyebrows went up. "How much better?"

"Lots." A solemn expression came over David's usually smiling face. "You know Mr. Innes said the monks up and left in 1921, without telling anyone where they were headed. Well, according to the monastery records, twenty-three monks are listed as having died in the four months before the last entry."

"That's interesting," Bo said, and his brow furrowed. "But I don't see what it has to do with anything. Many groups of monks kept very much to themselves even that recently, and often refused modern medical care. Lots of things could've killed them."

David nodded. "That's true. But we read all their death records. In every case, the cause of death was listed, or at least what they knew to be the cause of death. Died in his sleep, collapsed and stopped breathing during prayers, things like that. But with these twenty-three, the cause of death is listed as unknown. And, in each case, the burial place is also listed as unknown. With every other death, they have the exact burial plot recorded."

"Why would they list it that way?" Cecile wondered. "That's very strange."

"It is," Dean agreed. "And we wondered the same thing. But then in the last entry, we found something else. That entry said that they were thinking of leaving, and mentioned 'our missing brothers' as a major factor in their decision."

"And it doesn't say where they went?" Bo began pacing and twisting a lock of hair between his fingers. "Or what they thought happened to the missing men?"

"Not a word," David said. "That entry was the last."

The group stared silently at one another. Sam saw his own questions reflected in the eyes of his coworkers. What happened to the monks? Did they vanish like those three South Bay High teens had? And if so, where had they gone?

The possible parallels to what was happening at the school knotted Sam's insides. *We have to stop it. I have to stop it.*

It didn't matter to Sam that he had no idea how to keep another child from vanishing. All that mattered was that he had to do it, somehow. The thought terrified him.

Desperate for some sort of support, someone to understand what he felt, Sam shot a pleading gaze at Bo. No one knew better than Bo the burden of guilt and fear Sam still bore.

For a split second, Bo met his gaze. Then he blinked and turned away, and Sam felt more lost than he ever had.

♋

After the revelations from David and Dean, the rest of the afternoon flew by in a flurry of activity. David and Dean were told about the strange vibrations and sounds on the videos, and Andre was updated about the morning's findings. A call to Mr. Innes revealed that workmen had removed the brick barriers from the entrances to both side tunnels. The group decided to head to the school first thing the next morning to investigate the newly opened passageways.

At five-thirty, Sam turned off his computer and rubbed his eyes. His head throbbed and his neck ached with the tension of pretending nothing was wrong. Wincing at the audible pop of his knees, he stood, shrugged into his jacket and headed for the door.

"Bye," he called to Andre and Dean, who were the only ones in the office. David and Cecile had left earlier, and Bo had yet to emerge from his office, where he'd spent the past hour. "See you tomorrow."

"Hang on, I'll walk with you." Leaping to his feet, Dean clapped Andre on the back and hurried after Sam. "You don't mind, do you?"

Faced with Dean's friendly enthusiasm, Sam couldn't manage even mild irritation. "Sure," he said, returning Dean's smile. "I'm headed for the bus stop up the street, what about you?"

"Same." Dean held the door open for Sam, then bounced through and shut it behind him. "Only I think I've got farther to ride. I live over on Airport. Where do you live?"

"Just off Springhill." Sam hunched his shoulders against the rising wind as they descended the porch steps. "Wow, it got cold."

"Yeah." Shoving his hands in his pockets, Dean gave Sam a considering look. "You've seemed different this afternoon, Sam. Is everything all right?"

No. "Yeah, I'm fine."

Dean didn't say anything else, but his expression told Sam quite clearly that he didn't believe him. Part of Sam almost wished Dean would keep pushing. He wanted—no, *needed*—someone to talk to. Someone who could give him a clearheaded, unbiased perspective on what had happened with Bo. Someone who would understand without judging.

Someone who could help you forget him.

"No," Sam whispered before he could stop himself.

Dean blinked at him. "What?"

"Oh, um, nothing." Glancing up the street, Sam was relieved to see the headlights of the bus approaching. "This is mine. See you tomorrow, Dean."

"Yeah, see you."

As Sam hauled himself up the steps and dug the change out of his pocket, Dean called to him. "Hey, Sam!"

Surprised, Sam glanced down at him. "Yeah?"

Dean smiled. "Call me, okay? If you need to talk."

A fierce blush rose in Sam's cheeks. "Yeah, okay. Bye."

The door hissed shut, blurring Dean's face, and the bus lurched forward. Ignoring the driver's scowl, Sam slouched into an empty seat in the back. He closed his eyes and let his mind drift, wanting only to forget the whole lousy day had ever happened.

♋

When the group arrived at the school the next morning, they were greeted by a very put-out looking Mr. Innes. A large plastic bin sat on the steps beside him.

"Good morning," the principal called as they hopped out of the two SUVs and started toward him.

"Mr. Innes." Bo gave him a questioning look. "You didn't have to come just to unlock the place. You gave me a key, remember?"

"Certainly. However, I have been informed by the school board that since the side tunnels have been closed up for so long, they are officially considered hazardous. The only way the school board would allow you to come here today is if I stay here, and you all wear hard hats."

"Sorry, man." David clapped the older man on the back, earning himself a frown. "We'll be as quick as we can."

Mr. Innes gave him a withering look. "Please do. I had plans today. I'll be in my office, plotting the downfall of the school board."

"Okay, people," Bo said as Mr. Innes stalked inside. "Let's get our stuff and get started. We'll break into two teams so we can cover the ground faster. Andre, you and Cecile come with me, we'll take the one on the south end. David, Dean and Sam, y'all take the other one. Take notes, scope out possible camera positions, and see how the place feels psychically. We'll meet at the bottom of the stairs in one hour, or call on the radio if you're gonna be late. Got it?"

They all nodded. Sam wiped his sweating palms on his jeans and they trooped up the steps and into the school.

"Hey," Dean muttered, nudging Sam's shoulder. "What d'you think's down there?"

"How should I know?" Sam snapped, and instantly wished he hadn't. "Sorry. I haven't been getting much sleep lately and it's got me in a rotten mood." It wasn't a complete lie. His sleep had been quite troubled the past couple of nights.

"'S okay." Dean gazed thoughtfully at Sam for a moment before turning to narrow his eyes at Bo's back. Sam's pulse skidded to a halt, waiting for Dean to point at him and accuse him of being in love with his boss. But Dean said nothing, and Sam's heart began beating again.

Armed with hard hats, two-way radios and powerful flashlights, the team filed carefully down the steep, narrow steps into the main tunnel. It was even hotter than before, the air ripe and humid. It was like trying to breathe warm honey. Sam pulled at the collar of his sweatshirt.

"Goddamn," David gasped, dots of perspiration already popping up on his face. "I hope it's a little cooler in the side tunnels."

"Me too." Securing his hard hat on his head, Andre pulled a notepad and pen out of his jeans pocket. "I've got the notes covered, Bo."

"Good, thanks." With a quick smile at Andre, Bo surveyed the rest of the team. His gaze met Sam's for a heartbeat, then skittered away. "Remember, one hour, or call."

Bo turned and strode down the south leg of the tunnel, with Cecile and Andre scurrying in his wake. Resisting the urge to watch Bo's graceful figure as he moved away, Sam followed David and Dean down the north leg.

The tunnel grew warmer as they went. As they stepped through the ragged hole in the brick wall and entered the side tunnel, the temperature increased noticeably. The heat felt thick and viscous. The smell of mold and damp earth left a bitter tang on the back of Sam's tongue. He pulled the notebook and pen from his back pocket.

"Jesus," David swore, mopping his brow with the tail of the sweatshirt he'd taken off and tied around his waist. "What the hell's down here, a volcano?"

"Okay, I can't take this, y'all excuse me, but..." Shoving his flashlight into his back pocket, Dean tossed his hard hat on the ground and stripped off his thin sweater. An expression of blissful relief spread over his face as he tied the arms of the sweater around his hips and put the hard hat back on. "That's better."

Sam feigned interest in a gouge on the earthen wall. *I won't look, I won't look,* he promised himself, then immediately broke his silent vow by darting a glance at Dean from under his eyelashes.

The man was hot, no doubt about it. Hot, intelligent, open and giving, and an all-round good person. A perfect partner. The thought gave Sam a sharp pang for what he and Bo would never have together.

An elbow in his ribs brought Sam abruptly out of his thoughts. He blinked at Dean. "What?"

Dean smiled. "You're doing it again."

Sam licked his lips, trying not to notice Dean's clean, masculine scent, or the way his skin gleamed in the glow of the flashlights. "Doing what?"

"Thinking about him." Leaning closer, Dean dropped his voice down low. "I'm sorry, Sam. I'd make it better if I could."

"I know." Sam managed a halfhearted smile. "Thanks."

"Any time." Laying a hand on Sam's arm, Dean squeezed briefly before wandering over to where David crouched against the wall.

Sam drew a few deep breaths, composing himself before he joined them. He didn't want David to read the heartache on his face, and he didn't want either of them to notice his annoyingly persistent attraction to Dean.

"We could set up cameras at any point along here," David said, rising and brushing dirt off his hands. "Thank God for tripods. This damp air's gonna be bad enough, I hate to think what sitting on the ground would do to the cameras."

"Do we have enough extension cord?" Sam played his flashlight beam over the walls. Patches of fungus sprouted from the dirt, giving off a strong, musty odor. Sam wrinkled his nose.

David shrugged. "I hope so. I picked up some more on my way home yesterday, who the hell knows if it's enough. If not I guess we don't get any video."

Pointing his flashlight beam down the tunnel, Dean peered into the dense darkness. "I can't see the end of this thing, y'all. We should hustle if we want to get done with this in an hour."

"Yeah, the sooner we get out of here the better," David said.

"We still have to come back with the EMF detectors and thermometers and stuff," Sam reminded him. The thought was not pleasant.

"Don't remind me," David grumbled. "Come on."

The three of them plodded methodically down the tunnel, sweeping every inch of it with their lights to be sure they didn't miss anything. About ten yards in, a section of high, irregular ceiling and a significant narrowing of the passageway marked where the partial collapse of the tunnel had occurred decades before. The tunnel opened up again after one hundred feet or so.

Sam let his mind expand just a little, feeling cautiously for the sense of wrongness he'd felt before. It was there, a ribbon of cold menace winding through the heat of the tunnel. He backed off as fast as he could, slamming shut the strange door in his mind that let him connect with whatever inhabited the other side.

David glanced at him with a knowing look in his eyes. "You feeling it again?"

"Yeah." Sam's mouth felt dry and dusty, his head pounding from the brief contact with the thing. "It's strong here. I barely even tried, and I still felt it."

"You didn't have to try in Oleander House," David pointed out. "You, Andre and Cecile all felt it without trying at all."

"Yeah, but it's different here. More focused, or something. I have to reach out to it to pick it up, but when I do it's..." Sam tapped his pen against the notepad, trying to find the words to describe what he'd sensed. "It's sharper, and more localized. It's like there's a single point where it's coming from, rather than all over the place like it was at Oleander House. I'm definitely getting a stronger sense of it here than I did in the main tunnel."

Tilting his head to one side, Dean gazed thoughtfully at Sam. "That's interesting. I had no idea that psychic phenomena strengthened or dissipated proportionate to distance."

Sam shrugged. "I don't know if they do or not, normally. Maybe this is different because what Cecile, Andre and I are picking up here has an actual, physical source."

"The dimensional doorway, if that's what it is." Dean nodded, scratching his belly with one hand. "Makes sense."

"Guys, this is interesting, but can we move a little faster? I'm dying here." David mopped his flushed face again and gave Sam and Dean a pleading look.

Sam couldn't help laughing. Working with David and Dean, he decided, was the perfect way to forget his hurt, at least for a little while.

They hadn't gone much further when the tunnel began to curve to the right. David frowned. "I hope this thing doesn't start branching off. If it does, I—"

"Shhhh." Dean held up a hand, stopping David's protest. When he spoke, his voice was barely audible. "Y'all hear that?"

"What?" Sam whispered. "I didn't hear anything."

Listen, Dean mouthed silently, his gaze fixed on the place where the tunnel arced. Sam held his breath and listened. And heard it.

A movement. Scuffling noises, and something that sounded like muffled speech. Adrenaline rushed through Sam's veins, making the blood pound in his ears. He shot a wide-eyed glance at Dean and David.

"Someone's there," Sam murmured as softly as he could. "What should we do?"

David's Adam's apple bobbed as he swallowed. "Go see who—or what—it is."

"Crap," Dean breathed. To Sam's shock, Dean's hand clamped onto his left wrist, holding tight. "Didn't bargain on this, guys. I'm scared shitless."

"Me too." David drew a deep breath and blew it out. Flashlight held out in front of him like a weapon, he crept forward, hugging the wall. Sam followed, with Dean still clinging to his wrist.

Those were the longest seconds of Sam's life. His pulse raced as he wondered what waited for them around the bend. *Please don't be one of those things,* he silently pleaded.

"Ready?" David whispered.

"Fuck no." Dean pressed closer to Sam. His heart thudded against Sam's arm. "Let's do it."

They moved forward as a group. Sam held his breath, every sense on alert. They rounded the corner. In the distance, three lights bobbed above the ground. For a second Sam froze, shocked at the physical evidence that they had company in the tunnel. Then he realized what the lights must be, and laughed out loud.

"Sam," David hissed. "Be quiet."

"No, it's okay," Sam insisted, still laughing. "It's only—"

"Hey!" Andre's voice bellowed from where the three lights hovered. "That you guys?"

David groaned and leaned against the wall while Dean doubled over with laughter. Grinning, Sam started walking forward. "It's us, Andre. Y'all about scared us to death."

"Yeah, we thought you were other-dimensional critters." David ran a shaking hand through his hair. "Jesus."

"We thought the same about you guys," Cecile called.

Bo's laugh drifted down the tunnel, making Sam's breath catch. "Now that we know this is one tunnel instead of two, let's continue as before and meet in the middle."

"Gotcha, boss." David leaned against the tunnel wall, his smile fading. "I tell you what, I sure am glad that was them and not one of those things."

"Yeah, me too." Sam heard the faint tremor in his own voice and hated it. He wished he wouldn't react that way every time he thought of that night, the nightmarish creature appearing out of thin air and killing Amy right before their horrified eyes.

Dean's hand slid down Sam's wrist, twining their fingers together. Surprised, Sam turned to look at him. He'd forgotten Dean still had hold of his wrist. Dean squeezed Sam's hand, then let go without a word. Sam blinked back the prickling behind his eyelids and followed David, who was already moving down the tunnel.

"So," Sam said as he fell in step beside David. "Mr. Innes didn't say anything about there only being one tunnel. He made it sound like there were two."

"Maybe he didn't know. It's been bricked up for more than fifty years." Pointing his flashlight beam at the floor, David studied a long, narrow furrow in the dirt. "What's this look like to y'all?"

Sam crouched on the ground and peered closely at the deep scratch. Damp reddish earth lay loose on either side, and the bottom glistened with moisture. "It looks fresh. Like whatever made it was just here."

"Hm." Squatting beside Sam, Dean picked up a clump of earth and crumbled it between his fingers. "Yeah, it seems fresh all right. But we know no one else has been in here other than us, and the rest of our group hasn't been this far."

They looked at one another. Unease churned in Sam's stomach. "Rats, maybe?" he suggested, though he knew in his heart it wasn't.

"Maybe." David frowned, tapping his flashlight against his thigh. "Mr. Innes did say they found evidence of large rats in the other tunnel."

"That would be one hell of a rat," Dean observed. "This is, what, about two feet long?"

"And at least an inch deep." Rising to his feet, Sam glanced down the tunnel toward the lights of their coworkers. He didn't like the things he was thinking, but there was no point in keeping it to himself. *It's not like they haven't guessed anyway.* "No, this wasn't made by any rat. I think it was—"

A feminine cry cut off his words. He, David and Dean looked at each other, then took off running toward where the three flashlights huddled in a tight group about twenty yards away. Sam noticed the walls were lined with brick here, but didn't stop to consider what that meant. Not with Cecile's frightened cry still ringing in his ears.

"Hey!" David shouted as they drew closer. "What happened? Are y'all okay?"

Bo turned toward them. His face was pale, eyes wide. "Yeah, we're fine. Cecile found something."

Sam's insides clenched. *Not one of those missing kids. Please, not that.* "What?"

Taking a step back, Bo swept his flashlight beam into a shallow bay in the wall. Sam gasped. "Oh my God."

Lying against the crumbling, mildewed brick, with one torn strap and a broken zipper, was a backpack full of textbooks. The name stenciled across the front read "Arlene Ray".

Chapter Seven

David stepped closer, staring at the backpack. "Arlene Ray. That's one of the missing students."

"The latest one to disappear," Andre said. "I remember reading about it in the paper the day Mr. Innes hired us."

"We have to call the police." Cecile's voice shook. She pressed close to David, and he wound an arm around her shoulders. "What if she's down here someplace?"

Sam shook his head. "I don't think she's here."

"She's gone through the gateway, hasn't she?" Dean fixed a wide-eyed gaze on Sam. "Something took her."

"And the others." Crossing his arms over his chest, Bo glanced around at the rest of the team. "Cecile's right, we have to call the police. But don't anybody mention inter-dimensional gateways, or especially beings from those other dimensions."

"They won't hear it from me." Dean let out a dry laugh. "It's never good for the cops to think you're crazy."

"Maybe a couple of us should go call, while the others stay here," David suggested. "Just to make sure the bag doesn't, like, disappear or anything."

"I don't think it's likely to disappear," Bo said. "But I know what you mean. If we're really dealing with a dimensional portal, then we're flying by the seat of our pants here. Anything could happen." Bo's brow furrowed in thought. "Cecile, you and I can go call the police from Mr. Innes's office. The rest of you stay down here, but don't touch the bag or disturb the area around it. Gather whatever information you can by simply looking. I have a feeling that when the cops get here we'll be kicked out, for the rest of today if not longer."

Andre nodded. "We'll do what we can."

"All right. We'll be back as soon as we can. It might be a while. We'll probably need to wait for the police to arrive and bring them down here." With one last look around, Bo laid a hand on Cecile's shoulder. "Come on, let's go."

Cecile gave David a quick kiss, then she and Bo started off toward the South end of the tunnel. Sam watched them until they rounded the corner in the distance, then turned his attention to the backpack and the scooped-out place in the wall where it rested. There was something odd about it, something different that Sam couldn't quite put his finger on. When he realized what it was, he gasped out loud and took two steps toward the spot before he caught himself.

"What the hell, Sam?" Andre glared at him. "Don't mess with the evidence, man. I for one do *not* want to go to jail for interfering with a police investigation."

"Sorry," Sam mumbled distractedly, still staring at the place where the backpack lay. "Guys, look at the wall and floor where the backpack is. Do you see anything different about it?"

David crouched down and peered at the place for a long moment. "No, I don't see... Oh, hang on." Jumping to his feet, he backed up a few paces. Sam knew he'd figured it out when he let out a low whistle. "I see. Damn."

"What?" Dean cocked his head and narrowed his eyes at the spot. "I'm not getting it."

"David, you and Dean said the monks found a pit in the ground when they bought this property, right?" Andre's voice was slow and deliberate, excitement building in his eyes.

"Right," Dean confirmed. "But I don't—" His eyes went wide, jaw dropping. "Wait. The floor and wall are concave. Oh wow, this is it, isn't it? This is the pit the monks found."

"Sure seems like it. But let's make sure, huh?" David trained his flashlight beam on the ceiling. Sure enough, an irregular opening gaped almost directly above where the backpack lay. The beam illuminated a short stretch of rough-hewn burrow angling up into the darkness.

"I'll be damned." Taking a cautious step closer, Andre leaned over to peer into the dirt shaft. "I don't see any light coming from the other end. It seems to curve after a couple of feet, but still, if it was open at the other end we'd see light. It must be covered over with something."

"We should measure the tunnels before the cops get here," Sam said. "We need to figure out what's on top of this thing."

"Then we can do some poking around topside." Placing his flashlight and hard hat on the ground, Dean untied his sweater from around his waist and pulled it on. "I have a pretty accurate pedometer in my bag in the SUV. I'll run get it and we can do some quick and dirty measurements. They might not be one hundred percent perfect, but they'll be good enough."

"Good man." David clapped Dean on the back. "Run, boy, run like the wind."

Dean rolled his eyes as he put his hard hat back on. "Smart ass. Be back in a few." Smacking David on the arm as he passed, Dean snatched his flashlight off the ground and took off jogging down the tunnel the way they'd come.

"He's a good one," David declared, watching Dean's light shrink into the distance. "Smart as a whip, and full of great ideas."

"Good thing you talked Bo into hiring him. I was getting sick of interviewing unqualified people, frankly." With one last curious glance at the narrow opening in the ceiling, Andre focused his light on the walls and floor. "Don't know what makes people think that just because we investigate hauntings, we don't really need the qualifications we ask for in the ad."

"Yeah, that's irritating all right." Leaning close to Sam, who'd kept deliberately quiet during this exchange, David dropped his voice to a whisper. "Dean's into you, man."

"Oh really?" Sam murmured. "I hadn't noticed."

"Yeah, right." David snorted, dismissing the obvious lie with a wave of his hand. "I know you said he wasn't your type, but come on. There's no way you don't wanna hit that."

Sam chuckled at David's typically blunt assessment of the situation. "Yeah, okay, I wouldn't mind. And I did notice him flirting with me. I'd have to be blind not to."

"I knew it." David grinned, blue eyes sparkling. "So go for it."

"Why are you so interested in my love life?" Sam asked mildly, walking over to inspect a deep gouge in the dirt wall. "It's not like you need to live vicariously through me or anything."

"You're my friend, Sam. I want my friends to be happy, and you haven't been happy in a long time. Maybe Dean can change that."

That simple, honest sentiment brought a lump to Sam's throat. "I'll think about it," he whispered. "Thanks."

"Any time, man." David gripped Sam's shoulder in a sympathetic squeeze, then let go and stared at the piece of wall Sam was examining. "What the fuck's with all these scratches in the walls and floor?"

"There's more over here." Keeping carefully away from the pit containing the teenage girl's book bag, Andre walked over to join David and Sam. "The damn things are everywhere in this general area."

David's gaze was riveted to the wall a few feet away, where three parallel scratches marked the brick lining the pit and the walls. "You know what it looks like."

Sam swallowed hard. "Yeah."

Without a sound, Andre turned away and walked down the tunnel, far enough that Sam could only see his hand holding the flashlight. He didn't blame the man. Not when they all suspected the cause of those scratches and furrows had long, wicked claws of glassy black.

In the next half hour, Dean measured the entire length of the old tunnel, and David and Andre inspected every inch of the brick-lined pit. Using the digital camera Dean fetched from the SUV, Sam took pictures of the whole area. By the time Bo and Cecile returned with Mr. Innes and two uniformed officers, the four of them had documented the place as thoroughly as possible without touching anything.

After briefly questioning everyone, the police made them all leave, just as Bo predicted. Andre showed the officers the shaft leading toward the surface, then the group began the journey out of the tunnels. *At least we're not suspects this time,* Sam thought as he followed the rest of the group down the passageway.

"What else did y'all find while we were gone?" Bo asked, dropping back to walk beside David and Sam as they climbed the steps into the school hallway. "Not that that shaft in the ceiling isn't plenty."

"Andre and I looked over the walls, floor and ceiling as well as we could," David answered. "I don't know if you noticed it on your end, Bo, but the walls and floor are covered in furrows and scratches."

"Yeah, we noticed that too." Bo glanced at Andre, who was walking a few paces ahead. "I don't have to tell you what Andre thought of that."

"Same as us, probably," Sam murmured.

"Probably." Tugging on his braid, Bo looked over at David. "What else did you do?"

"Sam took pics, and Dean used his pedometer to measure the tunnel," David told him.

"We can pace it off outside in the courtyard," Sam added. "Then we can see exactly where the shaft from the pit comes out."

"I guess it's reasonable that the pit the monks found is still there." Bo tapped his flashlight against his leg. "But it's hard to believe the opening to the surface is still intact. Why didn't it collapse over the years?"

"Well, something's obviously covering it, or we would've seen daylight coming through. The monks must've built over it and planted grass on top or something." Spinning around to walk backward, Dean turned a questioning look to Bo and Sam. "Can we investigate the courtyard? Figure out what's hiding the pit?"

"Let's hope so." Shooting a quick glance at Sam, Bo jogged forward and touched Mr. Innes's shoulder. "Mr. Innes, we'd like to look around the courtyard, if that's okay."

The older man frowned. "Why?"

"We think the place where we found that backpack is the original pit that the monks found here when they bought the property," Bo explained. "We want to see what's above it. I expect the police will probably do the same once they finish in the tunnel, but we'd like to take a quick look."

"Very well." Mr. Innes sighed and shook his head. "I may as well give up on my antiquing trip."

Dean's eyebrows shot up. *Antiquing?* he mouthed, then swung his hand back and forth in a blatantly limp-wristed fashion. Sam bit the insides of his cheeks and decided they were all very lucky Dean still had his back to the principal.

"That's such a stereotype," Sam muttered as they followed the others down the hallway leading to the back courtyard. "All sorts of people collect antiques." He gave Dean a playful nudge with his shoulder. "Like you have any room to talk anyhow."

"Hey, my hobbies are all of the manly variety," Dean declared, turning around to walk forward again.

"Uh-huh."

"Motorcycle racing, moose hunting..."

"I'm pretty sure there are no moose in Mobile."

Dean pursed his lips. "Okay, when I say moose hunting, what I really mean is macramé. But it's *manly* macramé, dammit."

Sam laughed. "You lie like a rug."

Sidling closer, Dean gave Sam a purely filthy grin. "You could lay me like a rug."

Oh hell, Sam groaned inwardly. His cock liked Dean's suggestion far too much for comfort. He was about to politely insist that Dean not proposition him any more, when he reached the door into the courtyard and saw Bo standing just outside. The man was shooting furtive sidelong glances at Sam and Dean. His eyes blazed with jealousy, hurt and anger, but it was what lurked beneath the surface that hit Sam like a fist.

Shame, and fear. The same things that had kept Bo in the closet his whole life, and pulled Sam in there with him. Sam didn't know if the emotions playing across Bo's face were born of the fact that he'd broken up with Sam, or the fact that they'd been together to start with, but in the end it made no difference. The expression in Bo's eyes felt like the final nail in the coffin.

He'll never change. I have to move on with my life. And I know just how to do it.

Holding the door open, Sam smiled at Dean as they passed through into the winter sunshine. "What are you doing tonight?"

Dean shrugged. "Nothing much. Probably pick up some take-out, watch some TV. Why?"

"I was just wondering if..." Sam stopped and drew a deep breath. "I was wondering if you wanted to go out."

Dean blinked at him, clearly surprised. "Really?"

"Yeah." Trying to ignore the heat rising in his cheeks, Sam forced himself to hold Dean's gaze. "You're right, I need to get over...you know, him...and move on. I like you, you like me, so why not?"

Darting a quick look at the others, Dean leaned closer. "No pressure, Sam. I'm up for anything, you probably figured that out already. But we're friends first and foremost, and it never has to be any more than that if you don't want. I'm not looking for anything serious right now, and I know you're not."

"Definitely not." Feeling mischievous suddenly, Sam stuck his hand out and grinned. "So. Friends with privileges?"

"Hell yeah." Dean grasped Sam's hand and they shook. "Now let's see what's hiding in this courtyard, what about it?"

"Can't wait."

Sam kept a smile firmly fixed to his face as the group went to work finding where the pit lay. All the time, he felt Bo's gaze on him, tickling the back of his neck, but refused to let himself think of what that might mean.

♋

When the group left the school an hour later, it was with a subdued air hanging over them. Although Dean had measured off the proper distance not once, but three times, they'd been unable to find anything. Every time it seemed they were getting close to the right spot, they seemed to lose their way. It was puzzling, and horribly frustrating.

"I can't believe we couldn't find it," Sam groused, tossing the hard hat into the plastic bin still sitting on the front steps. "We had an exact measurement, why'd we keep..." He fumbled for the right words. "I don't know. Getting lost."

Yes, that's right. We got lost on the way. It was an odd thought, but it felt right. Sam didn't like that at all.

"Well the measurement wasn't really exact." Dropping his hard hat into the bin, Dean walked down the steps at Sam's side. "Pretty close, but not one hundred percent. That's probably what it was."

"Even so, we should've been able to find the place." Frowning, Sam shook his head. "It was weird, Dean."

"Maybe we can come look again."

"We can look around the courtyard again," Bo chimed in, making Sam jump with his unexpected presence behind him. "But the police have asked that we stay out of the tunnels for now."

Startled, Sam turned to look at Bo. "Why? I thought they were done gathering what evidence they could."

"They are, but they want to investigate the tunnels themselves." David sauntered down the steps and leaned with Dean and Sam against the side of the SUV. "I talked with the girl cop, Carrie—"

"Officer Wright," Cecile corrected, giving him a narrow look. "Now who's flirting, Casanova?"

David laughed. "You know you're my one and only, baby."

"Good thing for you." Standing on tiptoe, Cecile brushed a kiss across David's mouth. "You were saying?"

"Oh yeah." Pulling Cecile against his chest, David resumed his story. "So Car—I mean, Officer Wright, sorry—said they'd probably be done by tomorrow evening sometime."

"Too late to do anything much before the holiday," Andre said as he walked up to join the others. "Bo, why don't we plan on coming back here Friday to get EMF, EVPs and video? We have more research to do on this case, and there's a couple of other cases we need to do preliminary research on, plus we have permission to interview a couple of students who saw the missing kids before they disappeared. That'll keep us busy the rest of today and tomorrow."

"Good idea." Bo wound the end of his braid between his fingers, his gaze restless. Sam couldn't help but think Bo was trying not to look at him. "Let's get back to the office. We'll grab some lunch and divide up the work."

Sam watched Bo as the group dispersed, climbing into the two SUVs for the trip back to the BCPI office. Bo's gaze remained downcast, stray locks escaping his braid to shield his face from prying eyes. It made Sam ache to see Bo hiding like that, and to no longer have any right to hold him and kiss away his pain. He knew Bo was hurting. Just because Bo had broken it off with Sam didn't mean he felt nothing for him. In fact, Sam suspected Bo's fear of his own feelings played a large part in the break-up.

Not that it mattered. It was over, and they'd both just have to live with that.

Turning resolutely away from Bo, Sam climbed behind the wheel of the first SUV and started the engine. Beside him, Dean reached over and patted Sam's thigh. Sam returned the smile. Friends with privileges might be just what he needed.

♋

The afternoon passed quietly. David, Dean and Andre finished reviewing the video they'd taken Saturday at the school, while Sam, Cecile and Bo made phone calls and did internet research related to other cases they were considering.

At four o'clock, Bo emerged from his office looking stressed and tired. "Anyone who wants to take off now can. I'm wiped out, I'm heading home."

"Bye, Bo," Sam said as Bo shrugged into his jacket. "See you in the morning."

Bo stared at him, his expression unreadable. Sam held his gaze, unable to look away even if he'd wanted to. For a blistering second, Bo's eyes burned with a hunger that sent an electric jolt through Sam's bones. Then the veil dropped, hiding Bo's longing and need behind a wall of false indifference.

Bo cleared his throat. "Yeah. See y'all tomorrow." Yanking the front door open, Bo stalked outside and slammed the door behind him.

Sam glanced around. His coworkers didn't seem to have noticed how Bo acted. *Maybe they're used to him acting weird,* Sam mused. *They probably think it's because of Amy's death.*

He hoped he was right, if only because Bo would be horrified to know his employees were aware of the true cause of his dark mood.

Dean rolled his chair across the floor and leaned an elbow on Sam's desk. "Wanna get out of here? I'm done with my video."

"Go on," Andre said when Sam hesitated. "The rest of us will be heading out in a little while, I guess."

"Okay." Sam shut down his computer, stood and stretched his cramped muscles. "God, I'm more than ready to relax a little. This case is making me tense."

The case wasn't the only thing making him tense, but Sam wasn't about to share that fact with anyone else.

Sam and Dean donned their jackets and left the office in a flurry of goodbyes. "So," Dean said as they descended the front steps. "Where'd you want to go?"

"I don't know." He glanced at Dean as they strolled down the sidewalk to the bus stop, the late afternoon sunshine glowing through the bare branches overhead. "Now that I think about it, I haven't gone out anywhere since I moved here. I have no idea what sorts of clubs and restaurants there are."

"Lucky you met me, then, I know all the hotspots."

"Why does that not surprise me?"

"'Cause you're a smart, smart man." Pressing close to Sam's side, Dean slipped a hand into the back pocket of Sam's jeans, laughing when Sam squeaked and jumped. "Wow, you really are tense. Are you always like this, or is it because of your ex?"

"A little of both, I guess," Sam admitted with a sheepish smile. "I'd like to blame it all on him, but I can't. I'm a pretty reserved person most of the time."

"Not into PDA, huh?"

"Not really, no." Glancing at Dean, Sam searched his face for the anger he'd experienced from one or two former lovers who'd resented his public reserve. "Are you upset?"

Dean looked surprised. "Why would I be upset?" Pulling his hand from Sam's pocket, Dean tugged on his jacket sleeve. "The bus is coming, hurry up. Do you have a car?"

"A truck," Sam said, bemused by the way Dean shifted topics so suddenly. "Is your car still in the shop?"

"Yes, and we need wheels."

Sam grinned as they dug change out of their pockets and boarded the bus. "I guess you have an idea where to go, then?"

"Yep."

"You gonna let me in on it?"

Sliding into an empty seat, Dean grabbed Sam's wrist and tugged him down beside him. "I know a great place across the Bay, in Fairhope."

"That sounds like a long drive."

"It can be. We'll just avoid the main roads in town and take the Causeway over instead of the Bayway."

Scrunching up his brow, Sam tried to remember which road was which. Both crossed Mobile Bay, he knew that, but...

"The Causeway's the old road across the Bay," Dean supplied, laughter in his voice. "Highways ninety and ninety-eight. Most of the traffic's on the newer road, the Bayway, because it's wider and a shorter drive. But at rush hour, the Causeway's actually faster even though it's a longer drive. Plus you get a better view of the Bay from there."

"Sounds good to me."

"We'll be there just in time for sunset." Scooting closer, Dean lowered his voice to a seductive purr. "The place we're going is right on the water. We can sit by the big window and watch the sun set across the Bay. It's really romantic."

A wash of heat surged through Sam's body. Dean was so close, close enough for Sam to smell his skin, sunshine and sweat and spicy cologne. His lips were parted, his eyes brimming with undisguised lust. Sam stared into those eyes, so different from Bo's, and wished he could feel for Dean what he felt for Bo. Loving Dean would be easy. It would be good. But he didn't love Dean, not that way.

I may not love him, but I want him. And he wants me. And neither of us has any expectations.

It was enough to make up Sam's mind for him. Hidden by the bus seats and his own body, Sam slid a hand onto Dean's upper thigh and squeezed gently, letting his fingers creep dangerously close to Dean's crotch. He held Dean's gaze, watching his eyes glaze over. Dean's lips formed Sam's name, but no sound emerged.

"You want to shower and change before we go?" Sam asked, hoping Dean would say no. The man's heat-and-sweat scent drove Sam wild, and he didn't really want to trade it for the aromas of soap and shampoo. "I could pick you up at your place."

Dean licked his lips. "Naw, I'm good. You?"

Shaking his head, Sam smiled. "My stop's next. Let's grab my truck and go straight on over."

"Yeah." Dean leaned closer, his hand over Sam's on his thigh. "Christ, Sam."

Dean's rough whisper started a burning ache between Sam's legs. Sam ignored it. If he let his cock do the thinking, they'd end up making out on the bus, and Sam didn't think he was ready for that. "So where is it we're going?"

"It's a surprise." Lacing his fingers through Sam's, Dean straightened up in his seat and grinned. "You'll love it, I promise."

Sam laughed, a little breathlessly. "As long as you give me directions so I can get us there."

"Never fear, I am the king of directions."

They lapsed into a silence that was not at all uncomfortable. A few minutes later, the bus wheezed to a stop. When he stood and started down the aisle, Sam kept hold of Dean's hand. A few people glared at them, but most of the other passengers ignored them. Sam was relieved. Back in Marietta, he never would've dared to hold hands with another man in public. He'd figured the people here had seen such things enough that they no longer paid much attention. It was good to know he'd been right.

They walked the three blocks to Sam's building without talking, their fingers still casually intertwined. By the time Sam unlocked his apartment door and led Dean inside, Sam had decided he couldn't wait any longer to claim the privileges of their new friendship.

"Wow," Dean said, staring around with wide eyes. "This is a cool place. How'd you—mmph..."

His words were abruptly cut off when Sam shoved him against the wall and kissed him.

Chapter Eight

For a second, Dean went rigid with surprise. Then he moaned into Sam's mouth and melted against him, one hand curled in Sam's hair and the other winding around his waist. Dean's body fit perfectly against Sam's, warm and pliant, hips rolling in a search for friction. Hungry little noises bled from his lips as the kiss went deep.

"God, I want you so bad," Dean breathed, and bit Sam's ear.

Growling, Sam grabbed Dean's ass in both hands and squeezed. "Don't wanna go out anymore."

"Me neither. Oh shit, yeah, do that again..."

Sam obediently sucked up another purple mark at the juncture of Dean's neck and shoulder. "Bedroom," he mumbled, his mouth still pressed to Dean's skin. "Now."

"Hell yeah." With one more hard, hot kiss, Dean drew back, a finger still hooked through one of Sam's belt loops. "Which way?"

Taking Dean's hand, Sam led him through the door into the bedroom. As soon as they were inside, Sam tore off his jacket, watching as Dean did the same. Both garments were thrown unceremoniously aside, then Dean molded his body to Sam's, hands sliding around his hips to caress his ass. They kissed again, tongues winding together as Sam backed them toward the bed. His knees hit the edge of the mattress and he let himself fall backward across it, taking Dean with him.

Rolling over, Sam pinned Dean's body with his and buried his face in the man's neck, pressing tiny kisses to his skin. Dean writhed underneath him, hips canting upward and thighs spreading. His moans rode the air, and his hands roamed Sam's body with a great deal of skill and not an ounce of shyness.

Even through the lust fogging his mind, Sam couldn't help comparing Dean to Bo. Kissing Dean, touching him and drawing those sweet sounds from him, was a very different experience from doing the same to Bo. Dean smelled different, he tasted different, the noises he made were different. And Dean threw himself into kissing Sam with an abandon Bo had never shown. Sam understood the why of it—Dean was out. Very, very out. Bo was not. Plus Bo valued control in every area of his life. Dean clearly shot from the hip more often than not.

I've never made Bo lose control like this, Sam thought mournfully, even as he yanked Dean's shirt up and sucked one small pink nipple into his mouth. Dean arched against him, both hands fisted in his hair, soft keening sounds falling from his lips.

"Fuck me," Dean begged, his voice low and rough. "Fuck me, God please."

Sam closed his eyes. He'd have given anything to hear Bo say that to him. *But you never will,* he reminded himself. *Dean's here, he's hot and willing and expects nothing from you, and God knows you need a good fuck.*

Shoving the wistful thoughts of Bo firmly to the back of his mind, Sam sat up on his knees and went to work getting Dean's jeans undone. Once he had the button and zipper open, Dean toed his sneakers off, lifted his hips and helped Sam shimmy the tight denim down his legs.

Tossing the pants over his shoulder, Sam pushed Dean's thighs apart and stared at the thick, straight cock and tight balls he'd uncovered.

"I like how you're looking at me," Dean whispered. He ran his fingertips up and down his shaft, making the silky skin twitch. "Get undressed, so I can look at you too."

Without taking his gaze from Dean's prick, Sam stood and hastily shed his clothes, then crawled back onto the bed. Dean wrapped Sam in strong arms and long, graceful legs. Their lips met in another searing kiss. The feel of Dean's bare skin against his sent lust thumping through Sam's blood.

Following a sudden, irresistible urge, Sam kissed his way down Dean's neck, pausing to swirl his tongue in the hollow of Dean's throat before moving on. Dean cried out and squirmed as Sam's teeth dug into one nipple, his fingers pinching the other.

"Sam, yes," Dean hissed, his skin jumping under Sam's lips and teeth and tongue. "God...fuck..."

Sam could only groan his agreement, his mouth being busy with making Dean incoherent. He slid further down Dean's body, leaving wet kisses and reddened bite marks on the way. When he caught the sharp, musky scent of Dean's arousal, all his control vanished. Shoving Dean's thighs up and apart, Sam swooped down and swallowed Dean's flushed and leaking cock to the root.

"Ah, oh my *God!*" Dean cried, his upper body coming completely off the bed. "Yes, fuck yes."

Sam smiled smugly around his mouthful. He'd been half afraid he'd forgotten how to drive a man crazy with his mouth, after two months of not being allowed to even consider it.

Apparently he hadn't lost his touch after all, if Dean's broken, lustful moans and the persistent thrusting of his hips was anything to go by.

Sam licked and sucked and stroked until Dean was thrashing on the bed, legs splayed wide and hands clutching the sheets. When he felt Dean's cock swell in his mouth, Sam abruptly drew back. Raising his head, he grinned at Dean's shocked expression. Dean let out a pitiful whimper and pushed at Sam's head.

"Don't come yet," Sam said, struggling to get the words out past the need filling him to bursting. "Wait 'til I'm in you."

Dean's eyes went dark. "Yeah. Now. Sam, now!"

Luckily, that meshed perfectly with Sam's own thoughts. "Turn over," he said, running his palms up the insides of Dean's thighs. "Got to get you ready."

Dean scrambled to obey. Flipping onto his stomach, he drew his knees up under him and spread his legs. He twisted around to give Sam a smoldering stare. The way he licked his kiss-swollen lips pulled a groan from Sam's throat.

"God, you're so damn hot like this." Leaning over Dean's back, Sam snaked a hand between his legs, caressing the length of his prick. He pressed a soft kiss to the back of Dean's neck, smiling at the way the man shuddered under his touch.

"Mm. Christ, Sam." Dean ground his ass against Sam's groin, trapping Sam's cock between firm, warm cheeks. "Please. Please."

"Don't rush me," Sam whispered. "Want to rim you first."

"Oh fuck," Dean groaned. "Do it."

That was all the invitation Sam needed. Sitting back on his heels, he spread Dean's buttocks and just looked for a moment, letting the anticipation build. The sight of Dean's rosy little hole pulsing with need made his mouth water.

Bending down, Sam buried his face between Dean's ass cheeks and drew a deep breath of musky-sweet male scent. Dean moaned, thighs parting even further. Inflamed by the sight and sound and smell of Dean's desire, Sam swirled his tongue around the tight opening, urging it to relax, to let him in. Dean's body relaxed easily, and Sam plunged his tongue inside, savoring the sharp, rich flavor of skin and sweat and sex.

"Oh, oh fuck," Dean gasped. "Gonna come if you keep that up."

Sam didn't want to stop. He loved rimming, and it had been far too long since he'd been able to indulge. But Dean was teetering on the brink, and Sam wanted to be buried inside him when he came. Reluctantly, he drew away, humming with pleasure at the sight of Dean's hole open and ready for him.

"Let me get the lube and a rubber," Sam said, reaching to retrieve the necessary items from the bedside drawer.

"Hurry." Dean's voice was barely audible, muffled against the pillow under his cheek. "Can't hold out much longer."

Sam wasted no time rolling the condom on. That done, he opened the lube and coated his sheathed cock. "Ready?" he asked, pushing two lube-slick fingers into Dean's body.

"Yes. Now."

The lustful tremor in Dean's voice sent electricity sparking over Sam's skin. Holding Dean open with his thumbs, he lined up his prick and shoved himself in with one swift stroke.

"Fuck, yeah!" Dean cried, the muscles in his back rippling. "God, yes."

Sam sucked in a deep breath, holding still as he tried to keep the impending orgasm at bay. Dean's insides undulated around him, clutching his cock in snug living heat. *God, it's been way too long.*

Biting his lip, Sam began to move, slipping slowly out until only the head of his prick remained inside, then pressing back in again. Dean growled and pushed against him, and that was all Sam could stand. Holding Dean's hips in a punishing grip, Sam slammed into him, grinning when Dean's sharp cry told him he'd found the sweet spot. He changed the angle to nail Dean's gland with every stroke.

After long months without it, the feel of a hot, tight ass around his cock was like heaven. Sam knew he wouldn't last long, but he didn't mind and figured Dean wouldn't either. Only one thing, he thought, could make it better.

Closing his eyes, he let himself picture Bo bent over and spread for him, sobbing his name as he shot all over Sam's sheets. Bo's ass—*no, not Bo's, Dean's*—milked his cock in rhythmic waves.

His lips formed Bo's name when he came, and he hated himself for it.

Holding onto the condom with one hand, Sam carefully withdrew from Dean's body. He removed the used rubber, tied it off and tossed it toward the trash can beside the bed, keeping his gaze resolutely downcast. If he looked up Dean would surely read everything he felt in his eyes, and he couldn't face it.

"Sam?" Rolling onto his back, Dean sat up and laid a hand on Sam's knee. "Are you okay?"

Sam didn't answer. His throat burned with a sudden, overwhelming sadness. He'd been crazy to think he could forget Bo this easily. And to use Dean the way he had was inexcusable. He turned his back, closed his eyes and buried his face in his hands.

The mattress shifted. Dean's body pressed against his back, one arm sliding around his waist, long legs bracketing his hips. "I'm sorry, Sam," Dean whispered, lips brushing his ear, one hand stroking the sweaty hair from his face. "I'd make him come back to you if I could."

A shiver of unease ran up Sam's spine. "What?"

"Bo." Dean's arm tightened around Sam's waist. "It's all right. I won't tell anyone else."

For a minute, Sam remained tense and silent, shaking all over. His secret was out, his innermost heart laid bare to a man he'd just screwed through the mattress while imagining he was someone else. It was galling, it was mortifying, it was...

Good, he realized. It was an enormous relief to share his burden with someone. In spite of what had just happened between them, Sam sensed he and Dean were still friends. The gentleness in Dean's touch left no doubt of that.

Sighing, Sam relaxed into Dean's embrace. "I'm such a bastard, Dean."

Dean chuckled against his ear. "What, for thinking of Bo while you were fucking me?"

"Yeah." Embarrassment heated Sam's cheeks, even though Dean's tone held no hint of accusation. "How'd you know I was thinking of him?"

"You said his name when you came."

Sam winced. He hadn't realized he'd spoke out loud. "Shit. I'm sorry."

"Don't be. I would've been surprised if you didn't, to tell you the truth." Snuggling closer, Dean kissed the back of Sam's neck.

"I can't believe how nice you're being about this," Sam said.

"Hey, it's not like I didn't get anything out of it, you know."

"What could you have possibly gotten out if this?" Anger welled up in Sam's gut, anger at himself on Dean's behalf. "I used you, Dean. It was a terrible thing to do, why aren't you mad at me?"

"Good grief, how clueless can you get?" Letting out a long-suffering sigh, Dean unwound himself from Sam's body and crawled around to sit cross-legged on the mattress in front of him. "Sam, let me be far more blunt than should be necessary here. What I got out of this was twofold. One, I got an absolutely incredible fuck. Which is not to be taken lightly, let me tell you. I am a connoisseur of great fucks, so I can appreciate a high-quality ass pounding when I get one, and I just got one. And that's not even taking into account the extremely skilled and well-delivered rimming. Excellent work."

The grave seriousness with which this speech was delivered had Sam grinning by the time it was over. Which was probably the idea. "You said what you got out of it was twofold. Did you mean fucking and rimming, or was it something else?"

Dean took Sam's hands in his. "I got the satisfaction of helping you let off some steam and work out what you felt."

Shaking his head, Sam laced his fingers through Dean's. "What are you, Florence Nightingale or something? How do you manage to get any satisfaction out of me using you to work out my screwed up feelings?"

Dean's eyebrows disappeared under the thatch of damp, mussed hair hanging over his forehead. "Florence Nightingale? Well, yeah, I suppose. Only more manly. And less prone to wearing black dresses." He shrugged while Sam laughed. "What can I say, it makes me feel good to make other people feel good. Hell, it's even fun in a kinky sort of way to think of myself being used as a sex doll. Although," he added thoughtfully, "I really don't feel like you used me quite that way."

The smile faded from Sam's face. "What the fuck am I going to do, Dean? I'm in love with him. I thought sleeping with you would help me get over him, but I don't think it's quite that easy."

The teasing light went out of Dean's eyes, replaced by a surprising intensity. His fingers tightened around Sam's. "It doesn't have to be that way, Sam. You don't have to give up on being with Bo."

Sam let out a bitter laugh. "Yeah, actually, I do. He's the one who broke it off. He gave me no choice."

"There's always a choice. Don't you ever let anyone tell you there isn't."

Sam blinked, taken aback by the bite in Dean's voice and the fierce light in his eyes. "I...I don't—"

"You said you love him," Dean interrupted. "Do you, really?"

"Yes." Stung, Sam tried to pull his hands away, frowning when Dean wouldn't let him. "Let go of me."

"How does he feel about you?" Dean continued, paying no attention to Sam's protests. "Does he love you?"

"I, I don't know, he never..." Sam trailed off, hit by a sudden barrage of images in his mind's eye. Bo's fingers caressing his cheek, Bo's lips soft and trembling against his, the tender shine in Bo's eyes whenever their gazes locked across the room, before everything went wrong. The answer, Sam realized, was right there. His shoulders slumped. "He never said it. But I think he does."

"You love him. He loves you." Dean's eyes blazed. "So fight for him."

"It's not that easy," Sam stubbornly repeated.

"Why not?"

"Because. It just isn't."

It sounded petulant and childish, but Sam couldn't seem to help it. He felt a desperate need to shield himself from the wild hope Dean's words stirred inside him.

"Yes, it is." Leaning forward, Dean pinned Sam with a penetrating stare. "You love each other, Sam. What could be simpler than that?"

The man's certainty was infectious. Sam licked his lips, feeling his resistance start to crumble. "I'm scared. What if he won't have me? What if it's all too much and he won't try?"

"It'll hurt like fuck," Dean stated bluntly. "But you'll live, and eventually you'll find somebody else."

It wasn't exactly what Sam wanted to hear. He barked a humorless laugh. "I thought you were going to tell me there was no way he'd turn me down, that he'd run to me with open arms and we'd live happily ever after."

The corner of Dean's mouth hitched up in a wry half-smile. "I'm a cheerleader here, not a shameless liar."

Something about Dean's willingness to acknowledge the chance of failure made Sam feel better. "So do some more cheerleading. Tell me I can do this."

"You really can do it." Dropping his gaze, Dean stared pensively at his fingers and Sam's wound together. "It's a hard thing to do, going after what you want. *Who* you want. But if you don't try, you'll regret it for the rest of your life."

Sam gave Dean a sharp look. Deep sadness shadowed Dean's face, making him look young and vulnerable. Pulling a hand loose from Dean's grip, Sam cupped his cheek, stroking a thumb across his plump lower lip. Dean raised his head, mournful gaze meeting Sam's.

"Why do I get the feeling you gained this impressive wisdom through experience?" Sam asked.

"Like I've said before, you're smart." Turning his head, Dean pressed a kiss to the center of Sam's palm. "It was six years ago. My girlfriend left me because I was bi. I wasn't cheating on her or anything. She just couldn't handle knowing I'd slept with guys before."

Sam couldn't help feeling angry at the woman, even though he'd never known her and never would. "Don't take this the wrong way, but maybe you were better off without her, if she was that...well, that bigoted, to be frank."

"Maybe. Probably." Dean fell silent for a moment. When he spoke, his voice was soft and sad. "But I loved her, Sam. I loved her, and I let her go. I didn't fight for her. And every single day since, I've wondered what would've happened if I had."

Sam had no idea what to say. Wanting to take the sorrow out of Dean's eyes and not knowing how, Sam reached out and pulled Dean into his arms. Dean straddled Sam's lap, arms and legs wrapping around him, and laid his head on Sam's shoulder.

"I'm supposed to be comforting you," Dean mumbled, nuzzling Sam's throat. "Didn't mean to lay all my old baggage on you."

"Hey, you can come to me any time you need someone to talk to." Sam ran his hands in long, soothing strokes down Dean's back. "You helped me a lot tonight. I want to be there for you when you need help."

"Thank you." Raising his head, Dean gave Sam a hopeful look. "So, I helped you, did I?"

"Yeah."

"Does this mean you'll try to get Bo back?"

Sam swallowed. "Yes. You're right, I have to try."

"Good." Dean cradled Sam's face in his hands. "I should probably go."

"You don't have to."

"I know. And I appreciate that. But I should."

Disengaging himself from Sam's embrace, Dean slid off the bed and began retrieving his clothes from the floor. Sam did the same, watching Dean out of the corner of his eye.

"I'll drive you home," Sam offered once they were both dressed.

"That'd be great, thanks."

"It's the least I can do."

Crossing his arms over his stomach, Dean gave him a stern look. "Promise me you're not gonna angst over this, Sam."

"What, this crazy plan to get back the man I love, or the fact that I used you like a piece of meat?"

Dean shook his head. "You're angsting."

"It's hard not to."

Dean raised an eyebrow, and Sam laughed in spite of himself. "All right, I won't angst."

"That's my boy." Snatching his jacket off the chair where it had landed, Dean shrugged it on. He shoved Sam's jacket at him, grabbed Sam's wrist and tugged him toward the door.

Moved by a sudden surge of affection, Sam swept Dean into his arms and kissed his forehead. "You're a terrific guy, Dean. And a real hellcat in bed. I'm sorry we're not going to be any more than friends."

"Don't apologize to me. The last thing I need is a boyfriend cramping my style." Dean smacked Sam's butt and broke the embrace. "Now c'mon, get me home before I turn into a pumpkin."

Chuckling, Sam pulled his jacket on, made sure his wallet and keys were still in the pocket and followed Dean out the door.

♋

Sam spent a sleepless night staring at his bedroom ceiling, inventing and discarding one scenario after another of what to say to Bo. A bald declaration of his intentions would only put Bo on the defensive, and Sam knew it. But subtlety would never work. Bo was far too intelligent not to notice. Besides, Sam couldn't stand the thought of being less than honest with Bo.

In the end, he did the only thing he could. When he arrived at the BCPI office the next morning, hollow-eyed with exhaustion and more determined than he'd ever been in his life, he strode straight into Bo's office and shut the door behind him.

Bo stood at the window, arms crossed, staring out at the morning traffic. "What do you need, Sam?"

His voice was calm, but tension radiated from him. Squaring his shoulders, Sam gathered every ounce of his courage, walked around the desk and laid his hands on Bo's shoulders.

"I need you," Sam said. It wasn't what he'd planned to say, but it came straight from his heart, and he found he didn't want to take it back. "Please give us another chance."

Bo stiffened under his touch, but didn't move away. "It'll never work between us."

"No. I don't believe that." Leaning closer, Sam rested his cheek against Bo's hair and slid his arms around Bo's waist.

The fact that Bo didn't shove him away was enough to make him bold. "I'm in love with you, Bo. I can't just walk away."

Bo broke out of Sam's arms and whirled to face him, eyes wide and shocked. "What?"

"You heard me." Sam reached a hand toward Bo, then let it drop when Bo backed out of reach. "I love you, and I'm not going to let you go without a fight."

"You realize how disturbing that sounds." The way Bo's eyes softened belied the stern warning in his voice.

Sam shook his head. "I'm not a stalker, and you know it. I'd never try to force you into something you truly don't want."

"Then why are you?" Bo shot back, shoving a stray lock of hair impatiently out of his eyes. His hand shook violently. "I already told you that I want to break it off, and I told you why it has to be that way. Why can't you accept that?"

"Because I don't believe that's what you want. I think you love me too, and I think that scares you more than anything else."

All the color drained from Bo's face. He dropped his gaze to the floor. "We can't talk about this right now. We have work to do."

An odd calm came over Sam as he studied Bo's face. The war raging inside Bo was clear as day. *He needs time to think. I can give him that.*

Sam nodded. "David and Dean are probably going to the library for more research on the South Bay High property today. Cecile and I can go interview some of the students, if you want."

Bo glanced up, his relief palpable. "That'd be great. Thanks."

"No problem." Sam crossed the room and opened the office door. "I'm making some coffee, you want any?"

"No thanks." Chewing his bottom lip, Bo stared at Sam as if he wanted to say something but didn't know how. Sam waited with a patience he hadn't thought he possessed. "I don't understand, Sam," Bo burst out after a moment. "Why do you want to be with me? Why do you..."

He didn't finish the sentence, but he didn't need to. Sam knew what he was trying to say. "I don't know why I love you," Sam answered truthfully. "But I do. And that's why I want to be with you."

Lowering his gaze, Bo picked up a pen from his desk and rolled it between his fingers for a moment before laying it down again. "What you said before was true. What we were doing wasn't a normal adult relationship. I don't think it's fair of me to start things with you again unless I can at least give you what you want."

Shocked, Sam stared at Bo's profile. "You think what I said to you on Saturday was just about us not having sex?"

Bo didn't look up. "Wasn't it?"

"No. God, no." Sam ran a hand through his hair. "I mean yeah, I'm dying to get you into bed, and I'll admit I was frustrated. But sex can wait, honestly. What I was mostly upset about was that you're not ready to come out. That wasn't fair of me, I know that, and I'm sorry. I've never had a serious relationship before, and I've never had to see anyone in secret. I'm not very good at it."

Bo's mouth curved into a bitter smile. "No, you're not. But neither am I, so I'll forgive you."

Hearing the dry, pointed humor in Bo's voice lifted a huge weight from Sam's shoulders. He grinned, feeling lighter than air all of a sudden. "We both suck at relationships. We're perfect for each other."

Bo laughed. Pushing away from the desk, he walked over and slipped both arms around Sam's waist, tilting his face up in clear invitation. Cradling Bo's head in one hand, Sam kissed him, the touch soft and gentle. It felt like the most natural thing in the world, filling Sam with a wonderful sense of peace.

"Nothing good can possibly come of this," Bo declared, and bent to kiss Sam's neck. "Why can't I stay away from you?"

"Because you don't want to." Sam lifted his chin, shuddering when Bo's tongue pressed against his pulse point. "Because you know we should be together, no matter how difficult it might be."

"I'll end up hurting you." Snaking a hand under Sam's sweater, Bo pinched his nipple hard enough to make him yelp. "I don't want that."

"If you don't want to hurt me," Sam panted, thighs spreading as Bo's palm slid between his legs, "don't leave me again. I can handle anything but that."

Massaging Sam's swelling cock through his jeans, Bo bit delicately at the angle of his jaw. "What if leaving is the best thing I can do for you?"

"It isn't." Unable to think past the waves of pleasure, Sam grabbed Bo's wrists, pulling his hands away from his crotch. "Listen to me, Bo. I know you think you're hurting me by keeping us a secret, and by not going to bed with me. And I know I made you think that. But I've realized that even though those things are important, there's nothing more important to me than being with you. Whatever that means."

Bo stared at him, dark eyes brimming with fear and want. "What about my sons? I won't lose them, Sam. I won't. If it comes down to keeping them or keeping you, I'll choose them, no matter how much it hurts us both."

That stung, though Sam knew it shouldn't have. Bo couldn't be expected to favor Sam over his children. "I know that, and I understand, believe it or not. But I don't think it'll come to that. I think Janine's manipulating you, Bo. She can't possibly know about us, we've been too careful. And even if she did, I'm pretty sure it wouldn't be enough for her legally keep the kids away from you. Even cheating spouses get to see their kids, and you didn't cheat on her."

Closing his eyes, Bo leaned against Sam's chest, his head resting in the curve of Sam's neck. "I hope you're right."

"Me too." Sam wrapped his arms around Bo, holding him tight. Holding on for dear life.

Chapter Nine

By the time David and Cecile arrived twenty minutes later, Sam was hard at work on his computer. He glanced up and grinned at his friends.

"Hi guys," he said as the couple entered the office. "Cold today, huh?"

"I'll say." David shrugged his jacket off and hung it on the coat rack. "What the hell happened to that nice warm weather we were having?"

"It's November, sweetie. November's usually cold, even here." Handing David her coat to hang up, Cecile hurried over to the coffeepot and started to pour cups for herself and David. "What are you working on, Sam?"

"A list of questions. I talked to Bo earlier, we figured you and I could go out today and talk to the South Bay students whose names Mr. Innes gave us. David, you and Dean are doing some more library research today, right?"

"That was the plan, yeah." David wandered over to stand beside Sam. "Speaking of Dean, didn't y'all go out last night?"

A jolt of panic shot through Sam. He glanced at Bo's half-open office door. Bo had the phone receiver pressed to his ear, nodding as he scribbled something on a notepad. To Sam's relief, he didn't seem to have heard David.

"We ended up not going out," Sam answered, keeping his voice low. "We just sat and talked for a while. Hey, how'd you know that anyhow?"

"Overheard you asking him."

"David." Cecile gave her boyfriend a disapproving glare along with his coffee. "You shouldn't listen in on other people's conversations."

"Thanks, babe." Taking the Styrofoam cup from Cecile, David grinned, utterly unrepentant. "Hey, I was just glad Sam took my great advice." Leaning his free hand on Sam's desk, David dropped his voice to a conspiratorial murmur. "So. You, um...talked. How'd that go?"

Sam quirked an eyebrow at his friend. "You really want details?"

David paled. "Details?"

The temptation to tease was strong, but Sam took pity on him. "Don't worry, David, I wouldn't give you the details even if there were any to give."

It was only a small lie. Sam figured the real details were no one else's business, especially since he and Dean were not about to become a couple.

Before David could say anything else, the door opened and the man under discussion breezed in. "Man, it's freezing out there." Rubbing his hands together, Dean dipped his head at his coworkers. "Morning, y'all."

"Hi, Dean." With a mischievous glance at Sam, David moved over to his own desk and plopped into the chair. "Sam was just telling us y'all had a really nice talk last night."

Dean's expression didn't change at all. Sam was impressed.

"A very nice talk, yes," Dean agreed. "Is that fresh coffee?"

"Yeah." Leaning back in his chair, Sam gave Dean what he hoped was a casual smile. "I just made it about fifteen minutes ago."

"Fabulous." Dean crossed the room in a few strides, poured himself a cup and sipped it. He licked his lips, eyelids fluttering blissfully shut. "God, you have no idea how much I needed this."

"Didn't sleep much?" David asked, his face the picture of innocence.

Sam felt his cheeks go pink. Swiveling his chair around, he feigned deep interest in the list he'd been working on. *Please don't say anything,* he silently begged Dean.

"Slept like a baby, thanks," Dean answered cheerfully. "But I froze my ass off walking over from the bus stop. I will be *so* happy when my car's finally fixed."

Sam stared at the document on his computer screen without seeing it. Beside him, Dean sank into a chair and sat sipping coffee, making little pleasure noises that reminded Sam vividly of the previous night. If he hadn't been so worried about his face telling the world he'd had Dean in his bed, it might have bothered him that Dean evidently enjoyed mediocre coffee as much as sex with Sam.

The squeal of the front door opening was a relief. Sam looked up and smiled. "Hi, Andre."

"Hi." Andre unzipped his jacket and pulled it off, throwing it over the top of the coat rack. "I hate winter."

"You said it," David agreed.

Andre shuffled over to join the group, lowering himself into his chair with a sigh. "So what're we doing today?"

"David and Dean are going back to the library to do some more research on the history of the South Bay property," Cecile said. "Sam and I thought we'd go interview some of the students. I'm not sure what Bo's plans are."

"Bo's plans involve massive amounts of paperwork," Bo answered, walking in from his office with what looked like a stack of bills in his hand and a pen stuck behind one ear. "Andre, we have a pile of potential clients that we need to call, would you mind starting that for me? I can help you when I get caught up on the books."

"Sure thing." Holding a hand out, Andre took the list of names Bo handed him and set it on his desk. "We're all off tomorrow, so I guess we'll head back to the school on Friday, huh?"

At first Sam didn't know what Andre meant. Then he remembered. The next day was Thanksgiving. It would be the first time in his life Sam had spent a holiday alone. The thought was depressing.

"Yes," Bo said. "We'll meet here at eight a.m. Friday morning and head over to South Bay together. I was thinking we could do the whole tunnel as a group. That way we can get video, audio, stills and psychic readings all at one time. What do y'all think?"

"Sounds like a plan, boss-man." Draining his coffee cup, David hopped to his feet and nudged Dean's shoulder. "C'mon, let's go grab some breakfast before the library opens. I'm starved."

Cecile raised an eyebrow at him, but said nothing. Sam stifled a groan. By now, he knew David well enough to know he was going to grill Dean for information. *But not details,* Sam thought with a mix of amusement and irritation. He realized David was simply concerned about him, and he appreciated that. But he didn't want anyone else, even a close friend like David, to know what he'd done. Taking Dean to bed had been a mistake. He was lucky Dean was so perceptive and had such a huge, loving heart. Most men wouldn't have been so understanding, and he knew it. He much preferred to keep it between himself and Dean. Especially if he still had a chance to be with Bo.

Christ, my life's such a fucking soap opera. Sam bit back a laugh.

Shooting Sam a curious glance, Dean stood and stretched. "Okay. I want pancakes."

"What makes you think I'm buying?" David asked as they headed toward the door.

"You invited me. Therefore, you're buying. It's the rules." Tossing David his jacket, Dean pulled his own jacket on and zipped it up. "I just took this off. I'm not even thawed out yet."

"Don't worry, Princess, we'll take my car." David leaned over Cecile's desk and kissed her. "See y'all later."

Sam turned to Cecile as David and Dean left, Dean still complaining about the cold and David teasing him for it. "I guess we should wait a while before we go see the students."

"Definitely." Sliding open the bottom drawer of her desk, Cecile pulled out a sheet of paper with several names, addresses and phone numbers on it. "These are the students who've agreed to talk to us. They have their parents' permission, we just need to call ahead before we go to see them."

From the corner of his eye, Sam saw Bo lean against the wall and hook his thumbs in the front pockets of his jeans. He looked unbearably sexy. Sam had to fight back an urge to throw himself at Bo and kiss him until his lips bruised.

"Thanks for doing this," Bo said softly.

"Just doing the job." Sam flashed a quick smile at Bo. He hadn't intended to let his sudden lust show, but the way Bo's cheeks flushed told him he'd failed miserably at keeping it hidden.

"Um. Yeah." Bo licked his lips, dark eyes flicking down to Sam's mouth then back up again. "Okay, I, uh...I need to get back to the accounting stuff."

Andre stared as Bo turned and walked rather stiffly back into his office, swinging the door shut behind him. "Okay," he murmured, "is it just me, or is Bo acting very strange?"

Sam fought not to react. He shrugged and turned back to his partly finished list of interview questions, hoping the others wouldn't think anything of his silence.

"It's not just you," Cecile answered in a low tone. "He hasn't really been himself lately."

"Probably Janine." Andre's voice held an unmistakable note of anger. "I know Bo's having a hard time with the divorce, but I have to tell you, leaving that woman's the best thing Bo's ever done. She's never been good for him."

"Hm. I've only met her once, but I got that same feeling." Cecile let out a soft laugh. "David said I felt that because I'm psychic, and I could read her evil thoughts. I had to remind him my gift doesn't work that way. I can't read minds."

"You're just good at reading people, I think." Andre chuckled. "David's always hated Janine, since the first day he met her."

"Why?" Cecile asked. "I can't say that I liked her myself when I met her, but it was just a feeling. I had nothing on which to base it. I'm wondering what she did to make David dislike her so much."

Sam wondered the same thing. He figured his own experience with Janine was hopelessly tainted by his involvement with Bo. A more objective opinion would be interesting to hear.

Andre was silent for several long seconds. Curious, Sam turned his chair around. His friend's face was thoughtful. "Andre?" Sam asked hesitantly. "What is it?"

Glancing at Bo's closed door, Andre rolled his chair closer. "I shouldn't be telling y'all this at all, so keep it to yourselves, okay?"

"Sure." Sam leaned forward, elbows on his knees. "What?"

Cecile frowned. "I don't know, Andre. Is this something David told you in confidence? Because if that's the case I don't think you should be telling us."

"He never actually said not to tell anyone at all. Just not to tell Bo." Andre's voice dropped to a whisper. "He said the first time he met Janine, she propositioned him. And apparently she wasn't too happy when he turned her down and called her a bitch for trying to cheat on Bo, with one of Bo's friend no less."

Stunned, Sam stared at Andre. "Seriously?"

Andre nodded. "He said she acted like it was no big thing, like she did it all the time."

"And he didn't tell Bo?" Cecile's expression radiated disapproval. "I think he should have."

"We kind of went back and forth about that," Andre admitted, glancing at Bo's office door again. "But in the end, all he had to go on was her hitting on him that once. She never did it again, of course, and although we both kept our eyes peeled neither of us ever actually caught her at anything. So what would we say? You know Bo wouldn't have ended his marriage over one incident."

"Well, he's ending it over something now," Cecile pointed out. "I wonder if that has anything to do with it. Maybe he caught her out."

Sam kept quiet and schooled his face into a blank expression. As much as he would've liked to lay all the blame on Janine's possible infidelity, he knew better. In any case, Bo would've told him if he'd caught Janine in a compromising situation. The potential leverage it would afford Bo if she *had* cheated on him, however, did not escape Sam. He filed the idea away for future reference.

"I don't know," Andre said. "Maybe. Whatever his reasons are, though, it's a good move for him, in my opinion."

"I think you're right." The words were out before Sam had time to think about what he was doing. *Fuck it,* he thought, shoving the quick flash of panic impatiently away. He was sick of watching every word he said. "I mean, I don't really know her, but I got the same sort of feeling as you, Cecile. Like she wasn't good for him."

"And you want everything to be good for him." Cecile's voice was very soft. If it hadn't been for her sharp, searching gaze, Sam would've thought she was talking to herself.

He refused to look away from her. "We all want that, don't we?"

Cecile's smile was knowing and a little sad. "Yes, I suppose we do."

Andre looked from one to the other in evident confusion, but kept his thoughts to himself. "Okay. Well, I need to start looking into these investigation requests."

"I'll give it another hour or so, then call around and see what time we can go talk to some of the kids on this list," Cecile added. "I'll try to set up at least one appointment for later this morning, Sam. With any luck we can talk to all of the students today."

Sam nodded. "Great. I'll have our questions ready in a little bit."

The three of them turned back to their respective jobs, and Sam allowed himself to relax a little. As he typed, he thought about Cecile, and the sympathetic way she'd looked at him before. He'd wondered before if she suspected about him and Bo. Now, he was sure she did. To his surprise, it didn't bother him. He knew she wouldn't say anything, not even to David.

It suddenly hit Sam that Cecile was the second of his friends to find out about him and Bo. First Dean, now her. Somehow, the thought was comforting rather than frightening. Smiling to himself, he finished his list of questions and hit print.

♋

The first two students Sam and Cecile talked to weren't able to tell them anything they hadn't already heard about the missing students, or the rumors of what had taken them. Both had known at least one of the missing students in a waving-hello-in-the-halls sort of way, but weren't good friends with any of them. One boy had been in the tunnels once, but hadn't seen anything unusual.

Both kids spoke with breathless, horrified awe of the creatures that had been glimpsed by a friend of a friend, or the weird noises some students swore they heard in the courtyard during rare moments of quiet. Their tales sounded like the sorts of stories that always surrounded old, atmospheric buildings, growing through years of telling and retelling and gathering embellishments along the way.

The thing was, none of the stories involving South Bay were more than a few weeks old.

"This is really fucking weird," Sam said as he and Cecile climbed into the SUV, heading for the next interview. "Both of these kids can remember almost exactly when people started talking about things living in the tunnels."

"Yes. The day after the first disappearance." Turning in her seat, Cecile backed the SUV carefully out of the driveway then started down the narrow street. "Honestly, I'm not sure how much importance to attach to it. Stories are bound to spring up after something like that happens."

"That's true. But think about it for a minute. We're already pretty sure that there's a dimensional gateway in the tunnel, right?"

"As much as I hate to admit it, yes." Cecile sighed. "That scares me, Sam. Even though it doesn't seem to be as out of control as the one at Oleander House."

"No, it doesn't, does it?" Sam frowned, thinking of what Cecile said. Shaking off the disturbing possibilities that sprang into his head, he focused on regaining his previous train of thought. "Let's talk that over with the rest of the group later."

"Good idea." Cecile smiled as she turned onto the Cottage Hill Road traffic. "So. You were saying that we're pretty sure there's a gateway in the tunnel."

"Yes. And if that's the case, the rumors of things hiding in the tunnels would be more or less accurate."

"True."

"So here's an interesting thought." Twisting in his seat, Sam stared at Cecile's profile. "Why weren't there any stories before now?"

Cecile glanced at him, brow creased in thought. "That's a good question. Oleander House had a history going back over a hundred years, even though it was intermittent. This school has nothing like that, or at least it sounds like it doesn't. The students would know if it did, I'd think."

"David and Dean haven't mentioned any similar stories turning up in their research," Sam mused, rubbing his chin. "We can ask them when we all get back to the office."

Cecile was silent for a moment, a pensive expression on her face as she guided the SUV through the afternoon traffic. "What I'm wondering is, what does it mean?"

A theory had been forming in Sam's head. A profoundly disturbing one. He almost hated to voice it. But keeping it to himself wouldn't make it any less true.

"I think," he said reluctantly, "that the gateway is being controlled somehow."

"Controlled?" Cecile shot a wide-eyed look at him. "By who?"

Sam had force the words out. "By something from the other side."

The way Cecile's hands tightened on the steering wheel spoke volumes. She didn't have to speak for Sam to know she thought he was right.

They drove the short distance to the next student's residence in silence. Pulling up in front of a two-story brick apartment building, Cecile parked the SUV and shut off the engine. "This is the only other student whose parents would let her talk to us. Her name's Karen Redmond. Apparently she was dating Patrick Callahan, the first boy who disappeared."

"Maybe she saw something." Sam opened the door and hopped out, frowning as he and Cecile walked to the front door of the building. "I hope she didn't, though."

147

The sadness in Cecile's eyes told Sam she knew exactly what he meant. He hated to think of a teenage girl having to watch her boyfriend being dragged off by a creature like they'd faced at Oleander House.

In the building's small, dingy lobby, Cecile found the correct buzzer and pushed the button. After a moment, a man's voice answered, flat and tinny through the intercom. "Yeah? Who is it?"

"Cecile Langlois and Sam Raintree, from Bay City Paranormal Investigations," Cecile answered. "I spoke to you on the phone this morning, you said we could come by and talk to Karen."

A short silence followed. "Okay, come on up. Second floor, turn right from the top of the stairs. We're in 23B."

"Thank you." Letting go of the intercom button, Cecile took a deep breath. "Okay. Let's go."

They tramped up the stairs, found the apartment and knocked on the door. It was answered a matter of seconds later by a tall, thin man with a graying beard. He held a hand out.

"I'm Gene, Karen's dad. Nice to meet you both. Come on in."

"Thank you for letting us come over today, Gene." Cecile returned their host's smile. "I know it's an imposition, this close to the holiday."

"Not really. It's just Karen and me, since her mom died last year. You're not interrupting any plans." Gene's smile faded, sorrow clouding his face. "She's had a hard time of it. First losing her mother, then her boyfriend going missing. He's a good kid. I hope they find him."

Sam didn't know what to say. He shoved his hands in his pockets, wishing he wouldn't feel so uncomfortable in the face of other people's raw emotions.

148

To his relief, Cecile took control of the situation. "Gene, is Karen ready to talk to us?"

Gene nodded. "Sure. Y'all sit down, I'll get her."

Sam sat beside Cecile on a worn flowered sofa. Looking out the window behind the couch, he saw a large courtyard with a basketball court and a small rectangular pool. Dead leaves littered the top of the blue plastic pool cover. Two toddlers chased each other across the thin grass, shrieking with laughter. A young woman sat on a bench nearby, reading a book and glancing up every few seconds at the playing children.

It was a sweetly domestic scene, in spite of the general shabbiness of the place. It saddened Sam to think he would probably never have that for himself. For a while, he'd dared to hope he could have that with Bo. That they'd walk through Bienville Square hand in hand on fine summer mornings. Maybe take Bo's sons to the beach or the Gulfarium, smile and laugh and steal kisses while the boys played.

You'd probably be terrible with kids anyway. Sam turned away from the happy family scene outside the window.

It wasn't long before the door on the other side of the small living room opened and a teenage girl came shuffling through. She was petite, full-figured and pretty, with wavy reddish brown hair pulled into a disheveled ponytail and big, bright blue eyes that reminded Sam painfully of Amy. Her round cheeks were flushed pink, freckled snub nose red and blotchy as if she'd been crying. Gene stood behind her, hands protectively on her shoulders.

"Karen wants to talk to you alone," he said, sounding less than happy. "I'll be in my bedroom, okay, sweetie?"

"'K. Thanks, Daddy." Karen patted his hand as he kissed her cheek and left the room.

Cecile rose to her feet and smiled as she held out her hand. "Hi, Karen. I'm Cecile, and this is Sam. We're from Bay City Paranormal Investigations."

"Yeah, I know, Daddy told me." Karen shook Cecile's hand, then Sam's, her grip hesitant as if she wasn't sure she should be doing it. "Mr. Innes said y'all are investigating the school."

"Yes, we are." Cecile sat back down when Karen plopped into a chair. Sam did the same. "Mr. Innes tells us that many of the students have talked about seeing strange things in the tunnels under the school. Have you had any unusual experiences there, or heard about anyone else having them?"

"I've never been in the tunnels. Patrick..." Karen bit her lip, tears welling in her eyes. "He used to try to talk me into going down there with him. Not like skipping class or anything, just during lunch break and stuff. But I didn't want to. My friend Sharla said the tunnels were full of bugs. I don't like bugs."

"Karen, you don't have to talk with us if you don't feel up to it," Sam said gently.

Karen stared at him with wide, watery eyes. "No, I want to. I wanna tell y'all what happened to Patrick."

A jolt of adrenaline shot through Sam's veins. Exchanging a quick glance with Cecile, he leaned forward, clasping his hands together. "Were you with him when he disappeared, Karen?"

The girl's face crumpled. Snatching a tissue from a box beside the sofa, she blew her nose. "Yeah. I told the cops just exactly what I saw, but they didn't believe me. They thought I was, like, just traumatized or something, you know?"

Sam tensed. Beside him, he felt Cecile do the same. "What happened?" Cecile asked, her voice soft and calm.

Drawing her knees up, Karen rested her chin on them and wrapped an arm around her legs. Her knuckles were white. "We were walking to class together. We were going from the

150

Language Arts building to the main building, across the courtyard. And when we got near that big tree in the middle..."

She trailed off, staring at her toes. Her fingers trembled where they gripped her jeans. Concerned, Sam reached out and gently touched her hand. "Karen?"

The girl's eyes shifted and focused on Sam's face, full of shock and sorrow. "Something got him," she whispered. "Everything got kind of dark and fuzzy, then the ground opened up and...something came out. And, and it grabbed Patrick, and dragged him into the ground. And then it was gone, and Patrick was gone, and I looked but I couldn't find the place again." Karen drew a deep, shuddering breath, ending on a sob. "They won't find him. He's dead, I know it. That...that thing, it was...it was..."

Sam knew what it was. All the hairs on his arms stood up as a hard chill raced over his skin. Glancing sideways, he saw his own cringing horror mirrored in Cecile's face.

Slipping off the sofa, Cecile knelt beside Karen's chair. "Are you okay, honey?"

Karen didn't answer. "Do you think I'm crazy? Everyone else does."

The girl's blue eyes pleaded for understanding, and Sam felt a sharp pang of sympathy for her. She was utterly alone, burdened by a knowledge her teachers, her peers, and even her loving father couldn't understand or believe. Sam knew the feeling all too well, having experienced the cautious looks and malicious whispers in his own youth, before he learned to keep quiet about the strange things he'd see from time to time.

"You're not crazy," Sam told her, making sure his conviction was clear in his voice. "I can't be sure precisely what you saw, but whatever it was, we're going to find it. And we're going to do our best to stop it."

He hadn't meant to say that, but he didn't retract the statement. Even though the promise wasn't planned, it was sincere. Cecile turned to frown at him, but didn't contradict him.

Rising to her feet, Cecile laid a hand on Karen's shoulder. "We had several more questions, but I don't think it'll be necessary to ask them. Thank you for talking to us, Karen."

"Here's our number." Sam stood, pulled a business card from his pocket and handed it to Karen. "If you think of anything else you feel we need to know, or if you have any questions or concerns, call us. Okay?"

"Okay." Karen gave them a shaky smile. "Thanks. For believing me, I mean."

"Sure thing." Sam returned her smile, wishing he could erase that lost look from her eyes. No sixteen-year-old, he thought, should ever have to look like that. "We'll be in touch."

Gene emerged from the bedroom as they were leaving, making Sam wonder if he'd been listening in. He followed them silently out the front door. In the hallway, he shut the door, crossed his arms and gave them a stern glare.

"Listen," he said. "I know y'all are trying to help. But I'm telling you right now, I won't tolerate anyone encouraging these delusions of hers. She's been through enough without you people giving her the idea that she really saw this...this *thing* she thinks she saw."

Cecile started to speak, but Sam cut her off. "What makes you think it's her imagination? Is she in the habit of making up wild stories, or of seeing things that aren't there?"

Gene frowned, an angry flush rising up his neck. "I think you should both leave now."

"We're going," Cecile jumped in before Sam could say a word. "Thank you for letting us come over."

Clamping a hand firmly around Sam's wrist, Cecile dragged him toward the stairs. They walked down the steps and out to the SUV without saying a word. It wasn't until they were back on the road, heading to the office, that Cecile spoke.

"Would you care to explain to me," she said with remarkable calm, "just what the hell that was all about?"

Sam wanted to pretend he didn't understand the question, but he knew she wouldn't believe it. He sighed and leaned against the window. "That girl saw exactly what she says she saw, and we both know it. She's not crazy. She needs her father to believe her."

Cecile's expression softened. "I don't disagree with you, Sam. I feel as bad for Karen as you do. But you can't go around antagonizing the parents, and you *absolutely* can't make promises you have no way of knowing you can keep."

"I know." Sam stared at the paper cut on the side of his thumb. "I didn't intend to say that, it just sort of came out. But I meant it." Raising his head, he stared at Cecile as if he could make her understand by force of will. "We have to stop this thing, Cecile. And I think I can do it. I just have to figure out how."

Surprisingly, Cecile seemed to expect this. She nodded, never taking her attention from the heavy afternoon traffic. "We all have to figure it out. We're in this together, remember? You don't have to do this alone."

Sam's throat tightened. "I know," he said softly. "Thanks."

She smiled, reached over and patted his hand. The gesture reinforced what Sam already knew—he, Cecile and the others were a team. A family of sorts, after all they'd been through together. The thought was comforting.

He tried not to think of the fact that, even though Andre and Cecile both had psychic abilities that surpassed his own,

153

neither was psychokinetic. If the theories were correct, that meant only Sam had the power to open or close the gateway. The others would do everything they could to help him. He didn't doubt that for a moment. But in the end, it all came down to him.

If only he knew how to do what he had to do. He watched the city sweep past as they drove along and hoped he could manage it before another person died.

♋

When they arrived back at the office, they found their coworkers huddled around David's desk, all talking at once. Sam and Cecile glanced at each other.

"We're back," Cecile announced. "What's up?"

Straightening up, David bounded over and gave Cecile an enthusiastic kiss. "Hey. Me and Dean found out some really interesting things today, we were just discussing it. What about y'all, you learn anything good from the students you talked to?"

"We did, yeah." Sam shrugged out of his jacket, hung it on the rack and went to join the others. "But I think I want to hear whatever y'all found out first."

"Wait 'til you hear this." Dean grabbed Sam's hand and pulled him into an empty chair. "It's really amazing. Tell them, David."

Sam glanced at Bo, who was perched on the edge of the desk. The man's gaze shifted from Sam to Dean and back again. His eyes narrowed, and Sam's stomach rolled. If Bo found out he'd had sex with Dean, he'd never forgive him.

And whose fault would that be? Sam thought bitterly. *If you lose him for good over this, you've got no one to blame but yourself.*

Cecile's laugh cut through Sam's morose thoughts. "Yes, David, tell us."

"Okay." Moving back to his chair, David sat and pulled Cecile into his lap. "This time, we figured we'd have a look at the records of the South Bay property before the monks bought it. We thought we'd see if there were any records of disappearances like with the monks and with the students now."

"And what did you find?" Sam asked.

David rested his chin on Cecile's shoulder, his eyes sparkling with excitement. "We learned a lot about the history of the property. But what it comes down to is this—people have been vanishing from that property ever since the sixteenth century."

"And here's the really interesting part," Dean added. "The disappearances have happened at regular intervals. Every eighty-three years, for a few months at a time, and then it stops. The last one before the monks was the disappearance of an entire family. It was their house the monks found on the property. No one ever knew what happened to them."

A sense of looming revelation made Sam's pulse race. His gaze locked with Cecile's, and he knew they were thinking the same thing.

Not only did a dimensional gateway lurk in the tunnels under South Bay High, but its opening was no accident. It was just as Sam thought—something was controlling it. Something from the other side.

Chapter Ten

"What we were just talking about when you got here," Bo said, tugging on his braid, "was what exactly such a regular pattern of disappearances might mean."

Andre gave Sam and Cecile a considering look. "Why do I think you two might have some ideas?"

Sam glanced at Cecile. She huddled closer to David, brown eyes wide and solemn. "We do sort of have a theory, yeah," Sam acknowledged. "We think that the things from the other side are somehow controlling the gateway."

Bo looked startled, then his expression turned thoughtful. "Hm. That's an interesting thought. It fits, too. Nearly identical incidents every eighty-three years, with nothing in between, couldn't possibly be random. It stands to reason that the gateway is under some sort of control."

"But it could be that stuff has happened, and we just haven't found those records yet," David suggested.

"We didn't even find any folktales or anything about that site, though," Dean pointed out. "To me, that says people didn't experience strange things there in the times between the active periods. Hell, we only found a couple of accounts where anybody claimed to see anything unusual even while people were vanishing left and right."

"That fits with what we found out today," Sam said. "The biggest thing we learned from the student interviews was that these rumors of weird creatures living in the tunnels are only a few weeks old."

"The stories started up right after Patrick Callahan disappeared last month," Cecile chimed in. "He was the first one. We spoke with his girlfriend, Karen. She was with him when he vanished."

All eyes in the room homed in on Cecile. "What did she see?" Bo asked.

Cecile clutched David's hand tightly in hers. "She said they were walking to class across the courtyard, when suddenly everything turned, as she put it, 'dark and fuzzy', the ground opened up, and something came out and dragged Patrick back into the earth with it."

Andre's face went ashen. "Oh, fuck. That sounds like..."

He didn't finish the thought, but there was no need. The horrified expressions on his friends' faces told Sam they were all thinking the same thing.

"Before Patrick disappeared, the tunnels were just another place to go to smoke or drink or make out," Sam continued. "Just like when you were in school, Dean. Karen even mentioned that she'd refused to ever go in the tunnels because of the bugs."

Leaning back on his hands, Bo pinned Sam with a penetrating stare. "Okay, so, there were no stories about things in the tunnels until last month. After the first student vanished, the rumors started up. What sorts of things have the students seen and heard, exactly? Other than Karen's experience, poor kid."

"The two we talked to before Karen hadn't experienced anything themselves," Cecile told him, shifting in David's lap and winding an arm around his shoulders. "They'd mostly heard stories third and fourth hand. But the things they'd heard actually reinforce the theory that the tunnel contains a dimensional gateway. They were talking about seeing strange fogs in the tunnel, and hearing hissing or other frightening noises both in the tunnel and in the courtyard."

Frowning, Dean shoved his bangs out of his eyes and leaned back in his chair. "There's something I don't understand, though. The tunnel where we found the old pit was bricked up until we had it opened. If the students saw things in the main tunnel, how could it be the beings from the other dimension? It sounds like they were operating almost like a trapdoor spider, lying in wait and taking kids as they passed through the courtyard, rather than snatching them from the tunnel."

"I've been wondering that myself." Bo pushed away from the desk and started pacing. "Okay, here's a thought. Karen said that the ground opened up, right?" He glanced at Sam and Cecile, who both nodded. "We saw nothing but solid grass and concrete walkways when we explored the courtyard. I don't think there's an actual trapdoor, because I believe we would have noticed. There's just no way to hide such a thing from anything more than superficial investigation, and we were hardly superficial."

"If there's no trapdoor or something like that, then what do you think it is?" Andre asked, crossing his arms and raising his eyebrows at Bo.

Bo smiled, eyes glowing with the thrill of discovery, and Sam's chest constricted. He loved seeing that look on Bo's face, the childlike excitement that came from putting another piece of the puzzle in its place.

"I think maybe these beings can manipulate matter on an atomic, or possibly subatomic level," Bo told them. "If they can control a doorway between dimensions, I think it's reasonable that they would also have the technology—or, hell, the psychokinetic brain power—to rearrange atoms to create a temporary opening where there normally isn't one. Matter is made up of mostly empty space anyway."

"That might explain a few other things as well," Cecile mused. "You remember how we had so much trouble finding the spot in the courtyard where the pit would be, in spite of having Dean's measurements of the tunnel to go by. And Karen said that when she looked for the place where Patrick disappeared, she couldn't find it again."

"So you think these things might be able to camouflage their hiding place, is that it?" Dean's eyes shone with the light of pure scientific curiosity. "Wow."

Bo nodded. "I hadn't thought of that, Cecile. That's a good point."

"We were able to see every inch of the courtyard perfectly well, though. But we still couldn't find the spot. We felt like we kept getting lost." Curling one foot underneath him in the chair, Sam chewed his thumbnail as he worked out his thoughts. "Maybe it's a psychic camouflage rather than physical."

David's eyebrows went up. "You mean they just make people *think* they can't find it?"

"Kind of, yeah." Sam shrugged. "It's just an idea. I don't know, obviously."

"The big question here is, why?" Andre stared at the floor, a muscle in his jaw twitching. "Assuming this really is a dimensional portal, and that those fucking things are opening it at will, snatching innocent kids and most likely killing them, *why* are they doing it?"

A heavy silence fell. After a few tense seconds, Cecile's voice broke it, soft and hesitant. "I'm not sure we'll ever know, Andre.

They're intelligent, we know that, but their minds are so different from ours that I don't see how we could possibly understand their motives."

Andre didn't answer, but Sam knew he was thinking of Amy, just as Sam was. Just as they all were, even Dean who'd never known her and hadn't witnessed her death. Looking around at the people who had become his family, Sam had an idea. It terrified him beyond belief, but at the same time it felt like the right thing to do. He knew he had to try, if only to provide Andre with some sort of closure.

Drawing a deep breath, Sam straightened up in his chair. "At Oleander House, the thing communicated with me. I could sense what it was thinking. Or, well, some of it, anyway. Maybe I can do that again. Maybe I can get inside its mind, and find out why it's doing this."

In a shockingly quick movement, Bo pushed away from the desk and grabbed Sam's arm in a painful grip. Sam stared up at him, stunned speechless. "Bo, what—"

"No." Bo's voice was cold and clipped, his eyes hard. "You are *not* going to try to talk to that thing."

Torn between annoyance at Bo treating him like a child and a melting warmth at the man's obvious desire to protect him, Sam sputtered incoherently for a moment. "Don't you think that's up to me to decide?" he demanded when he got his voice back. "Don't you think—"

"No, I don't," Bo interrupted. "And neither do you, if you think for one second I'm going to let you risk yourself like that. No."

Sam shot furtive glances around the room as Bo started pacing, pulling savagely at the end of his braid. David and Andre gaped at Bo, clearly taken aback by his uncharacteristic outburst. Cecile watched Bo stalk back and forth across the floor, the corner of her mouth curled up in a knowing half-smile.

Leaning toward Sam, Dean reached over and gently squeezed his hand. Sam gave him a grateful smile.

"I don't plan on taking any unnecessary risks." Sam retrieved his hand from Dean's grip. "I just want to try, Bo. That's all."

Bo stopped and stood staring out the front window. "I know some of you have plans tomorrow. Why don't we call it a day? Be here at eight a.m. Friday and we'll complete the investigation of the old tunnel."

Sam had heard that tone before, and they all knew it brooked no argument. With a deep sigh, Sam swiveled around to switch off his computer. As everyone else collected jackets and other belongings, Sam felt Dean's hands on his shoulders.

"Have a good Thanksgiving, Sam," Dean said softly. "See you Friday."

"Yeah, you too." Sam turned and smiled up at Dean. "Thanks."

"Sure thing." Patting Sam's cheek, Dean backed away and headed toward the door.

"Dean," Bo said as Dean got his jacket down from the coat rack, "could you stay for a few minutes, please? I'd like to talk to you."

Dean's eyes widened, but he otherwise showed no reaction. "Sure, Bo." He flashed a wide smile at the rest of his coworkers. "See y'all Friday."

Nervously, Sam watched Dean follow Bo into his office. *He won't say anything,* Sam told himself as he tugged his jacket on. He trusted Dean to keep their tryst secret. Unless, of course, Bo asked him point blank if he and Sam had slept together. And therein lay the problem.

Sam knew Dean wouldn't tell Bo what had happened between them unless he had no choice. What Sam didn't know was whether Bo already suspected, and what he would do if he learned the truth.

♋

Sam spent a long, restless night in an agony of apprehension. His mind kept conjuring scenes of Bo dragging a confession out of Dean. The mental picture of Bo's face filling with hurt and anger knotted Sam's stomach. The worst part of it was that he didn't know which would upset Bo most—that he'd had sex with Dean, or that Dean knew Bo was gay.

Just before dawn, Sam gave up on sleeping. Kicking the covers aside, he dragged himself out of bed and shuffled into the bathroom. After relieving himself and brushing his teeth, Sam briefly considered lounging around in his underwear all day. He swiftly dismissed the idea as sad and pathetic.

Heading back into the bedroom, he put on a pair of well-worn jeans and a long-sleeved Radiohead T-shirt. His mother would've frowned and ordered him to change, he thought, smiling as he sauntered into the kitchen.

While the coffee brewed, he leaned against the counter, head swimming with exhaustion. He laughed, the sound rough and devoid of humor.

"Happy fucking Thanksgiving," he muttered to the dirty dishes in the sink.

A few minutes later, he settled into the chair by the window with a huge mug of lethally strong coffee. Outside, the faint light revealed a gray and dreary sky. It fit Sam's mood. Whatever happened, Sam knew he had no one to blame but himself. He accepted that. But it didn't make it any easier to face the possibility of losing his last chance with Bo.

Sam nearly jumped out of his skin when someone banged on his door, rattling it in its frame. Cursing under his breath, he glanced at the clock and frowned. *Who the fuck shows up at six in the morning on Thanksgiving?* He set his coffee mug on the windowsill and hurried to the door.

Peering through the peephole, Sam was startled to see Bo standing in the hall, lips pressed into a thin line and dark eyes shooting sparks. Sam's stomach plummeted into his feet. "Oh shit," he whispered as Bo raised a fist and started pounding on the door again.

"I know you're in there, Sam!" Bo shouted. "Open this fucking door right now."

For a second, Sam seriously debated whether letting Bo in would be wise. The man was clearly furious, and Sam didn't relish being on the receiving end of Bo's anger. He knew from experience Bo packed a powerful punch.

If he wants to hit you, he sure as hell has a right to, after what you did. Licking his suddenly dry lips, Sam slid back the deadbolt and swung the door open.

"Bo, I—"

"Shut up." Pushing past Sam, Bo swept into the apartment and turned to Sam with a dangerous fire in his eyes. "Did you?"

Sam saw no point in delaying the inevitable by pretending he didn't know what Bo meant. "Yes," he said softly as he shut the door. "It was a huge mistake. I'm sorry."

"You're sorry?" Bo let out a harsh laugh. "You're sorry. You told me it wasn't about sex, no, not at all, it was about us being together openly. And yet the minute I call it off, you fuck the first guy who'll have you. And you're *sorry.*"

"I am." Sam kept himself still, his voice carefully calm. "You have every right to be angry with me."

"Do I?" Shaking his head, Bo started pacing in a tight circle. "I don't know. I broke up with you, after all. Hell, I told you to go out with Dean. But I *am* angry, whether I have a right to be or not. I just can't stand the thought of you with someone else."

"Neither can I." Taking a cautious step forward, Sam brushed his fingers against Bo's upper arm. "What happened with Dean just proved to me that I don't want anyone else but you."

Bo jerked away from Sam's touch. He resumed pacing, gaze locked on the floor. Swallowing his hurt, Sam backed up and leaned against the wall, waiting for whatever Bo would do next.

"I had a feeling, you know?" Bo said, his voice low and ragged. "Just the way you looked at each other yesterday. I wanted to know. That's why I asked him to stay. So I could find out."

"You asked him?"

"No. I wanted to. But I couldn't. So I made up some bullshit about wanting to know how he thought he was doing so far in his job." Bo shook his head, his lips curling into a sad smile. "He saw right through that. Said he knew what was going on, that you and he had..." Bo's voice faltered. "He said that he was only a substitute for me. That I was the one you wanted, not him."

Sam stared, at a loss for words. He wanted to be angry with Dean, but couldn't find it in himself to feel anything but gratitude. Dean, he realized, must have told Bo in order to force the man into drastic action. *It sure as hell worked.*

"He's right," Sam confessed, watching Bo closely. "I used him, because I didn't know what else to do. I wanted to be with you, and I couldn't. I needed to forget you right then, so I took Dean to bed. But it didn't work. It didn't make me forget you, it just made me want you more."

Bo twirled the end of his braid around one finger. "I can't believe Dean wasn't angry with you."

"He knew what I was doing even before I did. And he told me if I loved you, I should fight for you." Sam deliberately left out the part about Bo loving him back. If it was true, he wanted Bo to say it.

"You said you loved me before," Bo whispered. "Do you?"

"Yes," Sam answered without hesitation. "I won't ask you the same. But, Bo, can you forgive me? Can we try again?"

Bo stood silently staring at the floor, and Sam's heart sank. He couldn't blame Bo for not being able to forgive him, but it hurt anyway. It took every ounce of strength he possessed to keep from falling to his knees at Bo's feet and begging him to give them just one more chance.

Sam had no idea how long they stood there like that, not looking at each other, not speaking. It felt like forever. Finally, Bo raised his head and stalked over to stand toe-to-toe with Sam. His eyes burned, and Sam could see the rapid pulse fluttering in his throat.

"I hate you for doing this to me." Bo's voice shook.

Sam blinked against the stinging behind his eyelids. "I'm so fucking sorry, Bo. I'd take it back if I could."

Bo raised a hand, and for a moment Sam thought he was going to hit him. He braced himself, holding Bo's gaze. When Bo laid his trembling palm against Sam's cheek, thumb caressing the corner of his mouth, Sam's knees went weak with relieved surprise.

165

"I thought I could live without you," Bo whispered. "But I can't. I can't. And I hate you for that. For making me love you."

A strangled sob burst from Sam's throat. "Christ, Bo..."

They moved at the same time, mouths fusing together in a hard, desperate kiss. Sam cupped Bo's head in one hand, using the other arm to pull their bodies together. He tilted his head to deepen the kiss, swallowing Bo's soft little moans. Bo clutched him close, one hand fisted in his hair and the other sliding down to knead his ass.

"God, Sam," Bo breathed. "I need you."

Electricity surged through Sam's veins. "Anything. Anything you want."

"Let's make love."

The raw need in Bo's voice made Sam's chest tight. "Are you sure? I don't want you to feel like you have to do anything you don't really want."

Bo's lips brushed Sam's jaw. "I've wanted this for a long time, but I was afraid." He pressed closer, the unmistakable evidence of his arousal digging into Sam's thigh. "I'm not afraid anymore. I'm ready."

The thought of making love to Bo was enough to bring Sam achingly erect in the space of a heartbeat. He kissed Bo again, very gently, hands stroking down Bo's back. "I'll make it good for you. I promise."

"I know." Bo groaned when Sam's hand slipped between his legs, tracing his hardness through the worn denim. "Just...let's go slow, okay? I've never... No one's ever done that, I haven't even...touched myself that way."

The fact that Bo was willing to bottom for him made Sam's head swim. As much as he wanted it, though, he wanted something else more.

"Maybe another time," Sam whispered. "Right now, I need you inside me."

A shudder ran through Bo's body. "Jesus." He leaned against Sam's chest, his heart pounding so hard Sam could feel it. "Take me to bed, before I fall down."

Taking Bo's hand, Sam led the way to the bedroom. His insides churned with a mix of desire and nervousness. He'd never been this anxious to please a lover. *It's being in love for the first time,* he thought as he pulled Bo into his arms again. *It changes everything.*

Bo's palms slid inside Sam's T-shirt. "Get undressed, Sam. Let me see you."

Obediently, Sam peeled his shirt off and threw it on the floor. Taking hold of the hem of Bo's sweater, Sam lifted it, nudging Bo's arms up so he could take it off. Once the garment was out of the way, Sam ran his hands over Bo's chest, thumbs catching on his hard little nipples. "God, you're gorgeous, Bo."

Bo groaned. His hips rolled against Sam's. "Pants. Off."

"Yeah."

Sam removed his own jeans first, wanting to put Bo at ease. Bo's gaze raked down Sam's body, hot and wanting. Reaching down, Bo yanked off his battered running shoes then started to undo his jeans. His hands shook. Staring into Bo's eyes, Sam saw a lifetime of unfulfilled need, overlaid with a sheen of fear. He knew that fear, had felt it himself the first time he had sex with another man. Fear of the unknown, of something he'd been taught to believe was wrong. He didn't want to see that look in Bo's eyes. Sam was determined Bo would never again associate sex with anything but joy and pleasure and love.

"Don't be afraid," Sam murmured, never looking away from Bo's wide eyes. Gently moving Bo's hands out of the way, Sam flipped the button of his jeans open and slid the zipper down. "I'm going to take care of you." He pushed Bo's pants slowly down over his hips, leaning in for a feather-light kiss. "If you want to stop, just say so. We don't have to do anything you're not comfortable with."

Bo gasped through parted lips when Sam's fingers traced up his shaft. "Oh..."

Nudging Bo backward, Sam lowered him onto the edge of the bed. He tugged the jeans the rest of the way off and tossed them aside, and Bo was naked, finally, bare and vulnerable to Sam's gaze. Sam pushed Bo's knees apart and knelt between his open legs. Bo's cock twitched against his belly, thick and dark and already leaking, making Sam's mouth water. Bending down, Sam brushed his lips across the head, tongue snaking out to taste.

"Oh!" Bo cried, hips jerking. "God, Sam..."

Dipping his head, Sam nuzzled Bo's balls, breathing deep to savor the scent of Bo's arousal. "You have no idea how much I've wanted to do this." Sam stroked Bo's thighs, loving the way the caramel-colored skin quivered at his touch. "How many times I've dreamed about sucking your cock."

Bo whimpered and spread his legs farther apart. "Please. God, please."

That was all the invitation Sam needed. He slid his lips over the tip of Bo's prick and down, swallowing him to the root.

"Ah! Oh God." Falling back onto the mattress, Bo thrust his hips up, shoving his cock down Sam's throat in one swift, sharp motion. Not that Sam minded. He was perfectly happy to relax his muscles and let Bo fuck his mouth.

Before long Bo was writhing on the bed, legs flung wide and knees bent up, hands buried in Sam's hair. His complete lack of inhibition came as a pleasant surprise to Sam, who'd expected to have his work cut out for him breaking through Bo's reserve.

When he felt Bo's shaft swell and pulse in his mouth, Sam pulled off with a pop. Raising his head, he grinned at Bo, who gaped at him in silent astonishment.

"D-don't stop," Bo gasped, trying to push Sam's head back down. "So close, please."

Sam pressed a soft kiss to the inside of Bo's thigh. "Let me rim you."

Bo's eyelids fluttered, his cheeks going wonderfully pink. "Oh Christ."

"I'll take that as a yes."

Rising to his feet, Sam moved up and gave Bo a long, lazy kiss, letting his lover come down a bit. When he felt some of the tension run out of Bo's body, he pulled back and settled on the floor between Bo's parted knees. He pushed Bo's legs up and just stared for a minute, licking his lips. Bo's hole clenched and relaxed as he watched, as if inviting him in. It was more than Sam could resist. He spread Bo open and flicked his tongue over the dusky pink skin.

"Fuck, you taste amazing," Sam declared, taking another taste. "Gonna tongue-fuck you 'til you come."

"Oh my God," Bo moaned, fingers bunching the covers as Sam's mouth closed over his hole. "Oh fuck, I've never... Oh... So good, Sam, yes..."

Sam bent happily to his task, spurred on by Bo's increasingly loud moans and half-formed pleas for more. Humming his pleasure, Sam worked Bo's hole relentlessly until the tight muscles began to relax. As soon as Bo was loose enough, Sam stabbed his tongue inside and wrapped a hand around Bo's cock.

"Fuck!" Bo cried, pushing his ass against Sam's face. "Oh God, Sam."

That's it, Sam thought, wriggling his tongue deeper as he fisted Bo's cock. *Come for me.*

As if reading Sam's mind, Bo came with a shout, his hole clenching around Sam's probing tongue. The feel and smell of hot semen coating his hand nearly sent Sam over the edge. *Not yet,* he sternly ordered himself. He wanted to come with Bo's cock buried inside him, watching the orgasm wash over Bo's face.

Letting his tongue slip out of Bo's hole, Sam wiped his hand on the sheet then crawled up and pulled Bo into his arms. Bo wound his body around Sam's and kissed him, surprising him again. He'd had plenty of lovers who'd refused to kiss him after he'd rimmed them.

"Good Lord, that was amazing." Bo smiled, raking his fingers through Sam's hair. "That's a hell of a talent you've got there, Sam."

Laughing, Sam snuggled Bo closer. "I love doing that. Now that I've made you come by rimming you, I can die happy."

"Oh, no. No dying, happy or otherwise. Not when we're just starting to make this work." Bo ran a hand down Sam's side, over his hip, and around to trace the length of his crease. The feel of Bo's fingertips on his most sensitive skin made Sam's hole pulse. A low moan slipped from his lips.

"You're so beautiful," Bo whispered, rubbing his cheek against Sam's. "No one's ever turned me on like you do. I'm going to be hard again in no time."

Sam rolled onto his back, spreading his legs to give Bo's fingers room to play. "Good, because I'm counting on you to fuck me through the mattress."

Sprawled on top of Sam's chest with one leg wedged between Sam's thighs, Bo stared down at him with uncertainty in his eyes. "I've never done that before. I'm not sure what to do."

"I'll talk you through it." Sam reached up to cup Bo's face in his hands. "Don't worry. You won't hurt me."

Bo laughed. "How'd you know that's what I was thinking?"

"That's what every gay man thinks the first time he tops," Sam told him, hips lifting as Bo squeezed his erection. "Oh Jesus, I'm not gonna last if you do that."

"Uh-oh. Can't let that happen." Bo moved his hand, leaving Sam torn between relief and disappointment. "Touch me, Sam. Get me hard again."

Sam was more than happy to obey. Worming a hand between their bodies, he curled his fingers around Bo's prick. Bo raised his hips to give Sam better access. His come-sticky flesh immediately started swelling in Sam's hand. Sam smiled at Bo's woozy expression. "I love how responsive you are."

"Uhhh," Bo moaned. "Never had anyone touch me quite like you do."

A swatch of glossy black hair came loose from Bo's braid, swinging down over his face and brushing Sam's cheek. The silky touch sent a jolt of need through Sam's body. The desire to see those long ebony locks lying loose on Bo's naked skin was suddenly irresistible.

"Take your hair down," Sam requested, pulling the rubber band from the end of the braid. "I love it loose."

Bo's laugh morphed into a breathless whimper when Sam rubbed a thumb across the head of his cock, pressing at the slit. "God, that feels good. Do it again."

Sam obliged, watching with hungry eyes as Bo's fingers worked his braid loose. Once unwound, Bo's hair cascaded over his shoulders, tickling Sam's chest and enclosing them both in a dark curtain. Sam pressed the fragrant strands to his cheek with his free hand. Smiling, Bo leaned down and captured Sam's mouth in a deep kiss.

By the time they broke apart, Bo's prick was once again rigid and dripping in Sam's hand. *Ready, willing and able.* The thought sent a sharp thrill through Sam's bones. Letting go of Bo's cock, Sam laid his palms on Bo's cheeks.

"There's lube in the drawer," Sam whispered. "Would you get it? You can reach it better than me."

Bo paled, but reached over and retrieved the lube from the bedside drawer. He held the tube in his hand, staring at it as if it might bite him. Sam stifled a laugh.

"What do I do?" Bo asked, eyes wide and serious. The question was so simple and heartfelt, Sam's urge to laugh vanished immediately.

"You have to get me ready." Taking the lube from Bo, Sam opened it and squeezed some onto Bo's fingers. "Start with one finger. I'll tell you when it's okay to add more."

Bo gulped. "I'm nervous, Sam," he said, his voice shaking. "I want this to be good for you."

Sam raked a hand through Bo's hair. "Trust me, Bo, there's no way this could be anything other than amazing for me. Now get busy fingering my ass so you can fuck me."

Bo let out a startled laugh. Nudging Sam's leg further out, Bo rolled up onto his side and slid his lubed hand between Sam's thighs. Sam felt a slick finger tentatively circling his entrance, and moaned.

"Is that good?" Bo murmured, watching Sam's face.

"Mm. Yeah." Sam bent the leg not trapped under Bo's body, opening himself as much as he could. "Put it in me."

Biting his lip, Bo pressed his fingertip against Sam's hole. There was a second of resistance, then Bo gasped as his finger slipped inside.

"Oh Christ, it's tight," Bo whispered hoarsely. Pushing in a little further, he wiggled his fingertip, drawing a ragged groan from Sam's throat as the invading digit brushed his prostate. "Wait, I feel something, is that—"

Bo's words were abruptly cut off by Sam's keening cry. Digging a heel into the mattress for leverage, Sam pushed his ass against Bo's hand, trying to get that exploring finger to hit his gland again.

"Guess that was it." Bo rubbed lightly across the sweet spot, taking evident delight in the way Sam writhed and begged for more.

"Another one," Sam gasped. "No, no two, put two more in me."

Bo looked uncertain, but did as Sam asked. It was a little clumsy, a little too quick, but Sam relished the tight burn. When Bo twisted his fingers, carefully exploring Sam's insides, Sam nearly came off the bed.

Bo went still. "Are you okay? Did I hurt you?"

It took a couple of tries before Sam managed to speak. "No," he panted. "It's good. 'M ready."

Closing his eyes, Bo drew a deep breath. His eyes fluttered open, burning into Sam's. "Condoms?"

"Drawer." Sam arched as Bo's fingers pumped in and out, stretching the loosening muscles and zinging over his prostate again and again. "Fuck, hurry."

Bo carefully removed his fingers from Sam's body, then plunged a hand into the still-open drawer and fished out a condom. Sitting back on his heels, he stared into Sam's eyes as he tore the packet open and rolled the latex sheath over his shaft.

The second the condom was on, Sam reached down and grabbed Bo's prick, pressing the tip against his slick, stretched hole. "In. Now."

Bo's apprehension shone in his eyes, but he didn't hesitate. Hooking his forearms under Sam's knees, Bo gave a push, and the head of his cock popped into Sam's ass.

"Oh *fuck.*" Bo fell forward onto his hands, driving himself deep inside Sam and bending him nearly double. Bo's face radiated shock. "God, Sam. Tight. Oh."

Burying his hands in Bo's hair, Sam pulled Bo down into a hard kiss. "You don't need to be careful," he whispered. "Fuck me."

Bo slid partway out, then pushed back in. A shudder ran through his body. His lips moved against Sam's, and Sam thought he heard his name as Bo began to move in earnest.

After almost a year without it, the feel of a hard, thick cock filling him nearly sent Sam right over the edge. He held release at bay with a massive effort. No way, he thought, was he coming until Bo was ready.

That proved more difficult than he thought it would. After a few slow, careful strokes, Bo let go and pounded into him, nailing his gland with every thrust. Sam clung to Bo as if his life depended on it, ankles locked around Bo's neck and fingers digging into his back.

"Oh...God...so close," Bo growled, his words rough and broken. "Come...come on...now, I'm...I'm gonna...oh, oh fuck..."

"Yes," Sam moaned. "Fuck yes, almost there."

It was the look in Bo's eyes, lust and wonder and tenderness, that finally tipped the balance for Sam, sending him spinning into the most intense orgasm he'd ever experienced. Bo's face blurred above him with the force of it.

With a sharp cry, Bo thrust into Sam twice more in rapid succession, stilled, and buried his face in Sam's neck, his shaft pulsing in Sam's hole as he came. He stayed like that for a moment, balls-deep in Sam's ass, every muscle tense. Then he collapsed onto Sam's chest, gasping for breath.

Sam unwound his legs from around Bo's neck, groaning as Bo's softening flesh slipped out of him. He removed the condom from Bo's cock, tied it off and tossed it at the trash can. Wrapping his arms around Bo, Sam petted Bo's back and showered his hair with tiny kisses. They lay that way for several minutes, not talking, just holding each other. Sam couldn't remember ever feeling so happy.

"Oh. My. God," Bo mumbled, lips still pressed to Sam's neck.

Sam chuckled. "Good?"

"Oh yeah." Bo raised his head and gave Sam a woozy grin. "I never imagined it would be like that."

"It was great for me too." Brushing the tangled hair away from Bo's face, Sam kissed his swollen lips. "You're amazing."

Bo blushed, which Sam thought was adorable under the circumstances. "I'd like to try it sometime. Getting, that is, rather than giving."

"We can definitely do that," Sam agreed. "So. What're you doing the rest of the day? You want to go out or something?"

"Maybe later." Laying his head on Sam's chest, Bo let out a contented sigh. "Right now, I just want to hold you."

Sam wasn't about to argue with that plan. Tightening his arms around Bo, Sam allowed his eyes to drift closed. Within minutes he sank into a deep sleep, with Bo slumbering warm and sated in his arms.

Chapter Eleven

When Sam opened his eyes, evening shadows stretched across the room. Yawning, he glanced at the clock. Five p.m. They'd been asleep for about ten hours. Part of him felt guilty for having slept the day away, without calling his mother or sister or even eating anything. But the practical side of him realized he'd badly needed the rest. He felt invigorated and clearheaded for the first time in weeks.

Bo was still dead to the world, face buried in Sam's neck, his breath warm and soft on Sam's skin. They'd shifted positions in their sleep, and Sam now lay spooned in Bo's embrace, back pressed to Bo's front, with Bo's arm tucked firmly around his waist. Sam snuggled deeper into Bo's arms with a contented sigh, careful not to wake him. The man clearly needed the sleep, and Sam intended to enjoy being held like that as long as he could.

Behind him, Bo moaned and rocked his hips forward, rubbing his erection against Sam's butt. Sam clamped a hand over his own mouth to keep from crying out, it felt so good. Shifting backward, Sam wriggled until Bo's rigid cock lay between his buttocks, sliding up and down his crease. *Good God, the man can fuck even in his sleep.* Sam groaned, gripped his own hard prick and started tugging on it.

Sam knew when Bo woke by his sharp, hissing breath and the sudden tension in his body. Batting Sam's hand out of the way, Bo took over jerking him off, humping Sam's back the whole time.

"Oh," Sam gasped as Bo's finger pushed into his slit. "Close. God."

"Yeah." Bo twisted his hand around the head of Sam's cock in a way that completely shorted out Sam's brain. "Come on my hand."

"Oh fuck," Sam groaned, and shot so hard semen spattered his face.

Sinking his teeth into Sam's neck, Bo slammed his cock against Sam's ass and came all over his back. Sam shuddered, delicious chills racing along his skin. He'd done more exotic things, but something about Bo rubbing off on his back felt wonderfully decadent.

"Mmmm," Bo hummed, kissing Sam's shoulder. "Good morning."

"Evening." Squirming in Bo's arms, Sam turned to face his lover. "It's five o'clock."

Bo craned his neck to look at the clock. "Actually it's ten after."

Sam laughed. "I haven't shot that fast since I was sixteen."

"Neither have I." Sliding a hand around the back of Sam's head, Bo pulled him close and kissed his lips. "This is amazing, Sam. Is it always like this between men, or is it just us?"

"I think it's us," Sam answered, winding Bo's hair between his fingers. "It's how we feel about each other. Gay sex is just like any other, I guess. Sometimes it's good and sometimes it's not. And being in love makes it so much better."

Bo traced the outline of Sam's mouth with his fingertips. "I've never felt this way before. Never."

Sam knew what he meant. He didn't want to talk about Janine. Not now, with Bo naked in his bed, the air heavy with the scent of male sex. But Bo obviously needed to make peace with himself over his relationship with Janine. If he needed to talk, Sam was determined to listen.

"Don't feel bad about her," Sam said, caressing Bo's cheek. "You said before that you weren't sure she'd ever loved you either."

"I know. And I don't feel guilty about it. Not anymore. It's just..." Bo trailed off, chewing his bottom lip. "It just seems like such a waste of so many years, for both of us. And when I think of our boys having to grow up in that environment, with parents who barely tolerated each other, it kills me. We had no right to do that to them."

"Well, you're not doing it anymore," Sam reminded him, and kissed the end of his nose. "Although she's obviously still badmouthing you to anyone who'll listen, including the kids." Sam frowned as a thought occurred to him. "If she doesn't love you, why is she fighting you so hard?"

"I don't know." Sighing, Bo slung a leg over Sam's hip. His fingers trailed up and down Sam's arm. "Come to think of it, she never fought the separation, and she never said she didn't want a divorce. It seems like she wants to hurt me just because she can."

Sam managed to resist the urge to call the woman an evil harpy. He didn't think it would help matters. "There's nothing she can legally do to you, Bo. You're a good father. Being gay is not a legal reason to keep your kids from you."

"You're right. I called my lawyer the other day, actually, and she said the same thing. She said I had nothing to worry about."

Sam blinked, surprised. "You came out to your lawyer?"

"Yeah." Bo smiled, cheeks pinking. "When I first went to see her about the divorce, she told me I'd better tell her anything Janine and her lawyer might bring up in the custody hearings. It took me a little while to work up the courage, but I did it. Nothing's more important than my boys. I'll do anything to keep them in my life."

"That must've been hard," Sam said softly.

Bo nodded. "It was. But Sarah—that's my lawyer—she'll be discreet. And she needs to know everything if she's going to help me keep my children."

Sam thought about that. "You should probably tell her about us."

"I know. I will." This time, Bo's smile held an endearing mix of shyness and mischief. "I think I'm going to enjoy being able to tell someone about us."

Those words made Sam feel warm all over. "Does this mean we can tell our friends? Other than Dean, of course, since he already knows." Sam didn't mention his suspicion that Cecile had figured it out as well. He wasn't sure, and he saw no point in worrying Bo with speculation.

"Dean's too perceptive for his own good," Bo grumbled, amusement sparkling in his eyes. "I don't know, Sam. I want to. But it might take me a little while to be ready for that. I hope that's okay."

Sam studied Bo's face. His eyes held a trace of anxiety, but not the borderline panic Sam had seen every other time he'd broached the subject of coming out. *Don't be picky, Sam,* he ordered himself. *He loves you. You're together, and he's willing to think about coming out at least. Don't push it.*

"It's fine," Sam reassured him. "You said you figured out that you can't live without me. I found out the same thing. I thought being out in the open was so important, and it *is* important to me. But not as important as being with you. We'll keep it to ourselves until you're ready."

Bo's smile lit up the darkening room. "Thank you."

Resting his forehead against Bo's, Sam stroked Bo's silky hair. "Anything you want, Bo. I love you."

Bo made a small sound in the back of his throat. For a second, Sam thought he was going to answer in kind. But he didn't. Instead, he wound his body around Sam's and kissed him, tongue darting quick and eager into Sam's mouth.

Sam responded with an equal passion. It wasn't long before he lay sprawled on his back with Bo on top of him, their cocks sliding together, magnificent friction sparking a fire in his body.

Sam didn't mind that Bo hadn't said those three little words. He'd said it once, and that was enough, for now.

♋

Full dark had fallen by the time Sam and Bo finally got out of bed, taking the lube and condoms with them. The shower they shared lasted somewhat longer than was strictly necessary, and Sam was walking rather stiffly when they got out. He wouldn't have changed a thing, though. Every time his backside twinged, he remembered what had caused it, and smiled.

Bo eyed him with concern as they turned on the TV and curled up on the sofa together to wait for the pizza they'd ordered. "You sure you're okay?"

"More than okay." Gingerly shifting his position, Sam looped an arm around Bo's shoulders and kissed his forehead. "It's just been a while, that's all. Takes a little getting used to."

"I didn't mean to make you sore."

Sam grinned at Bo's sheepish expression. "Sore from getting your ass thoroughly fucked—twice—is a good thing."

Bo's blush made Sam laugh. Trying without success to look stern, Bo smacked Sam's thigh. "Stop laughing at me."

With a great effort, Sam managed to look contrite. "Sorry. But you'll see what I'm talking about."

Bending his knees up, Bo leaned against Sam's shoulder. "Eventually. I don't think I'm ready for that just yet."

"That's fine," Sam said, ignoring the tiny twinge of disappointment. "No rush. Some men never bottom, it's okay if you decide you don't want to."

"I do want to." Tilting his head, Bo brushed his lips across Sam's throat. "When I was inside you, you looked like it was the best thing in the world. I want to know what that feels like, eventually. Just not yet."

"When you're ready, you let me know." Sam took Bo's hand, lacing their fingers together. "In the meantime, there's all kinds of fun stuff we can do."

Bo's eyes sparkled wickedly. "Such as?"

"Blowjobs," Sam said firmly. "We have to do that next."

"Oh, I definitely want to learn that particular skill." Smiling, Bo leaned over to kiss Sam's lips.

"Later," Sam answered, tangling his hands in Bo's hair. "I don't think I can get it up again today."

"But it's only been three times so far," Bo teased, and flicked his tongue over the corner of Sam's mouth. "You don't have one more in you?"

Chuckling, Sam nuzzled Bo's cheek. "Smart ass. Shut up and kiss me some more."

Bo obeyed, straddling Sam's lap and cupping his face in both hands. The kiss was deep and unhurried, all urgency burned away by their earlier lovemaking. By the time they pulled apart, Sam's body buzzed with a languorous desire, easily satisfied by Bo's soft, lazy touches as they held each other.

For a while they sat still and silent, Bo astride Sam's lap with his head resting on Sam's shoulder. Sam stroked Bo's hair and his bare back, relishing the feel of the man in his arms. He would be perfectly happy, he thought, to stay right there until the end of time.

A knock on the door roused Sam from his musings. "Pizza Palace," a bored voice called from the other side.

Sam patted Bo's ass. "There's our Thanksgiving dinner. Let me up."

"No, you stay put, I'll get it." Climbing off Sam's lap, Bo crossed to the door and flung it open before Sam could protest. "Thank you," he said, taking the box from the deliveryman and setting it on the counter. "How much?"

"Twenty-four fifty." The young man's gaze flitted to Sam, then back to Bo. His mouth fell open.

Bo dug a wad of bills out of his front jeans pocket and handed the young man two of them. "That's thirty. Keep the change."

"Thanks, man. Happy Thanksgiving." Cheeks flaming, the boy backed away, turned and fled.

Bo frowned as he shut and bolted the apartment door. "He was acting awfully strange."

"Yeah. I wonder what—" Sam stopped as Bo picked up the pizza and carried it to the coffee table in front of the sofa. "Oh my God," Sam said, laughing, "I know what was wrong with him."

"What?" Bo glanced down at his own bare belly. "It can't be because I'm not wearing a shirt."

"No, it's not that." Sam pointed at Bo's chest, just above his right nipple. "You have an enormous hickey."

Bo's eyes went comically wide. "Do you...do you think he..."

"Probably," Sam responded, answering Bo's unfinished question. "Don't worry about it, though. Even if he *did* figure out I was the one who gave you that love bite, he'll forget all about it before the night's out."

"I guess you're right." Shaking his head, Bo went into Sam's tiny kitchen and started rummaging through the cabinets. "It's a strange feeling, though. Having strangers just look at you and *know*. Do you have any paper plates?"

"Bottom cabinet next to the fridge." Sam licked his lips when Bo bent over to get the paper plates. The man had hands-down the best ass Sam had ever seen, the faded jeans hugging every curve and plane perfectly. "People don't just look at you and know you're gay. That guy figured it out because you're half naked, you have a gigantic hickey and we both look as well-fucked as we are."

"I know." Bo brought two paper plates over to the sofa, snatching a handful of napkins from the counter on the way. Plopping into the seat next to Sam, Bo piled super supreme pizza on the plates and handed one to Sam. "Damn, that smells good. I'm starved."

"Me too. Haven't eaten anything but you all day."

Bo choked on a mouthful of pizza. "Jesus, Sam," he wheezed when he stopped coughing. "Anyone ever tell you you're a dangerous dinner date?"

Sam laughed. "Sorry."

"No harm done." Taking another huge bite, Bo moaned and leaned back against the sofa cushions, eyelids fluttering as he chewed and swallowed. "God, that's good."

Sam's cock twitched lazily, too tired to take more than a passing interest. Leaning over, Sam stole a quick kiss, licking a trickle of sauce from Bo's lip. "You even eat pizza sexy."

Bo grinned at him. "You're good for my ego. I think I'll keep you."

Those words made Sam melt inside. Giving Bo a wide smile, he rested back against the cushions. "Good, because I sure as hell plan on keeping you."

Bo didn't say anything else, but his beaming smile said it all.

After a few minutes of flipping channels, Sam found a local TV station showing reruns of The X-Files. They settled in to watch while they ate, trading theories about extraterrestrial life and pointing out the admittedly few inaccuracies in the plots.

Sam was enjoying himself so much, he almost didn't notice the crawl that appeared at the bottom of the screen halfway through the third episode.

"Oh my God." Bo sat straight up, his plate falling off his lap. "Sam, look."

Sam frowned at the TV. "What? I don't—" Suddenly, he saw. "Oh no. Not again."

Slipping silently underneath Mulder and Scully's heated debate was one of the crawls the local stations used to report non-emergency breaking news. It read, *Fourth teen vanishes from South Bay High. Details at eleven.*

"The school's closed," Bo said, his voice soft and shocked. "What the hell happened?"

Sam shook his head, watching numbly as the crawl started over. "I don't know."

"We're going out there tomorrow." Scooting backward, Bo leaned against Sam's side as Sam put an arm around him. "We're going to have to be extra careful. You can't open this one, can you, Sam? Not like before."

Sam thought about that. "I don't know. I haven't tried. But it feels so different from Oleander House. I can't explain it very well, but it just feels... More controlled. Less random. And it doesn't feel like I can affect it. But, Bo, I think I have to try."

Bo's head snapped up from where it rested on Sam's shoulder. "What do you mean? You're not still seriously considering trying to communicate with those things, are you?"

"Andre and Cecile both got a sense of what that thing in Oleander House meant to do, but I *understood* it. No one else has shown any ability to connect with their minds to the extent I have." Lifting Bo's hand, Sam placed a gentle kiss on his palm. "If communicating with them is the key to closing the portal, then I have to do it. Before anyone else dies."

Bo fixed Sam with a fierce stare. "And what about you? What if you..." He stopped, eyes filling with fear. "Doesn't your life count?"

"Of course it does. Especially now." Reaching out, Sam pulled Bo into his arms, resting his cheek against Bo's hair. "Look, I promise I won't take any unnecessary risks. But I have to try. I could never live with myself if I didn't."

Bo let out a long sigh, his arms winding around Sam and holding tight. "We have no idea what will happen if you

186

deliberately plug your mind into one of those things, Sam. I'm afraid for you."

Sam didn't answer, because Bo was right. There was no way of knowing what might happen. But it didn't matter. Even though he was as afraid as Bo, Sam knew he had no choice. He had an ability to affect the barrier between the worlds, and he couldn't ignore that. Not when lives were at stake.

When Bo captured Sam in a deep kiss and the heat started to rise between them again, Sam was relieved. He didn't want to dwell on visions of what might happen when they entered the tunnels and he faced the portal. Tumbling onto his back and spreading his legs, Sam let Bo's touch take him away.

Chapter Twelve

Bo didn't spend the night, though Sam asked him to. He said he wanted to get home so he could call Janine's parents' house and talk to the boys. Clearly that was true, but Sam suspected Bo also didn't want their coworkers to see them arriving at work together the next day. Sam said he understood, kissed Bo goodbye and let him go without an argument.

To his surprise, Sam fell asleep early and slept like the dead, waking without need of an alarm at a quarter of six. He wolfed down coffee and cold pizza for breakfast, curled on the sofa where he and Bo had made love one more time before Bo left. The memory made him smile.

Feeling wide awake and energetic, Sam left for work early enough that he was the first to arrive. He let himself in and turned on the lights, then settled at his desk to mentally review his plan for the day.

The problem was, he didn't actually have a firm plan. Ever since Oleander House, he'd been researching the subject of dimensional portals and their connection to the human mind, trying to find a way to control his newly discovered abilities. So far he'd come up empty-handed. He'd run across a couple of people who claimed to be able to manipulate the inter-dimensional barriers, but those leads had both been dead ends. One couldn't provide Sam with anything but the vaguest speculation regarding how she did it. The other turned out to be a severe schizophrenic who refused to take his medications, rendering his entire story suspect.

"Go with your gut, Sam," he advised himself, ignoring the trickle of doubt seeping through the morning's excess of self-confidence. "You sent that thing in Oleander House back to its world and closed the gate without having any idea what you were doing. You can do it again, as long as you don't overthink it."

The squeal of rusting hinges drew Sam's attention to the front door. David made a face as he and Cecile entered, closing the door behind him. "That thing needs oiling. Hi, Sam, what're you doing here this early?"

"Talking to myself." Sam gave his friends a wide smile. "How was your Thanksgiving?"

"Filling," Cecile answered, patting her stomach. "Andre's sister invited us to spend the day with them. She made enough food for ten armies."

"Hey, a week's worth of turkey sandwiches is a Thanksgiving tradition." Plopping into the nearest chair, David slung his feet onto Cecile's desk and grinned. "What'd you do, Sam? I know you didn't go all the way to Marietta to see your mom."

The mental picture of himself, legs in the air and Bo's cock buried in his ass, sprang unbidden to Sam's mind. Heat rose in his cheeks. "I stayed at home and ordered pizza," he answered, truthfully enough.

"You at least called your mom though, right?" David asked, picking a piece of lint off his sweater.

"Um. No," Sam mumbled.

David shook his head. "Bad form, man. Very bad form, ignoring the parental units."

189

"Mom was spending the day with some friends from her church," Sam protested. "And I think my sister and her family were going to her in-laws house. I doubt they missed me much."

"You must be kidding." Cecile stared at him with such horror on her face Sam had to laugh. "It's not funny. I bet your mother's feelings were hurt."

That just made Sam laugh harder. His relationship with his family had been distinctly cool ever since that Easter Sunday nearly twenty years ago when he told them he was gay. That had been a turning point. They'd never openly excluded him afterward, but he knew they preferred his absence to his presence. The day he'd packed up to leave Marietta was the first time his mother had smiled at him in years.

Wiping his streaming eyes, Sam slouched in his chair and lifted an eyebrow at Cecile. "Trust me, her feelings were not hurt."

Cecile gave him a sharp look, but before she could say anything the door swung open again. Dean bounded in with Andre hot on his heels. Bo trailed behind them.

When Bo's gaze met his, Sam's stomach gave a funny little lurch. He smiled, knowing it looked goofy as hell and not caring. Bo grinned back, eyes shining.

"Good morning," Dean lilted. "Did y'all have a good holiday?"

As everyone else began talking at once, Bo shot Sam a furtive sidelong look. The heat in his gaze burned into Sam's skin, and it was all Sam could do to resist the urge to leap from his chair and cover the man with kisses.

"So who else saw the news last night?"

Andre's question silenced the chatter immediately. "We saw it," David spoke up, reaching out to take Cecile's hand. "Are they still gonna let us in today, after that?"

"What exactly happened?" Sam asked. "I only saw the crawl, I didn't stay up for the news."

"Neither did I." Darting a swift, wicked grin at Sam, Bo leaned against Cecile's desk. "The school's closed, did someone break in?"

"A group of boys snuck onto the grounds about one in the morning yesterday," Dean explained. "They aren't students there, but they'd heard the rumors and decided it would be fun to spend the night there, kind of like it was a haunted house or something."

"Crazy," Andre muttered, shaking his head.

Perching on the edge of Sam's desk, Dean continued the story. "One of the kids went missing sometime during the night. The others didn't see anything, but they couldn't find him anywhere when they were ready to leave, and he never showed up at his house for Thanksgiving dinner. His friends finally went to the police yesterday afternoon and told them what they knew."

Bo's expression gave nothing away, but Sam saw the fear in his eyes. The need to hold Bo right then was nearly irresistible. *I'll be okay,* he thought, wishing he could send his thoughts directly to Bo's mind.

"I don't think I need to tell you how careful we need to be today," Bo said. "I don't want any of us to be the next missing person."

"We stay together," Andre added. "No matter what. Cecile, you and I are going to have to keep our senses open. Maybe we can feel a change in energy or something before the portal opens. And Sam—"

"Sam can do the same," Bo interrupted, his voice stern. "We need all three of you."

Rising to his feet, Sam walked over to stand in front of Bo. "I'm going to try to actively sense the portal, and see if I can figure out a way to close it for good. I won't try to communicate with whatever's on the other side unless I have no choice. But, Bo, if that portal opens, I'm going to do what I have to in order to protect us all. Do you understand?"

Bo's throat worked. He turned away, heading into the back room. "It's about time to go," he called over his shoulder. "Let's get our gear together and hit the road."

The tension in Bo's voice was obvious. Glancing around as the group scrambled to gather their equipment, Sam saw Dean watching Bo with sympathy in his eyes.

"He's worried about you," Dean murmured, hanging back from the rest of the group as Sam walked up behind him.

"I know." Leaning closer on the pretense of picking up a pen from Andre's desk, Sam whispered in Dean's ear. "You're a bold, bad man, Dean. Thank you."

Dean grinned ear to ear. "Really?"

"Yeah." Sam felt that loopy smile curving his lips again. "We're together."

Letting out a little squeal, Dean squeezed Sam's arm. "Sam, that's great! I'm so happy for y'all."

Sam had no chance to reply, as David and Andre emerged from the back room at that moment, carrying bags of equipment. Glancing at Dean's hand on Sam's arm, David raised his eyebrows and grinned.

"Dean, you and Sam can get the rest of the stuff," Andre said as he brushed past. "Come on, I want to get started."

Sam hurried into the back room, with Dean behind him. Cecile and Bo stood in the back corner, talking in low tones while Bo rummaged through an equipment drawer.

"You two can grab the radios and flashlights." Cecile hefted a duffle bag onto her shoulder. "Andre, David and I have everything else."

"Sure thing."

Sam watched as she left the room. As soon as they heard the sound of the front door closing, Dean rushed at Bo and threw both arms around him in an enthusiastic hug. "Oh my God, Bo, I am *so* happy for you and Sam. This is fabulous!"

"Um. Thanks." Bo patted Dean's back, giving Sam a *what the fuck?* look over Dean's shoulder. Sam bit back a laugh.

Letting go of Bo, Dean stuck both hands in his jeans pockets and grinned. "Sorry if I embarrassed you, but I love to see the star-crossed lovers get their happy ending, you know?"

"Dean, you're a hopeless romantic," Sam observed, picking up the canvas bag containing the radios.

"It's what makes me so damn lovable." Grabbing the bag of flashlights, Dean started out the door. "If y'all want to have a quickie before we go, I'll keep the others off your back, just say the word."

"Thanks, but I think we should probably get going," Bo said dryly. "Dean? We'd like to keep this to ourselves for now, so please don't say anything to anyone else."

"My lips are zipped," Dean promised.

Looking amused, Bo scooped a package of flashlight batteries out of the drawer and dropped them into his backpack. As they followed Dean out the door, Sam slipped an arm around Bo's neck and kissed him. Bo's lips parted under his, tongue darting briefly into his mouth.

"I like being able to do that," Bo whispered with a smile.

Sam nuzzled Bo's cheek. "Me too. Come over to my place tonight?"

"No."

Sam blinked. "No?"

"No," Bo repeated. "Come over to mine. I'll make you dinner."

"Now there's an offer I can't refuse. It's a date."

"Good." Turning his head, Bo kissed Sam's palm, then drew away. "Let's go. The others are waiting for us."

They headed out of the office, and Sam locked the front door behind them. Climbing into the SUV with Bo and Andre, Sam thought about the night before, and the night to come. Memories and anticipation brought a smile to his face. He focused on those pleasant thoughts and tried not to consider too closely what might happen at the school.

♋

The South Bay High courtyard was still cordoned off with yellow police tape when the group arrived. Mr. Innes wasn't there this time, being out of town visiting family. Bo and Andre went to speak with the uniformed officer walking guard duty inside the school, while the others waited outside on the steps.

It didn't take long. The two returned within minutes. "We're good to go," Andre announced. "Let's sort out the equipment and get started."

"I'd like each of us to carry a radio, even though we're all staying together today." Plucking a radio from the bag, Bo switched it on and clipped it to the waist of his jeans. "Probably not necessary, but it can't hurt."

"Okay." Sam took the bag and began handing radios to each member of the team. "Channel two?"

"Yes. They all have fresh batteries, but check and make sure you have a full charge before we go in." Bo picked up a flashlight and turned it on. "Same goes for the flashlights, check them before we go into the tunnel."

The group spent a busy ten minutes checking and distributing equipment. Once everyone was outfitted, they trooped inside and gathered outside the tunnel door.

"All right," Bo said. "I have the EMF. Andre, ready with the video?"

"Check," Andre answered.

"Thermometer?"

David held up the special thermometer. "Got it."

"Great. Cecile, you have EVP, right?"

She nodded. "I'm ready."

"I'm ready to take notes," Dean sang out before Bo could ask.

Bo laughed. "Good, thank you." Switching on his flashlight, he grabbed the door handle and tugged it open. "I'll take the lead. Y'all stay close."

The team descended the stairs in silence. The heat was just as damp and stifling as it had been before. Sam wiped his sweating face on his sleeve.

"Why didn't you assign me anything?" Sam asked as they walked down the corridor toward the entrance to the old tunnel.

Bo shot him an eloquent glance. "If you insist on trying to steal control of this portal from those things, you need all your wits about you. I don't want you to have to think of anything else."

"That's not necessary, I can—"

"Yeah, I know." Hooking a hand through Sam's arm, Bo leaned close. "But humor me, okay? Unless there's still a chance I can talk you out of this."

"Sorry, you can't." Sam covered Bo's hand with his and squeezed, using his body to block the action so the others couldn't see it. "I swear I'll be careful, Bo. I want to keep my skin intact as much as you do."

Bo gave him a halfhearted smile. "If that's the best I can get from you, I guess it'll have to do."

"I'll be fine, don't worry." Squeezing Bo's hand once more, Sam let go and drew away, wishing he could do more to reassure his lover. He hated being the cause of Bo's distress. At the same time, though, it warmed his heart to have Bo worry about him. No one had shown such concern for his well-being in ages.

Since they'd already performed a thorough investigation of the main tunnel, the group headed directly to the older portion. As before, the temperature increased steadily as they neared the entrance to the original excavation. By the time they clambered through the broken brick wall, everyone but Cecile had stripped off sweaters and sweatshirts.

Cecile glanced from one coworker to another with an amused glint in her eyes. "You know, I think this might be considered a fringe benefit of the job."

"What?" Bo asked, switching on the EMF detector.

"The beefcake." Cecile grinned at them. "You guys definitely qualify as eye candy."

"Ooo, eye candy, I like that." Sidling up to Cecile, Dean bumped her hip with his. "You're not bad yourself, little girl."

She laughed. "Thanks. But I'm not half naked like the rest of you are."

"Feel free to strip down if you want, babe," David suggested with a leer. "We won't mind."

"I'm sure." Fishing a napkin from the pocket of her denim skirt, Cecile mopped the sweat from her brow. "I wish I could. It's hotter than ever in here."

"All right, people, let's focus." Bo pointed his flashlight at the EMF detector. "Dean, take down the initial readings. EMF's steady at five-point-oh-two."

"Got it," Dean said, scribbling on the notepad. "Temp?"

David let out a low whistle. "Ninety-eight. Damn."

"Yeah." Frowning, Bo glanced at Sam. "Anything?"

"Not yet. Hang on." Closing his eyes, Sam took a few deep breaths, stretching out his psychic senses. "I can feel the portal. Or, well, I believe it's the portal."

"I feel it too," Andre murmured. "It's like a hiccup in the energy of this place."

"I agree," Cecile added. "It's definitely there, but I don't believe it's open. I think the energy would be much stronger if it was."

Opening his eyes, Sam met Bo's worried, curious gaze. "I'd like to try something."

"What?" Bo's expression was apprehensive. "You said you weren't going to try to contact the beings from the other side unless you had no choice."

"No, I'm not, that isn't what I'm talking about." Playing his flashlight beam over the earthen walls, Sam tried to think how to explain his plan. "The portal seems to be closed right now. I'd like to keep it that way. As a matter of fact, I'd like to try to close it permanently."

"How?" Dean's eyes were bright with curiosity. "Do you have a theory about how it works?"

197

Sam shook his head. "No, not exactly. But I can sense the energy pattern, and I think I can close it."

"I'm not sure I understand," Cecile confessed, brows drawing together.

Chewing his thumbnail, Sam tried to come up with a workable analogy. "It's like I'm looking at a door, and I've figured out how to lock it. That's not exactly right, but it's as close as I can get. It's hard to explain."

Tilting her head, Cecile stared at him with narrowed eyes. "Actually, that makes sense now. Do you really think you can do it?"

Sam shrugged. "Only one way to find out."

Twirling the end of his braid between his fingers, Bo nodded thoughtfully. "It's an interesting thought, Sam. After we finish today's work, we'll do some research and work out a plan. Then we can come back tomorrow and give it a try."

Sam was anxious to get on with it, before anyone else went missing, but he knew Bo was right. They needed more information, and they needed a plan. Sam had no intention of risking his life, or the lives of his friends. Working out the details first was safer than rushing into it.

Bo's voice was calm and steady, but Sam saw the worry in his eyes. Worry for Sam, and for all of them. But the fact that he didn't reject the idea outright told Sam he saw the necessity of closing the portal if they could.

"Okay," Sam agreed. "A couple of us can watch the video and listen to the audio as soon as we get back to the office. We'll also need to compile the EMF and temp data, to see if there are any patterns."

"I'll do that," Cecile offered.

"Andre and I will work on a general plan, and revise it as necessary depending on what we turn up with today's data." Bo nudged David with his elbow. "You and Dean can take care of the video and audio."

"I'll do some internet research," Sam said. "If there's any literature at all involving inter-dimensional gateways and how to close them, I want to know it."

Bo gave him a smile that started a hot glow in his chest. "Sam, you read my mind."

All the witty retorts Sam would have given anyone else melted away in the warmth of Bo's smile, reducing Sam to tongue-tied silence. He shrugged and grinned, knowing he looked as lovesick as he felt and unable to bring himself to care. Bo blushed and hastily turned away, bending over his EMF detector.

He loves me, Sam thought, with a burst of pure happiness. The truth of it was huge. Overwhelming. Sam wondered if it would hit him in random moments like this for the rest of his life, making him feel light and giddy. Part of him hoped it would. The joy of being loved was as addictive as a drug. He never wanted to let go of that feeling.

The group made their methodical way down the tunnel, recording readings and impressions every few feet. Sam let his mind float free, following the trickle of alien energy winding through the humid air. The thread of it remained steady. After a couple of tries, Sam was able to relay his impressions to Dean without bringing himself out of the half-trance into which he'd fallen.

He smiled with detached amusement when he felt Bo's hand on his elbow, guiding his steps along the increasingly uneven ground. *Bo loves me.*

Sam wasn't sure how long it took them to reach the site of the old pit. It felt like no time at all to him, but the others were grumpy and tired, leading him to believe it had been quite a while. He didn't ask, not wanting to lose contact with the portal.

"Temp's one hundred and two here," David said. "Jesus H., y'all, what the fuck?"

"It's the portal," Sam replied, his voice sounding faint and dreamy in his own ears. "It wants to open. The energy it takes to keep it closed generates the heat."

Five pairs of eyes locked onto Sam's face, all wide with surprise. Sam didn't blame them. He was pretty stunned himself.

"How do you know that?" The light from the video camera washed Andre's face in blue, giving his skin a sickly hue that matched the shock in his voice.

"I have no idea. But it's true." Pacing toward the pit, Sam searched for the source of the energy he felt building in his skull. "It's changing."

He shouldn't have been surprised at the reaction his calm declaration caused, but he was. Blinking, he watched as his friends huddled together with their backs against the wall opposite the pit.

Grabbing Sam's wrist in an iron grip, Bo yanked him backward. "Hey!" Sam protested as he stumbled against Bo, jarring his connection with the gateway.

"What do you mean, it's changing?" Bo growled. His fingers dug painfully into Sam's wrist. "Is it opening?"

Sam frowned, letting his vision lose focus as he grasped at the psychic cord leading him to the other side. "I'm not sure. I think..."

Something niggled at Sam's mind. A disturbingly familiar feeling. Squeezing his eyes shut, he tried to think where he'd felt that before. When it came to him, his eyes flew open and he clutched at Bo's arm.

Bo's arm went around his waist, steadying him. "Sam? What is it?"

"It's them," Sam whispered. "Whatever they are, on the other side. They're in my head. They're showing me things, Bo, they're talking to me."

"What kind of things?" Dean asked, appearing on Sam's other side. He laid a hand on Sam's shoulder. "Maybe we should—"

If Dean finished the sentence, Sam never heard him. A sudden jolt of electricity slammed through Sam's body, driving him to his knees. *This isn't like before,* he thought as he fell forward, catching himself on his hands. *It didn't hit me like this.* The pressure in his chest, though, wringing the air from his lungs...*that* was familiar. Hands stroked his back and face, voices edged with panic asked him if he was all right, but he couldn't respond. Every ounce of his energy was focused on drawing the next breath.

"Sam! Can you hear me?" Bo's braid brushed Sam's temple, but his voice sounded muffled and far away. "Say something. Please."

The terror behind Bo's outward calm galvanized Sam into action. With a huge effort, he lifted his head and stared into Bo's eyes. "The portal," he gasped. "It's opening. Have to close it."

Bo and Dean were already hauling him to his feet before he finished speaking. A rasping, hissing sound filled the air. Sam homed his attention onto it, trying to grasp the shades of meaning flitting through it.

"No, Sam." Clamping his hands around Sam's arms in an iron grip, Bo tugged him away from the pit. "We're going. Now."

Sam didn't even have time to protest. As he watched, the air around the pit twisted and shimmered. The hissing grew louder, the temperature plummeted and space ripped open, spitting out not one but two reality-defying creatures that were all too familiar.

"Fuck!" Dean stumbled backward, pushing Sam and Bo behind him. His teeth chattered in the sudden frigid cold. "Is...is that..."

No one answered. There was no need.

A high-pitched wail broke from the smaller of the two beings, the sound piercing Sam's eardrums like a knife. From the corner of his eye, he saw his friends cover their ears and grimace. Images flashed through Sam's mind, images he didn't understand, and he realized with a shock he was picking up on a communication between the two creatures.

Amidst the chaotic pictures in Sam's head, the meaning behind the noises came through loud and clear, and he knew he was out of time.

Gathering all his strength, Sam shoved Bo and Dean out of the way and staggered forward. *Leave them alone!* he screamed silently at the things. *Go away! Go back!*

For a heart-thumping moment, Sam felt as if the fate of his world balanced on the head of a pin. Drawing a deep breath, he centered himself and prepared to send the creatures back where they'd come from.

As if in reaction to his intent, the smaller thing—a juvenile, Sam realized in a burst of insight—shot forward. It moved faster than anything Sam had ever seen. He whirled, grasped at it and missed, and watched in horror as it leapt on Bo.

Chapter Thirteen

Sam didn't stop to think. Scrambling toward Bo, he grabbed at the creature with his hands and his mind. He ignored the biting cold when his fingers sank into the thing, tuned out the shouts and sudden frantic activity of his friends. Nothing mattered but Bo, writhing in silent agony on the ground as the nightmare being sank its needle-like teeth into his thigh.

Somehow, Sam managed to pull the thing off Bo. Whether he did it by physical or mental force, Sam didn't know, and right then he didn't care. He glanced at Bo. His lover lay curled on the ground, face twisted in a rictus of pain, both hands clutching his right thigh just above the knee. Blood poured from between his fingers.

"Bo..." Sam half-turned, already reaching for Bo before he stopped himself. He wiped his palms on his jeans, fighting the need to scoop Bo into his arms and run.

"I've got it." Dropping to his knees beside Bo, Dean dug a small knife out of his back pocket. His wide eyes fixed on Sam's face. "Send them back. Close it."

Sam ruthlessly suppressed the helpless anger rising in him. Dean was right. He had to stop this. Now. Turning away from Bo and Dean and the rest of the group huddling around them, Sam focused his mind on the psychic umbilical cord linking the creatures with their home and followed it to its source. Without giving himself the time to think or to doubt, he gave a mental push.

The larger creature let out a furious screech and lurched toward Sam. Heart pounding, he redoubled his efforts. The tunnel seemed to bend, the walls angling inward. The creature's nebulous body twisted in a stomach-turning way and disappeared. Sam felt the reverberation of the portal closing in his head.

Sam stretched out his senses, feeling for any residual energy from the portal. There was nothing. Even the temperature remained down. Satisfied, Sam turned his attention back to Bo.

Bo lay on his back in the dirt, looking pale and glassy-eyed. The right leg of his jeans had been cut off at the groin. Dean leaned over Bo's injured leg, pressing his folded T-shirt to the wound with both hands. The white cotton was liberally splotched with red, and blood coated Bo's leg and pooled on the ground under him. Cecile knelt at Bo's left side, holding his hand in both of hers.

"Andre's gone to get the cops and call an ambulance," Cecile said. "David's looking for first-aid supplies."

"Okay." Sinking to the ground, Sam slipped his sweatshirt underneath Bo's head. He laid a hand on Bo's forehead. The skin there was hot and damp, matting stray tendrils of hair to his face. "Bo? How do you feel?"

"Hurts." Rolling his eyes up, Bo pinned Sam with a feverish stare. "Sam. The portal?"

"Closed. They're gone."

"Actually, the little one's not," Dean told him, sounding remarkably calm and not at all like the teasing person Sam had come to know.

Sam blinked at him. "What?"

"It stopped moving when the portal closed," Cecile explained. "And I can't feel it in my head anymore. Neither could Andre. We think it's dead."

"Good." Sliding his palm down to Bo's cheek, Sam cast a worried glance at Dean. "What did that thing do to him?"

"Bit him." Dean's voice was grim. "It bled a lot, but I think I've got that under control now. I think the big worry is going to be infection. There's already some redness and swelling spreading up and down the leg from the bite."

Fear shot through Sam, cold and nauseating. He glanced at Cecile, and saw the same horrifying realization in her eyes. *God, no. Not Bo, please not Bo.*

"Okay, what aren't y'all telling me?" Dean's eyes were wide and wary.

Bo's wheezing laugh startled them all. "Little girl got bitten at Oleander House," Bo said, his voice breathy and tight with pain. "It's why we got called to investigate. The bite got infected almost right away, and she died."

"You're not going to die. I won't fucking let you." Leaning down, Sam pressed a soft kiss to Bo's forehead. He didn't care who saw.

"'M not ready to die," Bo whispered as Sam pulled away. "Not now."

Sam's throat went tight. The sound of voices and running feet saved him from breaking down in tears. Drawing a shaky breath, he managed to pull himself together just as Andre and two police officers crowded around them.

"Ambulance is on the way," one officer told them as she knelt beside Cecile. "Your friend David and another officer are waiting for them out front. What happened here?"

"Bo was attacked by an unidentified animal. It's over there." Dean nodded to his right, where Sam saw a strange twisted lump, which had to be the thing that had bitten Bo. "It seems to have died."

Sam and Cecile looked at each other as the second officer approached the still form, pistol aimed at the thing. It hadn't occurred to Sam to point out the creature's carcass without mentioning where it had come from. *Clever,* he thought, giving Dean a tiny nod.

"Jesus fuckin' Christ!" the male officer bellowed. "Collins, come look at this fuckin' thing."

The female officer—Collins, Sam assumed—glared at her partner, but rose and went to look. "Good Lord. Shephard, we better get animal control. I don't know what the hell this thing is."

Bo reached up, grasping weakly at Dean's bare shoulder. "No," he breathed, the sound barely audible. "Don't let them. Need to…to study it…"

Taking Bo's hand, Dean squeezed his fingers. "Don't worry," he whispered. "I'll take care of it." Raising his voice, he called to the police officers. "Hey, guys? I have a friend who's a Biology professor at the University of South Alabama. I can take it to her, she has the facilities to study it. Would that be all right?"

The two officers looked at each other. Collins shrugged. "I guess. Animal control doesn't much like coming out to collect dead animals anyway."

"We'll get a bag or something to put it in," Shephard offered. Wrinkling his nose, he flipped the pistol's safety on and holstered it. "Damn ugly motherfucker."

At that moment, flashlight beams appeared from around the bend in the tunnel. Sam breathed a sigh of relief as David loped up, followed by another officer and two paramedics.

"All right, everyone please clear the area," one of the paramedics said, her voice calm but brooking no argument.

With a reassuring smile at Bo, Sam stood and moved back, along with Dean and Cecile. He leaned against the wall between Dean and Andre as the emergency medics worked over Bo, starting an IV line and examining his wound. Cecile went into David's outstretched arms. Her hands shook where she clung to his waist.

Within minutes, the paramedics had Bo loaded onto the stretcher and were pushing him down the tunnel toward the stairs. A clear plastic bag hung from a metal pole at the head of the stretcher, feeding fluids into the needle in Bo's arm through a short tubing. Sam and the rest of the team followed, jogging to keep up.

David turned a questioning look to Dean as the bottom of the steps came into view. "How are they gonna get him up the steps?"

"They'll fold the wheels and carry the stretcher," Dean explained. "They don't have to worry about jarring any broken bones or potential spinal injuries, so there's no need to wait for special rescue equipment. Getting him to the hospital quickly is the most important thing."

"How do you know all this?" Andre asked, voicing the question in the back of Sam's mind.

"I used to work in the emergency room as a nurse's aide. Learned all kinds of helpful things." Dean's mouth curved into a wan smile. "I kept my certification current until about a year ago."

Under different circumstances, Sam would've wanted to know more. He felt a vague curiosity, but it faded fast when the paramedics reached the bottom of the stairs and began to haul Bo up them one laborious step at a time.

It was all Sam could do to hold himself back when Bo cried out in pain. He crowded as close as he dared to the stretcher, peering around the paramedic's bulky shoulder to catch a glimpse of Bo's face. Bo's eyes were closed, his brow furrowed. His lips moved, murmuring something Sam couldn't hear.

The moment they cleared the steps and the paramedics unfolded the stretcher's wheels, Sam rushed to Bo's side. He took Bo's hand. "Hang in there, Bo. They're taking you to the hospital. You're going to be fine."

Bo's eyelids fluttered, but didn't open. "Sam. Don't leave me."

"I won't." Fighting tears, Sam kissed Bo's fingers. "Bo..."

They reached the front door of the school, and Sam was forced to move again as the medics lifted the stretcher down the steps. Sam followed them and stood behind the ambulance, watching as Bo was loaded into the back. One of the paramedics climbed in with him, while the other hurried around to the driver's side door.

"We're taking him to Mobile General," the man said as he heaved himself behind the wheel. "The emergency room's around back, just follow the signs. Y'all know how to get there?"

"Yeah," David answered, his eyes suspiciously wet. "Just get him there, and take care of him. We'll be along in a little while."

Watching the ambulance drive away, Sam felt desperate and helpless. He jumped when Dean's hand slid into his.

"Go get in the SUV, Sam," Dean said softly. "You're going with Andre and David to the hospital."

Sam let Dean lead him to the SUV and open the door for him. "What about you and Cecile?"

"We're going to collect that...that thing and take it to Dean's friend." Cecile gave him a watery smile. "We'll come on over as soon as we're done."

"Okay." Sam squeezed Dean's hand as Andre and David climbed into the front seat, with Andre behind the wheel. "See you there. Be careful."

Dean nodded, let go of Sam's hand and shut the door. Leaning his forehead against the window, Sam shut his eyes. His heartbeat pounded in his ears, drowning out the terse conversation from the front seat.

Please let him be okay. I can't lose him. Not now. Not like this.

Opening his eyes and gazing out at the city rushing past, Sam wondered if anyone was listening.

♋

Three hours later, Sam sat curled in a chair in the surgery waiting room at Mobile General Hospital, staring out the tinted window at an enclosed garden. Winter sunshine filtered through the bare branches of the trees, gilding the white angel statue in the middle of the garden. It was a peaceful spot. Sam wished that peacefulness would seep through the glass and into his mind.

He looked up when David shuffled over, carrying two cups of coffee from the coffee cart in the lobby. "Here you go," David said, thrusting a steaming Styrofoam cup into Sam's hands. "One extra-large high test. Heard anything?"

"Thanks." Holding the cup under his nose, Sam took a deep breath of espresso-scented steam. "Haven't heard a word yet."

"Figures." David sank into the chair next to Sam's with a deep sigh. "What about Dean and Cecile, have they called?"

"I just called Cecile," Andre answered, sticking his cell phone in his pocket. "There was a big wreck on Airport Boulevard, they're stuck in traffic."

"Ah, damn." Slouching in his seat, David took a sip from his coffee cup. "Did they find the phone number for Janine's folks?"

"No. It wasn't anywhere at the office." Andre sighed. "Bo's probably got the number at his place, or maybe it's just in his head."

"We'll ask Bo when he wakes up," Sam said, staring at the plastic lid of his cup.

Neither David nor Andre answered, but Sam felt their discomfort. He knew what they were thinking—what if Bo didn't wake up? Sam refused to consider that possibility.

When they'd arrived at the hospital, they'd learned that Bo was being rushed to surgery, though no one would tell them why. The only reason the nurse in charge had agreed to let them talk to the doctor after surgery was the fact that Janine, Bo's legal next of kin, was out of town and no one knew how to reach her. When David wondered why they didn't just ask Bo, he was told Bo had lost consciousness in the ambulance.

Sam had never felt more helpless in his life. The feeling hadn't faded with the passing hours, either. Shifting in his chair, Sam sipped his coffee without tasting it.

The waiting room door swung open and a tall, thin man in blue scrubs walked in. Sam looked up, along with everyone else in the room. The man in the scrubs frowned at a scrap of paper in his hand. "Mr. Meloy? Andre Meloy?"

Shooting a wide-eyed glance at David and Sam, Andre jumped to his feet. "I'm Andre Meloy."

The man gave a crisp nod. "I'm Dr. Shore. We've just finished Dr. Broussard's surgery. He's stable at present and doing well. He'll be going to the intensive care unit shortly."

"What sort of surgery did you do?" Andre asked. "No one would tell us anything, since we're not next of kin."

"His wife's at her parents' house," David added. "None of us knows their number, or Janine's cell number. We've got some friends trying to find the numbers, but no luck so far."

Dr. Shore's eyebrows went up. "Very well. I'll be happy to call her when you find the number."

"Can you tell us anything in the meantime?" Sam gave himself a mental pat on the back for sounding so much calmer than he felt.

"Your friend has Mr. Meloy here listed as emergency contact, so I think that will be all right." Perching on the edge of an empty chair, the doctor leaned forward and lowered his voice. "Dr. Broussard's wound had already developed an abscess by the time he arrived here, he was running a fever of one hundred and five, and his blood pressure was dangerously low. We took him straight to surgery to clean out the wound. The abscess was completely removed, then we washed the entire area with an antibiotic solution before closing. Luckily, the abscess was close to the surface, probably because the wound consisted of several parallel scratches rather than punctures. They were no more than half an inch deep, and the abscess didn't extend much beyond that depth."

David swallowed, looking a little green. "So, he's okay now? He'll be okay?"

Dr. Shore gave them all a long, solemn look. "Normally, I'd say definitely so. He's young and healthy, with no long-term health problems or immunosuppressive diseases, as far as we've been able to determine. Under normal circumstances, he should do just fine."

"But?" Sam wasn't sure he wanted to hear the answer, but he had to ask.

"But, these are not normal circumstances. This infection is like nothing I've ever seen. I'm told your friend was already developing localized signs of infection at the scene after being bitten by this unidentified animal. By the time he arrived here, not even half an hour later, he was in septic shock. No known infectious organism causes such severe sepsis so quickly. We're analyzing his blood to see if we can isolate and identify the organism behind this, and we're hitting him with broad-spectrum antibiotics to try and cover all the bases. But we're most likely dealing with an unknown quantity here, which means I can't predict what might happen."

Sam wanted to scream, but his throat was tight and aching and he couldn't make a sound. He stared at his feet, hoping the rest of the world couldn't see the anger and despair in his face.

"Can we see him?" David's voice shook. "You said he was stable."

"He is. He woke up in recovery, and was able to correctly tell us his name and the year, though of course he wasn't sure where he was." Dr. Shore smiled. "He did ask about all of you. He wanted to make sure you were all okay."

Andre let out a relieved laugh. "He would."

"Stay here, and the ICU desk will call you when Dr. Broussard is in his room. You'll only be allowed five minutes for this visit, since it's immediately post-op, so best to pick one person to go see him." Rising to his feet, Dr. Shore glanced at the scrap of paper he still held. "Speaking of which, is one of you Sam?"

Sam's heart leapt straight up his throat. "I am."

"Dr. Broussard would like to see you." Turning on his heel, the doctor strode briskly toward the waiting room door. "Have the nurse page me when you find the wife's number."

Silence hung thick and heavy in the wake of the doctor's departure. Tucking his feet under him, Sam took a long swallow of his cooling coffee. He could feel David and Andre staring at him, and knew they were wondering why Bo had asked for him when they'd been friends with him for far longer. Probably wondering if it had anything to do with the way Sam had kissed Bo's hand as the paramedics wheeled him along the hallway at South Bay High.

Sam longed to tell them, but he couldn't. Bo wanted to keep his secret for now, and Sam was determined to respect that. *You shouldn't have acted like that at the school,* he berated himself. *You were so fucking obvious, you might as well have "I love Bo" carved into your forehead.*

It was too much to think about right then. Sam kept his gaze fixed on the floor. Eventually, David and Andre started talking in low tones. Ignoring them, Sam steeled himself to wait for the time when he could see Bo.

It didn't take as long as he thought it would. No more than twenty minutes after Dr. Shore left, the volunteer at the waiting room desk came walking over. He looked up at her.

The elderly woman gave him a sweet smile. "You're Sam Raintree, right?"

"That's right." Sam glanced at David and Andre. Both were sitting ramrod straight, staring at the petite white-haired lady in the green smock. "What is it?"

"The ICU called. You may see your friend now." Moving to the big window overlooking the hospital lobby, she beckoned Sam over. He stood, his knees shaking, and walked over to her. She pointed at the hallway on the other side of the lobby. "Take that hallway to the B elevators. They're on your right about halfway down. Go up to the second floor and turn left from the elevator. The ICU is at the end of the hall. Just ring on the intercom, tell them your name and that you're there to see Dr. Broussard. They'll let you in and take you to his room."

Sam nodded, hoping he wouldn't forget her directions the minute he left the waiting room. "Thanks."

She patted his arm, faded blue eyes crinkling at the corners behind her glasses. "Don't worry. If you get lost, just follow the signs, or ask any of the hospital staff. They'll be happy to help you."

"Thank you," Sam repeated, forcing an anemic smile. Turning around, he met David and Andre's worried gazes. "I'll tell him y'all are here."

They didn't answer, but he knew how they felt. Wiping his sweating palms on his shirt, he walked out of the waiting room and began the journey to the ICU.

To his surprise, he found it without any trouble. The hospital was huge, the largest in the county, and he'd been certain he'd get lost on the way, but the volunteer's directions led him straight to the intensive care unit where Bo waited. Sam stood staring at the wide double doors, suddenly terrified of what he might see inside.

"You've only got a few minutes, dumb-ass," he muttered. "Don't waste even a second you could be spending with him."

Nodding to himself, Sam pressed the intercom button beside the door. "Yes? Can I help you?" a tinny voice responded.

Sam cleared his throat. "I...I'm Sam Raintree. I'm here to see Dr. Broussard."

"Oh yes. Come on in." The intercom cut off and the doors swung slowly open.

Drawing a deep breath, Sam forced his legs to move, taking him into the bright, busy room. His feet felt heavy and his chest tight. Following the directions on the sign beside the door, he stopped and washed his hands at a large sink, then went to the nurse's desk. A nurse with short graying hair and a kind smile met him there.

"Mr. Raintree? I'm Marlene, Bo's nurse." Laying a hand on Sam's elbow, she steered him toward a glass-enclosed cubicle on the far side of the round room. "Bo's kind of groggy from the pain meds, but he's awake and pretty lucid right now. He keeps asking to see you."

"Oh." Sam swallowed. His heart raced, making him feel dizzy and weak. "Can...can I just go in?"

"Sure. You have five minutes, I'll let you know when it's up." She frowned. "Are you all right?"

"I'm fine." Sam tried to smile at her and failed utterly. "Just worried, is all. Bo's a...a good friend."

Marlene gave a sympathetic look. "Of course. I'm right outside if you need me, Sam." Giving his arm a light squeeze, she walked over to the desk, leaving Sam alone in front of the curtained glass door.

"You can do this," Sam whispered. Steeling himself, he pushed the door open and walked in.

Bo lay with the head of the bed slightly raised, his eyes closed. White wires snaked out of the top of his hospital gown, connecting to a machine tracing the rhythm of Bo's heartbeat. It seemed abnormally fast to Sam. IV tubings dripped three different fluids into both of Bo's arms. The machines clustered around Bo's bed beeped and hummed.

Approaching the bed, Sam stared at Bo. His face was ashen and beaded with sweat, his hair damp and tangled where it had come loose from his braid. Beneath the thin sheet, Bo's chest rose and fell in rapid, shallow breaths. He didn't look any better than he had when Sam had last seen him.

Unable to help himself, Sam bent and kissed Bo's brow. The skin was damp and burning hot under his lips. "I'm here, Bo."

Bo's eyelids fluttered open. "Sam," he murmured, fingers clamping onto Sam's wrist. "Don't wanna die, Sam."

Shit. "You're not going to die. I'm not letting you go."

"'S poisoning me. They can't stop it." Bo stared up at Sam, eyes bright and feverish. "Just found you, Sam. Don't want to lose this."

Choking back the threatening tears, Sam pressed Bo's palm to his cheek. "Don't talk that way. You're going to be fine."

If Bo heard him, he gave no indication of it. "My boys. Sean and Adrian. Can't die without seeing them." Bo's face contorted. "Want to see them. Please."

"We can't find the number, Bo. Can you..." Sam stopped, fighting to control the quaver in his voice. "Can you tell us Janine's parents' phone number? So we can call and bring Sean and Adrian here to see you?"

Bo's eyes drifted closed, and for a terrible moment Sam was afraid he'd lost consciousness again. "In my cell," Bo slurred finally. "'S in the glove compartment."

"Which one? The SUV or your car?"

"SUV." Cranking his lids up again, Bo gave Sam the ghost of a smile. "Thanks. For coming. Wanted to see you."

"I'm not leaving. I'll be here any time they'll let me in. Everyone else is here too. We won't leave you alone." Sam pressed a soft kiss to Bo's palm. "I love you."

Bo didn't say anything. His eyes lost their focus, his hand going slack against Sam's cheek. Swallowing the sudden rush of fear, Sam brushed the sweat-soaked hair away from Bo's face with his free hand. "Bo? Can you hear me?"

No answer. Something rattled at the foot of the bed. Turning around, Sam saw Bo's feet shaking under the covers. Before he could process what was happening, the shaking spread like a wave up Bo's body. His eyes rolled back, his lips turning blue as Sam watched.

Terror bolted through Sam, sharp and sickening. Every machine in the room started screaming at once. Sam stared, horrified, as Bo convulsed on the bed. *Help, need help.*

Before he could turn the thought into action, the door burst open and the room filled with people. He was shoved unceremoniously out of the way. Stumbling backward, he leaned against the doorframe, numbly watching the frantic activity around Bo's bed. He had no idea what was happening, but he knew it wasn't good.

"Sir?"

Sam barely glanced at the young man who'd spoken to him. "Don't make me leave."

Obviously used to that sort of reaction, the man took Sam's arm and steered him firmly away from Bo's room. "He's in good hands. Let them take care of him."

Sam let himself be led, though he couldn't tear his gaze from the scrub-clad crowd huddled around Bo. "Can I stay here for a minute? I just want to know what's going on, and if he's okay."

Without a word, the man rolled a chair from behind the nurse's station desk and pushed Sam gently into it. He patted Sam's shoulder and hurried off to answer the insistent trill of an alarm in another room. Fighting back the need to jump up and run to Bo, Sam leaned back in the chair and forced himself to stay put.

It felt like forever before the crowd in Bo's room began to disperse. Sam anxiously watched as the staff exited the little cubicle. Each face looked grim, and no one would meet his eyes. A hard knot of dread formed in Sam's belly.

When Marlene came out, Sam leapt up. "Marlene? What happened?"

"He had a seizure, most likely caused by his fever. It's nearly one-oh-six." Sighing, she ran a hand through her hair. "His fever had started to come down right after surgery. The doctor's started him on some different antibiotics, plus an antiviral agent, and we gave him something to stop the seizures. At least he's still breathing on his own."

Sam grabbed the edge of the desk to steady himself against the wave of dizziness. "Is he awake? Can I see him?"

"I'm afraid not. The drugs used to stop the seizures are very sedating. He's sleeping right now, and he needs to do that. We'll update you the moment there's any change."

Sam stared through the glass into Bo's room. With the curtain partly drawn, he could only see the bottom half of the bed. He wished he could see Bo's face.

"When can I come back?" Sam asked, surprised at how calm he sounded.

"Four hours. You might want to go home and get some rest."

"No. I want to be here."

Nodding, Marlene steered him toward the exit. "I figured. There's a waiting room for the ICUs at the other end of this hall. You and your friends can wait there. And Bo's wife and kids, too, when they get here."

Sam suppressed the automatic anger and resentment he felt at the mention of Janine. *She's still married to him, and they have children together. Suck it up and deal with it.*

Stopping at the double doors, Sam managed a weak smile. "Thanks, Marlene."

"You're welcome." She took his hand and squeezed. "We'll take good care of him."

"I know." He felt like he should say something else, but he didn't know what to say. Whirling around, he shoved the door open.

The elevator was empty, for which Sam was profoundly grateful. He was shaking all over, his emotions out of control, and he didn't feel like facing a bunch of strangers. As he stepped out into the first floor hallway, he nearly ran right into Dean, who was walking past the elevator door at that moment.

"Sam. Cecile and I just got back, I was heading to the soda machine and—" Dean stopped short, eyes going wide when he saw Sam's face. Grabbing Sam's hand, he dragged him into a small alcove containing drink and snack machines. "What happened? What's wrong?"

Sam swallowed, trying to find his voice. "He was awake, he was talking to me, and then...he, he just...he started shaking, and he wouldn't respond to me. The nurse said he had a seizure, that...that it was probably his fever."

"What? But Andre told me the doctor said he was stable."

"He was, the nurse said his fever was down right after the surgery, but now..." Squeezing his eyes shut, Sam fought back tears. "What if he doesn't make it, Dean? I can't live with that. I can't."

"God, Sam. Come here." Dean put his arms around Sam's shoulders and pulled him close. Sam leaned against him, clutching his shirt. He couldn't cry, not here. But it felt good to be held.

After a couple of minutes, Sam felt sufficiently in control to face the rest of the group. Pulling out of Dean's embrace, Sam gave him a wan smile. "I found out how to get in touch with Janine and the boys. The number's in Bo's cell phone, in the SUV glove compartment."

Dean pressed his hand. "Great. Let's go find it. Andre can make the call."

As they walked across the lobby, Sam felt his composure returning, the old habit of hiding his emotions kicking in automatically. By the time he and Dean entered the room where their friends waited, he'd schooled his face into a blank mask. It wasn't perfect, but it was the best he could do. At least he wasn't screaming.

Chapter Fourteen

"Dammit." Snapping Bo's cell phone closed, Andre glowered at it before shoving it back in his jacket pocket. "Where the hell are they?"

With a sigh, Cecile shifted in her seat, leaning her head on David's shoulder. "You've left five messages. All we can do is keep trying."

"Yeah, I know." Andre rubbed a hand across his eyes. "I'm just afraid that..."

There was no need to finish the thought. They all knew what he was afraid of.

Andre had been trying to call Bo's in-laws for almost eight hours. So far he'd gotten the answering machine every time. As time ticked away and Bo's condition continued to deteriorate, they'd all begun to fear Bo's children wouldn't make it back in time to see their father before...

Don't think of it. That's not going to happen. Bo's not going to die. He's going to make it.

That mantra had repeated itself in Sam's head over and over ever since Bo had been bitten. At first it had helped. Soothed away some of his dread. But as the hours passed, a niggling voice in the back of his mind whispered that his hope was nothing but a lie. That he was going to lose the first person he'd ever truly loved.

The last visit to Bo's bedside, nearly four hours ago, had made the icy lump in Sam's belly a permanent fixture. Bo was unconscious, cheeks red and hot with a fever that refused to abate, his body twitching now and then. An oxygen mask was strapped to his face. Marlene had grimly informed them that if the oxygen level in his blood continued to drop, the next step would be a ventilator to breathe for him.

The whole group had gone to see him that time, by special permission from Dr. Shore. When they left, they were silent, but Sam saw his own fear reflected in their faces.

Glancing at the clock on the wall of the ICU waiting room, Sam realized it was nearly time for the next visiting period. He rose and stretched. On the other side of the room, the phone at the volunteer desk rang. "It's time, y'all," Sam said. "Who all's coming?"

"I'll stay here," Andre offered. "In case Janine calls back. Cell phones aren't allowed in the ICU and I don't want to miss a call."

What Andre said was true, but Sam suspected the man's willingness to stay behind had more to do with painful memories than anything else. Sam knew Andre had to be remembering Amy's death right now, and it couldn't be anything but sheer hell for him.

Nodding, Sam squeezed Andre's shoulder. "Okay. We'll let you know how he is."

As the group passed the desk, the white-haired man working there flagged them down. "You're with Dr. Broussard, right?"

Apprehension shut off Sam's breath. He clutched blindly at Dean's arm. Giving him a worried glance, Dean nodded at the volunteer. "Yes, that's right. What is it?"

The man smiled. "That was the ICU calling. Dr. Broussard is awake. They thought you'd like to know, but I guess y'all are heading there anyway."

Relief washed through Sam like a tide. He managed to keep himself upright by sheer force of will.

"Thank you very much," Cecile said, a wide smile on her face. "That's wonderful news."

Wrapping an arm around her shoulders, David kissed her temple. "It is. C'mon, let's go see him."

The trip down the hall to the ICU seemed to last forever. Sam chafed with impatience when they had to wait their turn to wash their hands at the big sink just inside the double doors. On the other side of the nurse's station, he could see Bo's room, the curtains still drawn across the glass door. He wanted to run right over, fling the door open and sweep Bo into his arms, hold him and touch him and reassure himself that Bo was really, truly alive.

Finally, all four of them were washed and ready to visit. Sam didn't mean to push ahead, but he couldn't seem to help himself. He was the first to enter the little room. The sight of Bo sitting up in bed, looking exhausted but wide awake, was the most beautiful thing Sam had ever seen. Without considering what the consequences might be, Sam crossed to Bo's bed, sat on the edge of the mattress and gathered Bo gently into his arms.

He heard the others come into the room behind him, heard David's surprised gasp, but it didn't matter. Nothing else mattered, because Bo's arms were around him, fingers in his hair and stroking his back, Bo's cheek was pressed to his. Bo was alive, and secrets had ceased to be important.

Eventually Sam drew back, letting Bo rest against the pillows. "Don't ever scare me like that again," Sam said, the seriousness of the statement softened by the huge grin he couldn't hold back.

"I'll try not to." Bo stared up at Sam. "I almost died."

Sam's insides clenched. "Yeah. You did."

For several long seconds, no one moved or spoke. Bo's gaze bored into Sam's. At the foot of the bed, the others stood still and silent. Sam held his breath. When Bo's hand snaked around the back of his neck, pulling him down to press their lips together, Sam's world tilted underneath him.

The kiss lasted forever and not long enough. When they drew apart at last and Bo whispered "I love you" against Sam's mouth, Sam thought he might float away.

"Okay then," David said, bringing Sam abruptly back to earth. "When did this happen?"

"It started at Oleander House." Taking Sam's hand and lacing their fingers together, Bo looked up at David, Dean and Cecile, who now stood on the other side of his bed. "I'm sorry I didn't tell y'all before, David. I was scared."

David shrugged. "I guess my feelings should be hurt, but they're not. It doesn't seem very important now. You're alive. Worrying about stuff like you not telling us you're gay seems kind of stupid at this point." He flashed a wide, wicked grin. "See, I told you office romance is a good thing."

Bo let out a raspy laugh. "So you did."

Leaning one hand on the bedrail, Cecile gave Bo a considering look. "I'd suspected something like this was going on. Is this why you're divorcing Janine?"

"It's what set the process in motion, yes. But our marriage has been a sham for years. It's better for both of us, and for the boys, if we break it off." Glancing around, Bo seemed to notice for the first time that Andre wasn't there. "Where's Andre? And did y'all get hold of Janine? I really need to see my sons."

Dean shook his head. "Sam found your phone, and Andre's been calling for hours. He keeps getting their answering machine. He stayed out in the waiting room, in case they call back."

The grief in Bo's eyes said he knew the real reason Andre had stayed behind. "They probably went to visit some other family members. Janine should have her cell phone with her, I'll call her myself."

"Andre tried the number listed in your cell," Sam told him, lifting his hand and kissing his fingers. "It was out of service."

"Yeah, she just got a new phone a couple of weeks ago. I never got around to programming the number in, but I think I remember it." Wrinkling his nose, Bo made an irritated sound. "I can't believe I didn't think to mention that to you before, Sam."

Sam didn't know whether to laugh or cry. "Bo, you were halfway delirious with fever. I'm surprised you even remembered where the phone was, never mind Janine's new cell number."

The corners of Bo's mouth curled into a sheepish smile. "I suppose you're right."

"Don't take this wrong," David said, "but why'd you get better all of a sudden?"

"I have no idea." Bo's brow furrowed. "Dr. Shore was in to see me a few minutes ago. He said it was almost like the infection just switched off all of a sudden. He couldn't explain it. Said he'd like to give credit to the drugs they were giving me, but he couldn't be sure. Hopefully they'll know more when the results of my blood and wound cultures come back. Oh, by the way, Dean, did you take that...thing to your friend at the college? The doctor wants to know what they find out from autopsy and lab testing."

"She's working on it now. She said she'd call me as soon as she has any results." Laying his hand on Bo's shoulder, Dean smiled. "I know I haven't been with this group long, Bo, but I consider you a friend as well as my boss, and I am incredibly happy to see you on the mend."

Bo's eyes shone. "Thanks, Dean. Hey, do y'all think you could keep this to yourselves for now? About Sam and me, I mean. I'm not going to hide who I am anymore"—Bo's fingers tightened around Sam's—"but I think we're both more comfortable practicing a little discretion in who we tell."

"So what you're saying is, you don't want Janine to find out," David clarified, blunt as usual. "That's cool. She'd totally use it against you."

Before Bo could answer, a young nurse with a long blonde braid appeared in the doorway. Her eyebrows went up at the sight of Bo and Sam holding hands, but she didn't comment. "Time's about up, y'all."

"Can't they stay for a little while longer?" Bo pleaded.

The nurse shook her head. "I'm sorry, no. But Dr. Shore said we could move you out of the ICU tomorrow, if you do all right overnight. After that you can have visitors whenever you want."

"We should really go and let Bo get some rest anyway," Cecile said. "Bo, we'll be back in the morning. Is there anything we can do? Anything you need?"

"You're already finding my kids. That's all I need." Leaning forward, Bo took Cecile's hand, pressing her fingers with his. "Thanks, all of you. For everything."

"Sure thing, boss-man." David's voice sounded suspiciously rough, but his blue eyes twinkled. "You and Sam probably want a minute. We'll wait outside."

David, Dean and Cecile left, the nurse trailing behind them. She shot a frankly curious look at Sam and Bo as she shut the door.

Sam chuckled. "Does David even realize what a closet romantic he is?"

"Probably not. Luckily for him, I think Cecile knows it quite well." Sitting up, Bo wound both arms around Sam's neck. "Nurse Nosy is going to make you leave any second now."

"I know." Sam ran his thumb over Bo's bottom lip. "Kiss me goodbye?"

In answer, Bo tilted his head and covered Sam's mouth with his. Sam let out a breathy moan when Bo's lips parted, tongue slipping out to twine with his. It was quite possibly the best kiss he'd ever had, in spite of the distinctly unromantic surroundings, because he'd come so close to losing Bo, and now Bo was back. He was going to be okay. Nothing could compare to that.

"Bye, Bo," Sam whispered as they broke apart. He rose reluctantly to his feet, Bo's hand still clasped in his. "I'll see you in the morning, as soon as they'll let me in."

"Okay." Smiling, Bo squeezed Sam's hand before letting his fingers slip away. "See you then."

Walking out that door was hard, but not as hard as it had been before. This time, he knew when he came back, Bo would still be there. It was a wonderful feeling. He'd never known what a magnificent thing a loved one's continued presence could be.

As they left the ICU, Dean nudged Sam with his elbow. "You look like you're on cloud nine."

"I am," Sam agreed. "God, you don't know how scared I was. I mean, I know we all were, but..."

"But you were even more scared than the rest of us, because you had more to lose," David chimed in, walking backward to face Sam and Dean. "I'm sorry, man. Must've been pretty rough, especially since you couldn't tell us. I know that was Bo's idea, too. He never did like anybody to be in his business."

"He's a very private person." Glancing over her shoulder, Cecile gave Sam a warm smile. "I'm glad you both feel comfortable sharing this with us, even if you keep it from the rest of the world. It's impossibly difficult to hide like that from the people who care about you."

"That's the truth," Sam said, with feeling. "I hope Andre won't mind. He's been friends with Bo longer than anybody."

"He won't," David confidently declared. "Andre's got a good head on his shoulders. He doesn't let the little stuff bug him. And believe me, compared to what he's been through since August, this is miniscule."

Sam knew David was right. Andre had suffered the worst sort of loss, and it had damaged him, but his love for and loyalty to his friends remained unsullied. He understood what a precious gift love was, and he would be happy Bo had found it, no matter who it was with.

The four of them burst through the waiting room doors together and hurried to where Andre sat slumped in a chair. The big man looked up, hope brightening his eyes as he caught sight of their smiling faces. David grinned. "Andre, have we got some news for you..."

♋

Janine and the boys showed up Sunday night. Sean and Adrian begged their father to come home with them, but Janine refused. Sam wasn't surprised. His dislike for the woman was stronger than ever, something he hadn't thought possible. Not once did she express any worry over Bo, or any emotion at all other than contempt. Sam wanted to strangle her, for the sadness in her sons' eyes as much as the way she constantly cut Bo down.

Janine's unwillingness to look after Bo gave Sam the perfect excuse to invite Bo to stay with him. Somewhat to Sam's surprise, Bo accepted. The way Janine's eyes narrowed when she found out stirred a nervous flutter in Sam's belly, but he ignored it. There was no possible way she could know about him and Bo. Only their friends knew, and they would never tell Janine.

Bo was released from the hospital the next day. They decided to stop at Bo's apartment and collect clothes and other necessities before going to Sam's place. To Sam's relief, Janine wasn't at the hospital when Bo was discharged. Not that he'd thought she would be.

"Thanks for letting me stay with you," Bo said, giving Sam a sweet smile as Sam guided his truck through the Monday afternoon traffic. "Maybe it's stupid, but I really didn't want to be alone."

"It's not stupid. After everything that's happened, I don't blame you a bit." Glancing at Bo, Sam shot him a suggestive leer. "It's not like I get nothing out of it."

Bo looked startled for a moment, then laughed. "Yeah, I guess you're right." His hand crept onto Sam's thigh. "I'm looking forward to that myself. There's still a lot you need to teach me about gay sex."

The sensation of Bo's fingers kneading his leg sent Sam's pulse racing. Licking his lips, he fought the urge to pull over and suck Bo off right there by the side of Airport Boulevard. The trill of his cell phone snapped him back to his senses.

Snatching the phone out of the cup holder where he'd put it, Sam flipped it open. "Hello?"

"Sam." Dean's voice bubbled with excitement. "Where are you?"

"Hi, Dean. Bo and I are on our way to his place to pick up a few things. What's up?"

"Get over to the college as soon as you can. My friend Laura—Dr. Trent, I mean—has some info for us about the thing that attacked Bo."

Twisting around to check his blind spot, Sam switched to the left lane. "I'll be there as soon as I can. Just let me get Bo settled at my place."

"Wait just a minute." Bo fixed Sam with a fierce stare. "What's going on?"

"Hang on a sec, Dean." Setting the phone carefully on his lap, Sam turned onto the narrow, run-down street where Bo's apartment complex was located. "Dean says his friend Dr. Trent at the college has some information for us about the thing that bit you. He said to get over there as soon as possible, and I told him to let me get you settled first."

Bo nodded. "Turn around. I'm going with you."

"Bo—"

"Don't argue. Let's go."

Sam sighed. "Come on, Bo, you just got out of the hospital fifteen minutes ago. Let me take you home to rest. I swear I'll tell you everything."

"Absolutely not." Crossing his arms, Bo gave Sam a determined look. "I feel fine, and I'd much rather hear what Dr. Trent has to say than hang around your apartment all by myself waiting and wondering. Turn around and go to the University."

His resistance crumbling, Sam shook his head and picked up the phone again. "You hear all that, Dean?"

"Yeah." Dean laughed. "You can't possibly be surprised he said that."

"No, I'm not." Pulling into an empty driveway, Sam turned the truck around and headed back the way they'd come. "Did you let David, Cecile and Andre know?"

"They were at the office with me when I got the call. We're on our way right now. Laura's office is in the science building, you know where that is?"

"No. Give me directions from the main entrance to the campus."

Dean rattled off the directions. Fishing a piece of paper and pen out of the glove compartment, Bo scribbled them down as Sam repeated them to him.

"Okay, got it," Sam said. "We'll see y'all there in a little bit."

"Great, see you there."

Sam broke the connection and clicked the phone closed. He shot a half-irritated, half-amused glance at Bo as he made the turn back onto Airport, heading toward the college. "Don't make me regret taking you."

"Yes, Dad," Bo answered dryly. "Seriously, Sam, I'm fine. Don't worry."

"Sorry. I just..." Sam stared out the window, concentrating on the traffic. "I keep seeing you lying in that hospital bed, Bo. I was so scared I was going to lose you. I'm having a little trouble getting past that, I guess."

For a moment Bo was silent. "I promise I'll tell you if I get too tired, or start feeling bad. Okay?"

"Okay." Sam smiled at him. "Thanks."

"Sure." Leaning closer, Bo caressed Sam's cheek. "I'm so glad we're together, Sam. You're exactly what I need in my life."

Warmth bloomed in Sam's chest. Reaching across the seat, he took Bo's hand, winding their fingers together. He didn't say anything, but he didn't need to. They understood each other just fine.

♋

Ten minutes later, Sam parked the truck in a miraculously empty spot right in front of the science building at the University of South Alabama. He hopped out, slammed the driver's side door, and jogged around to the other side just in time to help Bo step down onto the pavement.

"How's the leg?" Sam asked, closing Bo's door and locking the truck. "Is it hurting?"

"A little." Grimacing, Bo stepped gingerly onto the curb. He clung to Sam's arm as they headed for the door. "It's a lot better than it was, though."

"Good. Oh, and that reminds me, we need to stop at the drugstore and get some dressing supplies."

"They gave me some at the hospital before I left."

"I know, but it's only enough for a week. We might need more." Sam opened the door and held it open with his foot while Bo limped inside. "Besides, I want to get a different kind of tape. That stuff they gave you hurts like a bitch coming off."

Bo laughed. "Okay, Nurse Sam."

"Nurse Sam, huh?" Sam grinned. "I hope you don't expect me to wear a white dress."

"Now there's an interesting visual." Casting a quick glance around the empty hallway, Bo leaned over and planted a light kiss on Sam's neck. "I think I prefer you as yourself, though."

"Good. I could get into some roleplaying occasionally, but I draw the line at costumes." Sam slowed, perusing the room numbers as they made their way down the hall. "Here it is, 175."

Sam pushed the door open, and they walked into a large room that smelled like formaldehyde. A counter with several sinks in it ran the full length of the room, underneath a bank of windows that let in the late November sunshine. Two rows of lab tables took up most of the room. An open doorway to their right led to a small, cluttered office.

David, Dean, Cecile and Andre huddled at a table in the corner, along with a middle-aged woman Sam assumed was Dr. Trent. Dean looked up and grinned as they made their way across the room. "Hi y'all. C'mon over. This is my very good friend Dr. Laura Trent. Laura, this is Sam Raintree and Dr. Bo Broussard."

Laura came forward with one slender hand outstretched. "It's very nice to meet you both. Dr. Broussard, how's that bite doing?"

"Call me Bo," he said, smiling as he shook her hand. "It's doing okay now, thanks."

"Does it seem to be healing normally?" Laura gave him an apologetic look. "Sorry if this sounds nosy. Professional interest, you know."

"I understand completely." Hobbling over to the table, Bo eased himself onto a tall stool. "It's healing well, I think. There's no sign of infection at this point, and I'm feeling back to normal other than being just a bit tired."

"That's good." Opening a file that lay on the table, Laura shuffled through the papers and pulled out a sheaf of notes and several photos. "I'd like to explain to you all what I found."

"We're all ears." Andre leaned his elbows on the table, gaze fixed on the doctor. "What was that thing, and how did it make Bo so sick so fast?"

Sam slipped an arm around Bo's shoulders. The reminder of what had happened brought out Sam's protective instincts toward Bo.

Laura tapped a short fingernail on the tabletop. "I don't know what it is."

"What do you mean?" David asked. "You told Dean you had information for us."

Dean smacked David's arm. "Be nice."

Laughing, Laura brushed a dark blonde curl out of her eyes. "It's fine, Dean. David, I have what I think is some very interesting information for you. I don't know what this thing is because it's a completely new species. Or rather, one that's previously unknown to science."

"Oh." Shooting an apologetic look at Dean, David leaned a hip against the table. "Go ahead, Doctor."

"First of all," Laura continued, "I was unable to perform an autopsy. The creature doesn't seem to have internal organs. Either that, or I was unable to access them using traditional techniques. It's difficult to explain."

"What about lab results?" Cecile wondered. "Were you able to learn anything from those?"

Laura nodded. "Yes. The animal's teeth secrete a substance containing both a microbe and an inorganic chemical. I was unable to positively identify either. Whatever the chemical is, it seemed to work as an adjunct to the microbe. The microbe alone died out quickly in culture, but when we added the chemical, it practically exploded out of the dish. It completely used up the growth medium within a few minutes."

Bo blinked. "Dr. Shore told me my blood cultures grew out some kind of unknown organism. They sent it to the Centers for Disease Control in Atlanta."

Laura gave him a solemn look. "You're very lucky to be alive, Bo."

"So why am I alive?" Resting his head against Sam's side, Bo wound the end of his braid through his fingers. "By the sound of it, I should be dead. I almost was. So why aren't I?"

Flipping through the stack of papers, Laura dug one out and scanned it. "I'm not entirely sure, to tell you the truth. I repeated the culture yesterday. The microbe alone behaved in exactly the same way as before, dying within a few hours of being planted in the growth medium. But this time, when we put it in culture along with the chemical, nothing happened. No growth whatsoever. When I checked it again first thing this morning, all traces of the microbe were gone."

"What happened to it?" David asked.

"I don't know for sure," Laura admitted. "But it seems as though the microbe has a limited lifespan. Almost as if it contains a genetic off switch. Either that, or the chemical acts as both an on and an off switch, if that makes sense."

"So basically, the only reason the infection didn't kill Bo was that it switched itself off for some reason before he died." Sam clutched Bo closer. "Christ."

Andre frowned. "I'm glad it switched off, but why did it? Any ideas?"

"None at all. Hopefully I'll be able to learn more with further tests." Picking up the stack of photos, Laura handed them to Bo. "Those are the pictures I took while attempting an autopsy. Anything jump out at you?"

Bo examined the photos one by one. In the silence, Sam could hear the sounds of students exiting another classroom, talking and laughing as they walked past Dr. Trent's room. It seemed odd that others went about their normal lives, utterly unaware of the nightmares lurking on the far side of their reality.

"Here." Holding out one of the pictures, Bo pointed at a close-up of something Sam couldn't identify. "These two structures just behind the teeth look almost like a snake's venom glands. Considering your lab findings, it would be reasonable to hypothesize that they are in fact analogous to venom glands."

"Exactly what I thought," Laura agreed. "And?"

"And, if that's more or less what they are, they're very small."

David looked confused. "So?"

"So, if this was a snake, I'd say it was a juvenile." Bo shrugged. "Of course there's no way to know that, unless we manage to catch several more and study them."

Cecile shuddered. "No thank you."

Sam said nothing, but he vividly remembered how certain he'd been of that very thing at South Bay High. The implications of it swirled in his mind, maddeningly elusive.

"Laura knows where we think this came from." Dean stared directly at Sam, as if he knew what Sam was thinking. "We can trust her."

All eyes in the room focused on Sam. He swallowed. "You're right. It's a juvenile."

Twisting around, Bo frowned at Sam. "How do you know?"

Sam didn't want to say. It bothered him how easily the horrible things had connected with his mind. "I think I got it from that thing's mind," he confessed. "I don't know if it told me on purpose or not. But I'm pretty sure that's where it came from. It didn't feel like my own conclusion, if you know what I mean. It felt like something that came from another source."

"Oddly enough, I think I get you." Andre scraped at a gouged place in the top of the lab table. "I felt something kind of like that, only not as strong. Like I could sense the presence of the thing in my mind, but couldn't pick up on what it was thinking. If it thinks at all. Who knows?"

"But what does it mean?" Cecile burst out. "Assuming it's a juvenile, so what?"

Brow furrowing, Dean chewed on his thumbnail. "There's a connection there, something about the timing. Something about the disappearances every eighty-three years. Something..." Suddenly Dean's eyes went wide. "Oh my God. Oh shit. Oh *shit.*"

"What?" David nudged Dean's shoulder when he didn't answer. "Come on, man, let us in on it."

Dean blinked. "Okay, listen. For a few months every eighty-three years, people have disappeared from that spot, for as far back as records have been kept."

"Yeah," David agreed. "We figure the critters have some sort of control over the portal, to make it open on such a regular schedule."

Nodding, Dean swept on. "When those things came through on Friday, there were two. One large and one small. The large one hung back and the small one attacked, right?"

"Right." Picking up another photo, Bo examined it. "But what does that—" He broke off, set the picture on the table and looked up at Dean. "Oh. I see."

"What?" David asked, clearly frustrated. "Somebody please clear it up for us slow people, huh?"

"They were hunting," Sam explained, his voice faint as he suddenly remembered the strange pictures flitting through his mind just before Bo was attacked. "The adult brought the juvenile out to hunt."

"It must be part of a breeding cycle," Dean added, his face pale. "They breed, then they take the juveniles through the portal to hunt."

Cecile sank onto a stool. "Good Lord."

"I'll continue to run tests, of course. I still have the body, though it's already quite desiccated, more so than one would normally expect. But we know nothing about this species, so I suppose we should have no expectations. Especially if it's truly from another dimension." Her expression stunned, Laura shook her head. "I can't believe I'm actually having a serious conversation about this."

Tightening his arm around Bo, Sam could feel the man trembling. "Is there anything else?"

"Isn't that enough?" David swiped a hand across his eyes. "This is some fucked up shit."

"That's the extent of my findings so far," Laura confirmed. "I'll be in touch with any further results, of course."

"And we'll let you know if we think of anything else that might shed light on your findings." Getting a firm grip on Sam's arm, Bo stood. "Thank you, Laura. We really appreciate your help."

"It's my pleasure. What scientist wouldn't want to study a creature from another dimension?" Taking the hand Bo offered, she shook it. "Let me know if there's anything else I can do."

"We will, Laura, thanks." Grinning, Dean threw his arms around her in an enthusiastic hug. "See you later, hon."

As they left the room, Sam slipped his arm around Bo's waist. Bo glanced around nervously at the students in the hall, but didn't protest. Sam was glad. He felt an irresistible need to protect Bo, after the revelations in Dr. Trent's classroom.

"It's okay, Sam," Bo murmured. "I'm okay. And you closed the portal."

"Yeah, but did I close it for good?"

"I think you did," Andre said. "Cecile and I went back to the school yesterday. We didn't feel a thing."

Sam gave him a sharp look. "You didn't tell me you were going. I would've gone with you."

"You needed to stay with Bo, for yourself as much as for him." Smiling, Cecile slipped a hand through Sam's free arm. "I think the really telling thing is, the tunnel's cold now."

Sam considered that. "Hm. So, if I was right about it taking energy to keep it closed, the cold would indicate that it's closed for good."

"That's what the other two-thirds of the psychic crew think," David said.

"Think about it," Dean added. "The tunnel's been hot for at least as far back as the monks, because that's why they couldn't keep their stuff there. And it was hotter during our investigation than I remembered it being when I was in school. So here's the theory. Keeping the portal closed takes energy, which generates heat, which made the tunnel stay hot all the time. When the portal's activated or whatever for taking the juveniles out to hunt, it takes even more energy to keep it closed, thus the increased heat."

"The fact that the temperature dropped dramatically when the portal opened lends credence to that theory," Bo mused. "And if that's the case, the fact that it's cold in the tunnel now might indeed mean the portal's gone for good."

"That's assuming we're right about any of this," Andre reminded them. "We don't know anything, not really."

Leaning against the side of the truck as Sam opened the door, Bo voiced precisely what Sam was thinking. "Then let's hope we're right."

Epilogue

Stuffing a sweatshirt into his duffle bag, Bo glanced around Sam's bedroom. "I think that's the last of it."

"No, *this* is the last of it," Sam corrected, coming in from the bathroom with Bo's brush in his hand.

"Thanks."

Sam watched mournfully as Bo stuck the brush in the bag and zipped it. "You don't have to leave."

It was Saturday morning, five days after Bo left the hospital, and Bo was preparing to return to his own apartment. Sam was less than thrilled about that for lots of reasons, not least of which was he'd grown used to waking up with Bo in his bed. The thought of going back to sleeping alone was depressing. Plus he worried about Bo being alone, even though he seemed perfectly healthy other than a slight limp.

"I know," Bo said. "And I'm more grateful than I can say for all you've done for me. But I really should go."

"Everybody we work with already knows about us."

"True. But Janine doesn't, and I don't think she should find out."

"Your lawyer said she has no legal grounds to use that against you," Sam persisted, following Bo as he limped around the bedroom checking for anything else he'd left. "Move in with me, Bo. Please."

Laughing, Bo wound his arms around Sam's neck and pressed their bodies together. "Every time you ask me that, it gets harder to say no."

Sam grinned. "Move in with me."

"No." The love shining in Bo's eyes took the sting out of the word. "I'm not worried about her using our relationship to take Sean and Adrian away from me. Not anymore."

"Then what are you worried about?" Pulling the rubber band from the end of Bo's braid, Sam unwound the long ebony locks and ran his fingers through them. "Why won't you move in with me? Or at least stay a little longer, until your leg's completely healed."

Bo sighed and nuzzled Sam's neck. "I don't need help any longer. Janine's a damn good journalist. If I keep staying here, and especially if I move in, she'll figure out that you're not just helping me out, and that we're more than coworkers and friends. And she may not be able to use that to take the boys from me legally, but she'll use it to turn them against me somehow."

"They love you, Bo." Nudging Bo's head sideways, Sam kissed the pulse point in his throat. "They won't be swayed that easily."

"They're just children. I know they love me, but they're with her all the time other than short visits. She has a lot of influence over them." Bo's hands wandered down to trace the outline of Sam's nipples through his thin shirt. "God, I don't want to talk about this right now."

"Then don't talk." Sam flicked Bo's earlobe with his tongue. "Make love to me one more time before you leave."

Bo's soft moan reverberated up Sam's spine in a way that did nothing at all for his concentration. "Mm. No. Not this time."

Something in Bo's voice made Sam's knees weak. "Why not?"

Laying a hand on Sam's cheek, Bo leaned close and kissed him, the sweet slow caress of his lips and tongue sending a rush of heat through Sam's blood. When they pulled apart, Bo's eyes burned.

"Let me suck you," Bo whispered. "I haven't yet, and I...I want to try."

The mental picture alone was almost enough to make Sam come in his jeans. He reined himself in with an effort. "Are you sure?"

"Yes." Blushing, Bo hung his head and gazed up at Sam through a veil of hair. "I keep dreaming of having your cock in my mouth. I want to know how it'll feel. How you taste when you come."

Sam had to close his eyes against the whirling in his head. "God, Bo. I want you to. But the tests aren't back yet."

Sam had gone to his doctor that week for HIV and hepatitis testing. Both considered it more of a formality than anything else, since Dean was the only other man Sam had been with in months. But they'd agreed it was necessary, and Sam didn't want to expose Bo to unnecessary risk. Bo hadn't had sex for over a year before Sam came along. Being a regular blood donor, his blood was tested every couple of months, and he was clean.

Bo's grin held an irresistible combination of shyness and teasing. "I won't swallow, if it makes you feel any better."

Sam had to laugh. He'd been swallowing Bo's spunk all week.

"It would, actually." Slipping both hands down to cup Bo's ass, Sam kissed the end of his nose. "Let me undress you."

"That would be nice." Bo's breathing was already becoming ragged. "As long as I can return the favor."

"Definitely." Burying one hand in Bo's hair, Sam captured his mouth in a deep kiss while working his buttons open with the other hand.

They kept kissing as they undressed each other, kicking their shoes off and inching toward the bed. Sam's head was spinning, his heart thudding so hard he wondered if the rest of the building heard it. When they fell onto the mattress, tongues and limbs tangled together, both their shirts lay discarded on the floor and Sam's jeans were already halfway off.

Taking care to keep his weight off Bo's injured leg, Sam rolled Bo underneath him. "I still can't believe this is really happening."

"What?" Bo bit Sam's neck. "God, get those jeans off."

Sam groaned and arched his neck to give Bo better access. "I can't believe you're really here, in my bed."

Bending his good leg, Bo hooked his toes in the V of Sam's undone zipper and shoved his jeans down to his ankles. He cradled Sam's face in his hands. "Sometimes I can't believe it either. It was never like this with Janine. Never. I didn't know it could be this good, with anyone."

Lacking the vocabulary to accurately explain how he felt, Sam bent to kiss Bo. He slipped a hand into Bo's jeans, freeing his erection. Bo moaned into his mouth.

"Can't wait any more, Sam." Catching Sam's lower lip between his teeth, Bo flicked it with his tongue. "Need to suck your cock."

Hearing Bo say that made Sam's groin ache. Pushing off Bo with great difficulty, Sam sat up on his knees. "Sit with your back against the headboard, it'll be easier on your leg that way."

Bo squirmed out of his jeans and underwear, then scrambled backward and rested against the headboard. "Come here."

The anticipation in Bo's voice set Sam's skin on fire. Yanking his tangled jeans off his ankles, Sam crawled forward to straddle Bo's lap. He rose onto his knees, the tip of his rigid cock brushing Bo's chin.

Bo licked his lips. Wrapping a hand around Sam's shaft, Bo slouched until his lips brushed the leaking tip. His gaze locked with Sam's as he opened his mouth and slid Sam's prick inside.

"Ooooh, oh God," Sam groaned. "Jesus, Bo, that's good...so good..."

Bo hummed, sending luscious vibrations shooting up Sam's spine. Biting his lip, Sam curled his fingers around the top of the headboard and fought the urge to thrust down Bo's throat.

Bo couldn't take Sam more than halfway in, but the way he used his hand in concert with his mouth more than made up for it. He was a quick study, picking up on Sam's every reaction and using the knowledge to make Sam's body thrum with pleasure. It didn't take him long to figure out that Sam loved just the barest hint of teeth. When Bo's teeth scraped across the underside of his glans, catching on the flared edge, it was all Sam could do to keep from collapsing into a writhing heap on Bo's lap.

Leaning back a little, Sam watched Bo's head bobbing at his crotch. A strand of glossy black hair tickled Sam's balls every time Bo sucked him in. The sight of Bo like that, eyes closed and lips stretched around his shaft, made Sam feel hot all over. He laid one palm on Bo's head, petting him like a cat.

It wasn't long before Bo had Sam teetering on the brink. "Christ, Bo," Sam whispered, his voice low and rough. "So good. Your mouth, God... Dreamed of this..."

Pulling off of Sam's prick, Bo gazed up at him with lust-hazed eyes. "Come on my face, Sam."

Bo's words were all it took. With a cry that had to be heard by half the building, Sam came, splattering Bo's cheeks and coating the hand still stroking Sam's cock. Bo leaned forward to lap up the last drops leaking out of the slit. Something about that seemed unbearably erotic to Sam.

Oh my God, Bo just sucked me off. The knowledge would've been enough to bring Sam to orgasm again, if he'd had another one in him at that moment. He sagged into Bo's arms, sitting next to him and snuggling against his chest.

"Was it okay?" Bo sounded nervous.

"Oh my God, that was amazing," Sam told him, with absolute sincerity. "You're a natural, Bo."

Laughing, Bo lifted Sam's chin and kissed him. "Good. I was afraid I'd do it wrong."

Picking up a corner of the blanket, Sam used it to wipe the spunk from Bo's face. "First of all, there's no such thing as a bad blowjob." He returned Bo's kiss, tasting the tang of his own semen when Bo's tongue snaked into his mouth. "Second of all, you didn't do a thing wrong. Like I said, you're a natural."

"I'm glad, because I loved doing that." Bo smiled, caressing Sam's cheek. His fingers felt wonderfully cool against Sam's heated skin. "It's a powerful thing, making someone feel that good."

"Yes, it is." Sam nudged a hand between Bo's legs, grinning at Bo's needy moan. "Now it's my turn to do it to you."

"Oh God," Bo groaned. Squirming until he lay flat on his back, Bo opened his thighs wide and curled one hand around his cock. "Suck me."

Sam didn't need to be told twice. Batting Bo's hand out of the way, he dove in and swallowed Bo's cock to the root. Bo whimpered and began to thrust, fucking Sam's mouth hard, one hand fisted in Sam's hair. Sam hummed around his mouthful.

Bo gasped when Sam swallowed around the tip of his cock. "Oh, oh Sam. So close."

An idea struck Sam, and he ran with it. Popping a finger into the corner of his mouth, he wet it then pressed the tip against Bo's hole.

He looked up at Bo, asking permission with his eyes.

A shudder ran through Bo's body. "God, yes. Do it."

After days on end of loving attention from Sam's tongue, Bo's sweet little pucker opened like a flower with the slightest pressure. A few soft strokes was all it took for the tight muscles to relax enough to let Sam's finger slip inside. Sam's strangled moan echoed Bo's when Bo's body gripped his finger like a vise.

"Oh God, oh God, oh God," Bo chanted, legs lifting and spreading as Sam probed deeper. "Oh, that's...oh...God, almost...oh..."

The way Bo's cock swelled and pulsed in Sam's mouth told him how close Bo was. Gently twisting his finger, Sam felt for that one little spot...

"Fuck!" Bo cried, fist tightening in Sam's hair. "Ohfuckohfuck..."

Right there, Sam thought, feeling smugly pleased with himself as Bo thrashed underneath him. Rubbing the magic spot in firm circles, Sam hollowed his cheeks and sucked for all he was worth as Bo's cock shoved in over and over. A few more hard thrusts, and Bo went still, the tip of his prick against the back of Sam's throat.

"Fuck, Sam," Bo sobbed, and came. Sam swallowed the hot, salty fluid, feeling like a god.

"Good Lord." Bo let out a contented sigh. "Sam, you outdid yourself. C'mon up here."

Letting Bo's cock slip out of his mouth, Sam carefully withdrew his finger, making Bo whimper. Sam crawled up to lie down beside Bo and pulled the man into his arms. "Did you like that?"

"Very much." Draping his injured leg across Sam's thighs, Bo snuggled against him, one arm tucked around his middle. "I had no idea prostate stimulation felt that good. It was...God, I don't even have the words."

"It's okay, I know what you mean."

"Yes, I suppose you do." Bo kissed Sam's collarbone. "Sam?"

"Hm?" Sam combed his hand lazily through Bo's hair. The way the long satin strands flowed between his fingers fascinated him.

"What happens now?"

"You could move in with me," Sam suggested, kissing Bo's brow.

Bo pinched Sam's nipple, making him yelp. "Sam..."

"Yeah, I know. Sorry."

Propping himself on one elbow, Bo gazed solemnly into Sam's eyes. "I'd like to, one day. Just not yet."

Sam smiled at him. "I know. It's fine. We're together, and that's all I need right now."

Bo traced Sam's jaw with his fingertips, his eyes shining. "Thank you for that."

"You're welcome." Drawing Bo's face down to his, Sam collected a soft, sweet kiss. "So what did you mean? When you said 'what happens now'?"

"I actually meant about the portal. Or, well, other possible portals, I guess." Bo kissed Sam's chin.

"What about them?"

"Do you believe the one at South Bay High is closed?" Nuzzling Sam's cheek, Bo rolled on top of him, straddling his hips. "Do you think there are others?"

Sam shivered with pleasure as Bo's fingers plucked at his nipples. "I...I think the one at the school's gone. At least I didn't pick up any sense of it—oh shit, Bo, do that again—I, I didn't sense it when I went over there yesterday. Jesus, you're turning me on again."

"That's the idea." Shimmying down Sam's body, Bo snagged a nipple between his teeth and tugged. "What about others?" he mumbled, moving over to worry the other nipple.

Sam's ability to think was rapidly degenerating under Bo's determined onslaught. Furrowing his brow, he made a mighty effort to focus. "Um. I, I think there's definitely others. We—God yes—we, uh, we've already encountered two in the last few months. Gotta be more." He arched against Bo's mouth.

Bo raised his head. "Why is it that we've managed to run up against two inter-dimensional gateways in four months, when we had no idea they even existed before that?"

Sam blinked at him, trying to shift his mental gears from *sex* to *shop talk*. "I haven't thought about that."

"It's been bothering me." Dipping his head, Bo delicately licked Sam's nipple, the one he'd been biting moments before. "Andre felt the one at Oleander House almost right away, just like you did. He'd never felt that on any of our other investigations." He caressed the inside of Sam's thigh. "And for that matter, Oleander House was your first time experiencing a portal as well, wasn't it?"

"Yeah." Sam opened his legs, obeying the gentle urging of Bo's hands. "What do you think that means?"

Settling between Sam's thighs, Bo wedged his hips against Sam's groin. "I don't know. But I have this feeling the portals are multiplying. Or the barriers between realities are becoming more unstable. Whatever it is, I don't like it."

Unease curled in Sam's belly. Reaching up, he framed Bo's face in his hands. "Let's not talk about that right now. Make love to me before you go."

"I like that idea." Bending down, Bo brushed his parted lips against Sam's. "I love this. Love you."

"Love you," Sam echoed, running his hands up and down Bo's bare back.

When Bo's hungry mouth claimed his, Sam let the passion of it drown out the uneasy thoughts of dimensional portals and the things on the other side. He knew what his plans were regarding the gateways between worlds—find them, and close them. He'd made that promise to himself in those endless hours waiting to see if Bo would live. No one, he'd decided, would ever endure that kind of agony again if he could help it.

"Sam?" Bo drew back enough to give Sam a curious look. "What are you thinking about?"

Sam gazed up at him, into those beautiful dark eyes that he loved. "You. Kiss me again."

Smiling, Bo did, and the rest of the world went away.

They made love in the light of the afternoon sun pouring through the window. It was lazy and languorous, the desire rising slow and sweet between them, ending in mutual release that left Sam feeling boneless and utterly content. Pulling Bo close, he cuddled his lover against his chest.

I could get used to this, he thought, and closed his eyes.

About the Author

Ally Blue used to be a good girl. Really. Married for twenty years, two lovely children, house, dogs, picket fence, the whole deal. Then one day she discovered slash fan fiction. She wrote her first fan fiction story a couple of months later and has since slid merrily into the abyss. She has had several short stories published in the erotic e-zine Ruthie's Club, and is a regular contributor to the original slash e-zine Forbidden Fruit. To learn more about Ally Blue, please visit http://www.allyblue.com/. Send an email to Ally at ally@allyblue.com or join her Yahoo! group to join in the fun with other readers as well as Ally! http://groups.yahoo.com/group/loveisblue/

Look for these titles

Now Available

Willow Bend

Love's Evolution

Oleander House:
Book One of the Bay City Paranormal Investigation series

Eros Rising

Hearts from the Ashes
(print collection which includes Eros Rising)

What Hides Inside:
Book Two of the Bay City Paranormal Investigation series

Coming Soon:

Fireflies

Twilight:
Book Three of the Bay City Paranormal Investigation series

When you've lost something, it's always in the last place you look. Quinn's found Billy. Does he want to keep him?

Sex and Sexuality
© *2007 Willa Okati*

A newly-hired professor at a mountain college, Quinn is determined to put the past behind him. No more longing after men, not when he's turned his life around and even found a woman who's almost his fiancée. He's on the straight and narrow now—that is, until Billy comes along.

A force of nature, Billy sweeps Quinn off his feet and into a pair of welcoming arms. But does Quinn want to go back to being what he was, or does he dare to walk the path again after being interrupted? In the end, it's all about sex and sexuality...

Available now in ebook and print from Samhain Publishing.

*On the streets of old San Francisco darkness threatens
to consume a vampire's soul, and one man's love is all
that stands between good and evil.*

Soul of the Night
© *2007 Barbara Sheridan and Anne Cain*

The truth of his vampiric nature a carefully guarded secret, Kiyoshi Ishibe wanders alone in the shadows of the past. Banished from Edo in disgrace, the once famous kabuki actor Ryuhei Nakamura also journeys in loneliness. Both souls find one another in the night, each man filling the emptiness of the other.

But temptation and desire brings out the worst in Kiyoshi, triggering a fascination with the blood of a killer known as the Poisoned Dragon. As this interest quickly spirals into an obsession, everything Kiyoshi and Ryuhei have come to treasure is in danger of being lost...forever...

Soul of the Night includes 9 original illustrations by Anne Cain.

Available now in ebook and print from Samhain Publishing.

GREAT
cheap
fun

Discover eBooks!

THE FASTEST WAY TO GET THE HOTTEST NAMES

Get your favorite authors on your favorite reader, long before they're out in print! Ebooks from Samhain go wherever you go, and work with whatever you carry—Palm, PDF, Mobi, and more.

Samhain
publishing, ltd

WWW.SAMHAINPUBLISHING.COM